A NOVEL

SURVIVING
MINIMIZED

ANDREA WHITE

RIVER GROVE
BOOKS

Published by River Grove Books
Austin, TX
www.rivergrovebooks.com

Distributed by River Grove Books

Design and composition by Greenleaf Book Group
Cover design by Greenleaf Book Group

Publisher's Cataloging-in-Publication data is available.

Print ISBN: 978-1-63299-194-2

eBook ISBN: 978-1-63299-200-0

First Edition

To Bill

TABLE OF

CONTENTS

PART THREE

PART ONE

CAPTURED IN
ONE BOUNCE

Even with his oxygen mask on, Zert Cage caught a whiff of moldy tomatoes, plastic, grease, and rotten eggs. Using the masher stick, he packed his overripe and oily load into the barrel of his trash rifle. When he pumped his gun, the loader gave a satisfying slurp.

He aimed at the gloomy building that his friends had claimed as their headquarters and pulled the trigger.

Bam!

The shot fell short. The red mash splattered an old column and slid downward to the street.

He ducked behind a rusted triangular sign labeled "Caution. Radioactive" and waited. But there was no answering fire.

Bizarro. Had Eckle and his crew stood them up? He glanced over his shoulder to search for Cribbie. His best friend should have caught up with him by now. They'd been slinking down opposite sides of the street using the signs and junked vehicles for cover.

Only a tumbleweed of plastic rolled toward him, propelled by the breeze from the Enviro-fans. Even though Public Protection Warden Honest Goodman had declared this area safe twenty years ago, the street was still abandoned. Black soot streaked the faces of the crumbling buildings, and the potholes had grown large enough to swallow kids whole.

The sound of footsteps on broken glass came from the alley as a shadow fluttered in its depths.

Zert held his breath and watched a figure lurch out of the darkness. He dipped his hand into the trash bucket to grab a handful of the squishy, stinky stuff that he'd harvested from a broken g-pipe. He reloaded and turned toward his target.

The thing in his sights wasn't human. It was a creature with curled horns and curly hair. He lowered his gun as an abandoned designer animal tottered toward him.

The poog, a poodle-goat blend, began licking up the trash on the sidewalk. *Poor starving beast.*

Zert was searching his pockets for leftover nibbles when something clattered close by. He tightened his grip on his gun. A few meters away, Cribbie was climbing up the side of a rusty purple lifter, using its air vents as stairs. The lifter was an ancient model with thick wheels for driving on the road, a rusty propeller on top for flying to the Up Cities—where all the rich people lived—and a bulky magnet-box for docking in the sky.

Zert felt a gasp catch in his throat as he saw Cribbie reach the roof and straddle the propeller. It wasn't the steady way his friend aimed his rifle at the bombed-out building, or his wispy blond hair blowing in the night breeze. It was his O-mask flopping around his neck.

Zert would be grounded for life if his father knew he was waging a trash war . . . *during* the Quarantine . . . with Cribbie, the friend his father disliked *the most*. But at least he hadn't broken his father's most important rule. He ran his finger under the elastic strap of the oxygen mask that cupped his mouth and nose.

Cribbie hadn't exactly dared him. *But enough.* It wasn't as if he were in any danger. Despite what his father believed, he was thirteen—not a kid anymore—and he knew how to take care of himself.

Zert yanked off his own O-mask. For the first time in months, he tasted the chemicals, dust, sweat, and garbage of Low City DC on his tongue. The thick night air tickled his nose. *Crunchy.* It felt great.

Cribbie began pumping his rifle. He must have located their friends' hiding place inside the gloomy building.

Too bad Cribbie's ammo was gray, moldy bread. It spewed into a beautiful, high arc. Like Zert's, though, the shot fell short and splatted onto the sidewalk.

"Come out, cowards!" Cribbie yelled.

Silence.

"Have you spotted them yet?" Zert yelled, even though he could already guess the answer. The black trash sack that Cribbie wore over his clothes was still slick and clean, like his own.

"Nah," Cribbie said as he clambered down from the roof. "I'm starting to think Mr. Etc. stood us up." Mr. Etc.—Cribbie's nickname for Eckle.

The shaggy poog stumbled toward Cribbie. Red scars pockmarked the animal's face and ears. Its red, milky eyes oozed pus and blood.

"Cribbie," Zert yelled to his friend. "That poog's got Superpox!" He jammed his O-mask back over his nose and mouth, yanking the straps tighter to make sure it was sealed.

Cribbie dropped his trash rifle. It clattered to the ground as he grabbed his mask. He had barely gotten it back in place before the poog swayed past him onto the street.

Boing. Boing.

The sound came from behind him, and he felt his knees start to wobble. He didn't have to turn around to know who was coming. A trampo. Policemen earned their nickname from the spring-powered shoes they wore, shoes that allowed them to bounce as though they were on trampolines and which propelled them into the air.

A strong hand gripped Zert's arm.

Zert's heart did backflips in his chest as he turned to face his bad luck. Policemen never listened, never gave kids a chance to explain. They just hauled them down to Teen Jail and booked them. Then . . . well, he couldn't think about that.

The trampo nodded at Cribbie. "Game's up, son."

Cribbie ran toward them and launched himself at the trampo's knees.

As the trampo crumpled to the ground, he let go of Zert's arm. But in the furious tumble, Cribbie ended up underneath the fallen trampo.

"Why you nasty little . . . ," the trampo yelled. He scrambled to pin Cribbie, who was squirming to get away.

"Old Man!" Cribbie called out Zert's nickname. "Run!" The words, muffled by his mask, sounded as though shouted from behind a thick wall.

Zert picked up his rifle and ran. The black potholes yawned wide, as if they would gobble him up as he raced down the street.

Out of nowhere a second trampo bounced into his path. The partner.

Zert couldn't see the woman's face, only the tension in the square of her shoulders, the anger in the set of her jaw, and the strength in the expanse of her chest.

As Zert searched for an escape route, the partner bounced up and nabbed him. She wrenched his rifle out of his hand and threw it onto the ground. A pair of magnetic cuffs appeared as if from nowhere. "Hands in front," ordered the cop.

Zert gasped. His lungs struggled to bring in enough air.

"Name?" the trampo said as she slapped the cuffs over Zert's wrists.

"Zert Cage," he wheezed. Somewhere nearby, the poog bleated.

"Old Man!" he heard Cribbie yell from the distance. "Run!"

The trampo held Zert's hand over the identity reader until it beeped. "Zert Cage, you're going to Teen Jail."

Zert bowed his head. His dad was going to kill him.

2

NEW WORLDS

"It's a BIG opportunity. You and Zert should come with me." Marin smiled. "He's got to be miserable with the Quarantine and all." The sign on his forehead—"World's Greatest Adventurer"—flashed in green letters.

Jack Cage took a sip of his vita-coffee. His brother-in-law had arrived a few hours ago the way he always did, with no advance notice, pitching another crazy idea.

"Zert can get vaccinated if you guys come," Marin said. Both his grin and the sign on his forehead slid into off-mode.

Jack rubbed his upper arm, tracing the scar from his Superpox vaccination, still bumpy after twenty-five years. He'd gotten it when he was in the army. But that was before the market price for a single vaccination had skyrocketed to five hundred thousand credit coins—more than he could earn in a lifetime.

Oxygen masks substantially reduced but didn't eliminate the risk of catching Superpox. So the best alternative for his son and the billions of others who weren't vaccinated was virtual isolation. That's why tonight he'd left Zert sleeping soundly in their apartment. It was dangerous for his son to go outside, even just to a diner down the street.

"Zert gets to visit with my regular customers," Jack said. "I don't let them inside the store unless I know they're vaccinated. He's not as bored as the kids who are totally cut off."

"If you don't come, I might never see you guys again," Marin said.

"You *can't* be serious, Marin." Jack paused. "You're the only family Zert and I have left." His brother-in-law's slight build and sizable nose didn't remind him of anyone. But he could never look into Marin's blue eyes ringed with green without thinking about his own wife, dead these seven years.

"I saw your store," Marin said, ignoring his plea. "You're struggling. You could use a fresh start."

The deeply discounted prices. The bare shelves.

Jack smiled at the server as she poured more of the green, vitamin-rich coffee into each of their cups. "Thank you, Glade."

"Excuse me for interrupting, Jack," she said. Her flat, clean cheeks had no implants or designer freckles, but her lips were unnaturally red with Permanent Lipstick, which never wore off.

That was a slip-up. Everybody who worked at the Old Timey Café was supposed to look truly old-fashioned. But he understood. It was 2083 after all, and the owner, Papal George, wasn't likely to find young women willing to renounce all modern beauty products just so they could look as if they were from the 2050s.

"What is it, Glade?" Jack said.

"I didn't recognize your friend at first." She smiled at Marin. "Aren't you Marin Bluegar? Weren't you the first explorer on that show, *New Worlds*?"

Marin's foreboard flashed on—except for the broken exclamation point at the end. Only a line of bumpy skin on his forehead marked where it had once lit up.

"Yeah, that's me," Marin said, grinning.

Jack took a sip of hot coffee. He had forgotten this annoying aspect of being with his brother-in-law: the fans. Especially the young girls. Marin had never married. Flowers, his dear departed wife, always claimed her brother was too selfish to be a good husband.

"Do you really do all that stuff?" Glade asked, her tongue bumping up excitedly against the gap in her front teeth as she talked.

"I sure do," Marin said.

Jack suppressed a smile. Marin had once admitted to him that he used stunt doubles for the dangerous scenes on the show. "Insurance requirements," he'd said. "I'm too valuable."

"I haven't seen you on the tube lately. When's your next show?" Glade asked, patting her long black hair.

"I've been taking a break," Marin said. The lights on his forehead died away as he picked up his coffee cup.

Jack knew it was a forced break. Marin's career had stalled.

"But I'll be back next season," Marin said. "It's going to be a BIG one."

Glade leaned closer to the table and aimed her smile at Marin.

"Thank you, Glade," Jack repeated to put an end to the flirtation. "I haven't seen Marin in a while, and we have a lot to talk about."

Glade cast one last long glance at Marin before swishing away.

"You were saying?" Jack said, turning to his brother-in-law.

"This plan I'm working on is perfect for Zert," Marin said. "And you. You both need this."

With his free hand, Jack reached for the payment screen in the tabletop. The total flashed when he punched the button. Marin—who always spent money faster than he made it—was almost certainly broke. "OK, enough teasers. What's the plan, Marin?" he asked as he held up a crypto credit coin for the screen to scan.

"I'm heading west to live off the land. Miles from here. Back to nature," Marin said.

Jack glanced out the window at the street. The artificial moon was flashing an advertisement for PeopleColor so large and so bright that it could easily be seen down here, six hundred kilometers below its orbit. "There's no place like that left," he said.

"If you're game, there are always new worlds to explore," Marin said. But his voice—usually full of excitement—came out flat. That was the opening to the *New Worlds* show.

"You know me, Marin. I'm a homebody. I'm staying where I am," Jack said as his I-ring lit up.

A picture of a gray, windowless building filled the screen of the com-device that he wore on his index finger. It had to be the loneliest-looking place on earth.

The bold black words "Teen Jail" appeared at the top of a line of endless steps leading to the entrance. "What the . . . ?" Jack's voice trailed off.

3

STUCK BUTTS

Teen Jail was a warren of tiny cells packed with kids waiting for their parents—somebody, anybody—to take them away.

Zert and Cribbie sat in a cell, stuck on opposite ends of a metal bench. They were stuck. Really stuck.

When they'd been brought in, a robot matron—dressed like a woman cop—had fit them with black magnetic belts that wrapped around their waists, extended down their butts, and came all the way up to their belly buttons where the belts locked. About a centimeter thick, the belt was made of orange metal mesh. It looked fragile, but no matter how hard he struggled, it wouldn't give.

Zert's butt was pinned to the bench so securely he couldn't even squirm. His rear end felt as dead as a lump of chewed-up gum.

He checked the back of his hands for the hundredth time. He didn't spot any blisters. But the light was bad in the cell.

He wanted to ask Cribbie if he had seen what had happened to that poor, sick poog. But he didn't want to think about the animal's sad, pus-filled eyes.

He lifted his hands to take another peek for red spots, and as he did, he and Cribbie locked eyes.

"Don't worry, Old Man. You didn't get close enough." The

place on Cribbie's forehead where the trampo had bopped him was a red dome the size of a dodo egg.

Zert nodded as he heard the chime—the signal that the holorehabilitation program was about to begin. Not again! They had listened to it five times already, and they'd only been in jail for two hours. Throughout the cluster of cells, kids began stomping their feet and yelling things like, "Shut up!" "Make the holobum stop," and "That ol' blister makes me ill."

Zert watched as a figure of a man materialized in the corner of their cell. He appeared real, but he was only made of light.

"I was a kid once," the holobum started. Zert plugged his ears to block the grating voice, but it was no use. "A normal kid just like you," the holobum droned. "Then, I robbed a gum salesman and ended up in Teen Jail. Look at me now." He pointed his skeletal finger at the bags under his sunken eyes and the clumped hair topping his misshapen head.

When the bum opened his mouth to show his rotten teeth, Zert turned away.

"I'm going to get Eckle for this," Cribbie said.

But Zert didn't turn to face him. He felt bad looking at Cribbie's bruised forehead.

"I know exactly where he lives," Cribbie boasted, hatching a plan. "He's in one of those ground-floor caves." He slapped the metal bench with his open hand as he said this.

Cribbie was trying to drown out the holobum's sermon, but he was only making things worse. Cribbie's plans for revenge against Eckle called for Zert to play a major role.

"We'll sneak out," Cribbie said. "And when we get out of here . . ."

Impossible. After this, his father would never let him out of his sight again. He'd be stuck inside the apartment in the back of the store for the rest of his life.

But Cribbie *had* tried to save him from the trampo, and for that, Zert was in his debt—big time. Zert put his head in his hands and breathed in the smell of trash.

Cribbie said, "We'll cover Eckle and his gang with the stinkiest, ripest trash ever."

This hard metal bench had him in its grips all right, but it wasn't nearly as bad as being stuck between his father and his best friend.

The guard, a slight man, limped by their cell.

"Can't you turn the tube off?" Cribbie yelled as the guard passed by.

The guard looked as though he had just drunk a bottle of PeopleColor. Like the ad said, "Turn your skin any color you want it to be," the guard's skin matched his blue law enforcement uniform. The uniform was covered with pockets and compartments that held a stun gun, magnetic handcuffs, a zapper, water tablets, buttons to activate a camera, a heart rate monitor, and a laser light bomb.

"My friend's sick of listening to that holobum," Cribbie said to the guard.

The guard wrenched his neck in a quick twist, and Zert watched his forehead light up in red script: *Shut up.*

"PLEEEEZZZZ, SIR, PLEEEEZZZ," a kid's voice called out from the cell next door.

The guard marched down the length of the hallway with his foreboard facing the prisoners. As he passed each cell, the kids quieted.

"Next, I stole a few identity chips," the bum whined. "They didn't magnet me up in Teen Jail *that* time." He paused. "*That* time . . .*"

Zert shuddered, dreading what was coming next.

The bum started coughing. The sound was so real and viral sounding that Zert's own throat tingled with imagined moist lumps of phlegm. The bum seemed almost as sick as that poog had been.

Kids in the cells groaned and sighed in unison.

Doctor GoodHealth had drilled the symptoms of Superpox into everyone. Red, itchy blisters, almost too small to be noticed, popped up on the victim's hands or arms. The blisters swelled into welts. The welts erupted into boils. By the time the victim developed a hacking cough, the boils would be bursting.

Zert took advantage of the light from the holo-imagetube to push up the sleeve of his shirt and view the patches of freckles on his arm. Some freckles looked like couples hugging. Others like colonies of ants. One bloated one resembled a cloverleaf.

He checked his hands. His thumb was wide, perfect for pushing the toggle sticks in zoink ball, and his fingers were long and skinny enough to also play the deflector position. If he got lucky, he might be able to get a scholarship to stay in school. *If* he got out of this scrape.

"You can blast Eckle with some good ol' Italian trash, and I'll flatten him with some spoiled meat," Cribbie said. "We'll stake out his place until he leaves. OK, Old Man?"

Old Man—Cribbie's nickname for him because over their long friendship of two years, once or twice Zert had refused to go along with one of Cribbie's daring plans.

"OK, Cribbie," Zert said. He wasn't sure who he hoped would shut up more: Cribbie or the bum. At least the bum wasn't interactive, demanding promises he couldn't keep.

Footsteps sounded in the hallway. Steady, familiar footsteps. Footsteps that didn't rush. Footsteps that demanded respect. And as bad as his cell was, those footsteps meant that his life was about to get worse.

Before he could decide which excuse to use, his father was there, walking down the hallway toward the tightly spaced bars.

It would be easy to pretend that he wasn't related to Jack Cage.

His dad's face was all angles, unlike his own, which was round. His father's nose was pointed, while his refused to grow beyond a stub. His father's eyes were the blue of glacier ice he'd read about in books; his were an ordinary brown. Not only that, his father's skin was spotless, while daisy-chains of freckles crossed Zert's cheeks and nose, traveled up his fingers, and—he'd been told—laid a train track on his back.

"That's him," his father said through clenched teeth. He had on his blue jeans with the broken front loop and his red T-shirt with the Cage & Sons' logo.

"I told you so, Mr. Cage. Our DNA testers don't make mistakes," the guard said.

His father didn't answer. He just narrowed his eyes and glared at Zert through the bars.

Zert looked down at his shoes, polka-dotted with specks of garbage. He waited for his father's lecture.

"Don't we have enough problems, Zert, without you making more?" his father asked from the other side of the bars.

"We just snuck out for an hour," Zert said.

"I don't want to hear your excuses," his father said. His voice was weary in a way that made him sound . . . old. His shoulders, usually strong and erect, were slouched. "What you did was dangerous."

"But there haven't been any cases of Superpox for weeks and weeks," Zert mumbled.

"You know the epidemic isn't over yet," his father said.

Boy, did he know. The memory of that poog flashed in his head.

The guard pulled a thin black cylinder out of his pocket. It was the guard's identity wand containing his DNA, World Council Identity Number, blood type, and who knew what else. He waved it over the lock and it clicked open.

His father started to step into the cell, but the guard motioned for him to stay where he was.

The guard bent over Zert and waved his identity wand over the magnetized belt. It opened and fell softly onto the bench with a metallic whisper.

The guard turned to his father. "How about the other one? The Vermin kid. Do you know where his parents are?"

Cribbie usually beat up kids who called him *vermin*, but magnetized to the bench, he could only growl. "Not vermin. *Vimen*."

Zert's father shook his head. "Glorybeth Vimen, the boy's mother, isn't around much, but there's an older brother . . ." The guard turned his back on the cell, and the two adults began conferring.

Glorybeth Vimen didn't have a job. She didn't buy chips for Cribbie and his brother, Roal, to eat. She didn't do anything a mother was supposed to do.

Zert stood up and shook his butt to get the feeling to return. He stopped when he saw Cribbie snickering.

"Dead Jell-O," Cribbie said.

"Exactly," Zert said. *Uh-oh*. He was about to leave, while Cribbie had to stay. "Roal will be here soon," he told him.

"I'm not worried, Old Man," Cribbie said, staring at the back of his hand. He started scratching it.

The guard escorted Zert and his dad through the open jail door. Zert looked back at his friend, then down the long hallway.

Freedom.

4

A BITE OF
THINGS TO COME

There was nothing else to do but press his forehead against the warm glass of the front window.

Across the street, seven holostatues of liberty stood as tall as the rooftop. Their green bases were as wide as the trunks of the "Instant Trees" that grew a few meters every night. If only he could run through those holostatues of liberty and feel the dense light invade all his brain cells.

But it was day 123 of this Q—the third quarantine in his lifetime—and he was stuck inside. He might be trapped in the store forever.

He glanced over his shoulder at his father. Stubble covered the bottom half of his face. He was hunched over his net worth calculator, as if he expected only bad things to happen.

It wasn't only their looks that were different. His father was definite and clear about everything in life, while Zert could count on one hand the things he knew for sure.

One: He missed his mother.
Two: He wanted to be a veterinarian when he grew up.
Three: Snow Blakely was the cutest girl at St. Lulu's.
Four: His father was all he had.

"Dad, I'm sorry I snuck out," Zert blurted out. "Please, say something."

"Maybe if I sell the store," his father mumbled to himself, "I can raise the money for an attorney. But . . ." his voice trailed off.

Sell the store? Zert glanced at the sign on the window.

CAGE & SONS
Ultimate Xtermination Service
Family Owned and Operated since 2020

His great-grandfather had started the store. Both he and his father had been born here. It was a part of who they were.

Felony vandalism. That was the charge against him. No way could his father afford to get him a good lawyer. But his dad would try anyway. Jack Cage, fourth generation owner of Jack's Ultimate Xtermination Service. Army sergeant during the Antarctica Wars that pitted China and Russia against the old United States. Professional worrier. Miniature wolf breeder. All-around nice guy.

Turning away from the window, Zert walked over to the corner and bent down next to a row of cages against the wall. Only one was occupied.

Chub, a miniature wolf the size of a rabbit, got her name from her soft belly that seemed to beg for a tickle. She pressed her white chest against the cage and poked her snout through the bars.

As a side business, his father used to buy twenty of these designer animals from the factory every month and sell the lot, but his father hadn't restocked since the Quarantine, and now, Chub was the only one left. She was just supposed to be merchandise, but Zert loved her anyway.

He uncoupled the magnets and the cage door flew open.

Chub tore out and ran circles around him.

"Hi, girl," Zert said. "I'm happy to see you too." He paused. "Sit," he said.

Chub sat on her haunches with her tail wagging from side to side. Her ears stood tall, and she looked expectantly at him. Her hair was fluffy, and she smelled like the mint soap that he'd washed her with yesterday.

Miniature wolves had a reputation for being harder to train than dogs, but Zert had never had any trouble. "Good, Chub. At least *you* love me." He rubbed her head. "Let's go feed Okar."

As Chub followed at Zert's heels, the sound of her claws clattering against the floor mingled with the clicks of his father's net worth calculator.

Zert passed the shiny boxes of their best-selling products: the Xterminators. The Xterminators were just vacuums on wheels that sucked up roaches and other insect pests—as long as the insects weighed less than a couple of spools of thread. The Xterminators were cheap and the city was overrun with roaches, so they sold well. Or they used to before the Quarantine.

His father didn't even look up when Zert walked by.

His father didn't understand what it was like to be a prisoner. He had gotten vaccinated in the old days when the vaccine was cheap. He could come and go as he pleased.

His uncle's voice floated down from the attic. "Plenty of holo-imagetube coverage for sure . . . It's a go, all right. I'm trying to figure out an exit strategy. But I might use doubles . . ." He paused. "Sure. I'll let you know. Later."

"Going on another adventure?" Zert called up to Uncle

Marin. He hadn't had a chance to talk to his uncle last night. Zert had been too busy pretending to be asleep so he could sneak out.

"Yeah," his uncle's voice boomed down from the attic. "I'm trying to convince your dad that you two ought to join me."

"How crunchy would that be?" Zert said. Chub heard the excitement in his voice and howled, a miniature version of a real wolf howl.

His father looked up and gazed at Zert.

"I'm sorry, Dad," Zert moaned. "I understand we don't have the money to go anywhere."

"We need to talk, Zert," his father said. "But before our appointment with the judge, I've got to figure out if we have any options. Give me another hour." He looked back down at his net worth machine.

"Yes, sir," Zert said. The sight of his father working so hard might have made him feel hopeful. *If only the bank loans weren't past due.*

Zert passed the table stacked high with unsold boxes of roach perfume. "Perfume your toilet bowl and watch them drown." He murmured to Chub, "Quiet," and began tiptoeing toward another line of animal pens.

The cage for ypersteroid rats was floor to ceiling and the width of Zert's arm span. It boasted a brightly colored rat city, a trampoline, a wheel, and a lookout tower. "If you want to sell Xtermination services for rats, you've got to make people afraid of what they can do," his father claimed. Large enough for fifty rats, the cage held only one now: Okar.

Zert had named Okar after the inventor of dense light, Okar Accomody. His science teacher called Okar Accomody "a visionary." Even before dense light was used to make the first lifelike hologram, Okar Accomody understood the important role that light-based beings would play in the world.

A visionary like his namesake, Okar always sensed when Zert was coming to feed him and waited by the door. Today was no different. The rat squatted near the door and peered up at him through the bars of the floor-to-ceiling cage.

Back when they had fifty ypersteroid rats in the cage and appointments for thirty Xtermination demonstrations a week, Zert had written the sign that now hung on the front of the cage: "Blowout sale. Buy one treatment. Get one free." It seemed like so long ago, but it was just before this latest quarantine had ruined Jack's business and put Zert's life on hold.

Peeking out from under the worn sign, Okar didn't look like a rat superstar. He was no bigger than Zert's hand. But his perfectly formed and toned body could actually do amazing things.

Zert could recite his father's spiel by heart. "*Ten years ago, a pharmaceutical company began the illegal dumping of chemicals, and these ypersteroid rats began to plague Low City DC. The chemicals they consumed gave them unusual powers.*" And so on and so on. But one part of his father's pitch *really* scared customers: "*These rats will eat anything. Your clothes. Your wiring. Your silver . . . Your parakeet.*"

Not Okar, though. Okar was sweet.

Zert took a broom and dustpan off the peg in the wall, stepped inside the rat's cage, and breathed in the smell of wood chips. He closed the door behind him so that Okar wouldn't escape.

Chub pressed her nose against the door to the cage and pawed the floor.

"I'll brush you in a minute," Zert promised as he dropped a handful of pellets into Okar's blue bowl.

Okar, a flash of brown fur, raced toward him and stuck his head in his feed.

Zert began sweeping up the leavings. He opened the lid on the wall and dumped the contents of the dustpan into the g-pipe. *Swoosh.* It sucked up the trash and transported it to one of the nearby recycling centers. Their g-pipe was a silver tube bracketed to the wall, not like the kind in newer buildings that was embedded into the wall so it couldn't be seen.

Okar crawled onto his trampoline and bounced upright. From there he jumped onto the watchtower and hung by his tail from a pole. To show off, he swung back and forth like a pendulum.

Zert stood on tiptoe, reached up, and rubbed Okar's nose. "Good night."

Okar opened his mouth to reveal his pearly teeth. Zert had no time to pull back before the rat lunged at him. It was like someone had snapped him hard with a fat rubber band. He winced.

"Ouch!" Zert yelled, backing out and slamming the door of the cage.

"What's wrong?" his father called.

"Okar bit me," Zert said, looking down at the red blood trickling out of his cut.

"Really? He's never bitten anyone before," his father said.

Zert stuck his throbbing finger in his mouth. "He just did."

"I guess Okar's in a lousy mood. He's penned in and all alone," his father said, "like someone else I know."

Righting himself, Okar glared down at him from the platform circling the pole, as if they weren't friends but strangers who lived in different worlds.

Little did Zert know that just one week later, he'd be in a different world. And in that far-off place, rats weren't anybody's friend.

5

LOCKED UP FOREVER

"On," his father ordered the holo-imagetube.

Theirs was a discount model. It wasn't disguised as a chandelier like the fancy ones. It was just a black box with tubes dangling from it. "Local justice channel. Interactive mode," his father told the holo-imagetube.

Zert sat next to his dad on their purple couch. When his mother bought the couch at the bargain store a long time ago, it had been covered in pink balls of puffy fabric. But over the years, the balls had fallen off and the springs had pushed through the upholstery. Now the couch looked like it had Superpox. Still, he wouldn't let his father give it away. He could still catch a whiff of her scent. *Maybe. Yes, he could.* He could smell flowers—that was her name—and pickles—her favorite snack.

From the ceiling in the dark corner of the room, a beam of light rayed down from the hololaser tube. Zert drummed his fingers against the arm of the couch, waiting for the tube to turn on.

"Local justice channel. Interactive mode," his father repeated.

A man wearing black robes lit up in the corner of the living room. He had straight white hair and bright blue eyes, eyes that inspired trust because their size, shape, and color had been engineered to do that. Zert knew that the judge had not been born with that appearance; his facial features were a favorite design of judges, lawyers, and politicians. Black lights on his forehead flashed his name—"Gorightly"—and a message—"Justice for All."

"World Council vs. Bezert Cage. Will the defendant please announce his presence?" Judge Gorightly said in a deep voice.

Zert stiffened, trying to sit straight and tall like his father. His father elbowed Zert and whispered, "Remember, plead guilty."

"Present, your honor," Zert said, swallowing.

"And do you have a guardian or parent with you?" Judge Gorightly said.

"His father, Jack Cage, is present, your Honor," his father said, standing. Then he quickly fell back down on the old couch, which protested with a sharp squeak.

"Bezert Cage's crime, defacement of public property and felony vandalism, carries a minimum sentence of six months in Teen Jail," the judge said.

Six months!

His father let out a sigh and began popping his knuckles.

"And a maximum of twenty years," Judge Gorightly finished, his voice as matter-of-fact as if he were ordering a slice of zero-calorie pizza.

"Twenty years!" Zert and his father shouted in unison.

Zert turned to his father. "But I'm only thirteen."

His father kept gazing at the judge.

"Dad," Zert whispered urgently, "if I miss that much school, I'll never get to be a veterinarian."

"Does Bezert Cage plead guilty or innocent?" Judge Gorightly said.

"Innocent!" his father shouted as Zert opened his mouth to answer.

"But you said . . . ," Zert hissed to his father.

"Will Bezert Cage be represented by counsel?" Judge Gorightly said.

"I don't have the funds, sir," his father said. "My son made a mistake. But twenty years?"

Out of the landscape of his face, the judge's steely eyes bored into them. "Felony vandalism is no mistake," he said.

"My son is a good kid," his father finished lamely. "Even six months is harsh."

Zert squirmed on the couch next to him. He may have been thirteen and his father forty-eight, but he knew more than his dad did about this judge and the legal system. He knew that his father's protests were useless.

"Bezert Cage will have his time in court. I'll appoint a public defender to represent him," Judge Gorightly said.

His father scooted to the edge of the couch. "Do you have a son, Judge?" he cried.

Judge Gorightly ran his fingers through his straight white hair. "Irrelevant."

"I've never been away from my son for a whole week, sir. Six months is a lifetime," his father said. "Please, sir." He paused. "Mercy."

Zert's face felt hot. He had never heard his father beg before.

"J. Cage," Judge Gorightly said, "your son was in the company of a juvenile who assaulted a police officer."

"Assault?" his father asked, turning to gaze at Zert.

Zert looked down at his clenched hands. He hadn't mentioned that Cribbie had tackled the trampo. He hadn't wanted to worry his father more than he already had.

"Ah, J. Cage." Judge Gorightly tapped his finger against his head. "I thought so." He smiled for the first time. "I'm not sure that you know your son."

His father nudged Zert's leg.

Zert looked up into his father's flushed face. "Cribbie was trying to help me."

"My clerk will message you Bezert Cage's court date this week," Judge Gorightly said. He looked down at his I-ring. "Next case," he said into his communicator.

The judge's image faded, and the corner of the room stood empty again.

Zert turned away and thrust his head into the crease in the couch so he wouldn't have to see his father stomp out. But he couldn't block his ears, and his father slammed the door so hard the walls of the small room shook.

›››

The store's doorbell sounded. It was a recording of the yelp of a woman surprised by a roach, the squeak of an ypersteroid rat, and the whoosh of a g-pipe vacuum.

"I'll get it," Zert said. He had been training Chub to roll over in the wide-open space between the door and the counter. "It's probably Dorpus Thoougar." Dorpus and her pet dodo, Marsh, were regular customers.

He headed toward the door. Chub's claws clicked against the floor as she trotted after him.

"Wait. It's too dangerous," his father called out from behind the counter. "I heard at the jail: There's been an outbreak of Superpox nearby. Let me get it."

The door rattled as the visitor pulled against the lock. Through the window in the door, Zert could only see the holostatues of liberty across the street. But as he drew closer, following his father, he was able to make out a figure standing outside. It held a glow ball, like the one in his old Boy Scout kit.

The light from the ball lit up the fleshy boils and leaking pus that mottled the figure's face.

"Go away!" his father yelled through the glass. "My son's not vaccinated."

"I think I caught *it* last night," a familiar raspy voice said. "From that poog."

"Cribbie!" Zert cried, stepping out from behind his father.

"Don't worry, Old Man," Cribbie croaked through the door. "I'll be OK. I just wanted you to know why we're not going after Mr. Etc. yet." He dropped the glow ball but didn't seem to notice. Zert heard the ball bounce, bounce, bounce toward the street.

"Where are you staying?" Zert asked through the glass as he watched the glow ball hit a bit of uneven pavement across the way and roll back toward the door.

Cribbie turned toward the street. His head hung down between his broad shoulders. He started shuffling away, as if he had weights in his shoes.

"Dad, help him!" Zert cried. He pressed the button on the side of the door, and the magnetic field clicked as it disengaged. The door swung open, and air from the street wafted in. He caught a whiff of curry from Mystery Meat Restaurant, grease from the Old Timey Café, and trash from the overflowing barrels in the alley.

Chub stuck her nose out the door and sniffed the glow ball.

His father simultaneously grabbed Chub back and reached up to grip Zert's shoulder—hard.

"Tell me the truth" his father said through clenched teeth as he slammed the door shut. "Did you wear your mask last night?"

"I did," Zert said. "But . . . ," he stammered.

"But what?" Jack demanded.

"I took it off," Zert admitted. His voice sounded small, like a child's. "For just a second," he added in a firmer tone.

His father bent forward as if someone had punched him in the stomach. "*Zert. You could DIE.*"

6

BEWARE OF UNCLES BEARING GIFTS

Zert squinted to keep the tears from spilling out. "I heard on the news that there hadn't been any new cases for weeks. I didn't think . . ."

His father's grave expression didn't change. "That's right. You didn't think."

"Dad, you can lecture me later. Right now, will you please help Cribbie? Please!" Zert begged.

Thump. Clomp. Thump.

His uncle was hurrying down the attic stairs.

Without a backward glance, his father opened the front door and went out onto the street. He walked in that way he had, not hurrying but with a firm step.

Uncle Marin stepped off the staircase and joined Zert. His uncle had a hooked nose, "Star-Bright" white teeth, tanned skin that he got from drinking "Healthy Tan" PeopleColor, and pale blue-green eyes. He was dressed in red pajamas that were sheer and soft looking, but faded, as if they had been washed a million times. "What's wrong, Zert?"

"My friend," Zert began, feeling his voice shake. This was unreal. The poog. Cribbie must have caught it last night. The incubation period for Superpox was twenty-four hours. That meant . . .

"Is your friend sick? I heard something about Superpox," Uncle Marin said.

Nodding, Zert pushed up his shirtsleeves to see the back of his hand. He found the same old game board of freckles.

The door opened, and his father stepped back inside. His face looked even sadder and grayer than it had when he had come to Teen Jail to pick him up that morning. He thrust his hands deep into the pockets of his jeans and stood there, silent.

"Did you find him?" Zert asked.

His father shook his head.

"So what's going . . . ?" Uncle Marin asked.

"Zert's friend," his father said quietly to Uncle Marin. "This juvenile delinquent he hangs out with—"

A firecracker exploded in Zert's head. "Cribbie's not a juvenile delinquent!" he yelled.

"—has Superpox," his father finished. His father's jaw tightened in a way that meant he had been right. That he was always right. That Zert knew nothing, and he knew everything.

"I'm sorry," Uncle Marin said. "One of the many hazards of living in Low City DC."

When Zert turned to gaze at him, his uncle's face went blank. But not before Zert glimpsed a hint of a smile.

"Did you look for him, Dad?" Zert asked his father.

"I tried," he said. "He must have ducked into one of the alleys." His father paused and shook his head. "I shouted his name. He doesn't want to be found, son."

Zert moaned.

His father stepped closer.

Zert closed his eyes as he waited for the check he knew was coming. His father grabbed Zert's wrist and started examining his skin. *Blisters to welts to boils to* . . . If his father found a blister on him, he would likely be dead within forty-eight hours.

After a few moments, Zert pushed his father's hand away. "Stop. I don't want to know."

His father exhaled. "You're clear."

Zert exhaled and waited. His father had already grounded him and taken his I-ring, so he couldn't call Cribbie to find out what was going on. He couldn't call anybody. He was trapped in here when Cribbie might be . . . No, this couldn't be happening to his best friend.

His father and Uncle Marin stood facing each other. They were having one of those unspoken adult conversations.

After a few moments, Uncle Marin was the first to break the silence. "You can escape all of this," he said. He sounded like that salesman on the holo-imagetube who made Zert want to buy not one but a hundred glow balls. "And protect your son."

His father scratched his stubbly chin. "You're *sure* Zert can get vaccinated if we go?"

"I am," Uncle Marin said. "One-hundred-percent sure."

Zert looked from one person to the other.

His father's eyes took on a lost gleam. The one that reminded Zert that his mom had died too young.

"I could hire a lawyer, but then we couldn't afford to eat. I don't know any other way to keep him out of jail and get him vaccinated," his father said.

"So you'll do it?" Uncle Marin said.

"What choice do I have?" his father sighed. His eyes circled the store, gazing at every display, and Zert felt as if he could read his thoughts. His father seemed to be thinking: This is my life. This was what I built.

"Let's go," his father said, finally.

"Where are we going?" Zert asked. His father hadn't said, "Let's go" like he did when he decided to go to the zero-calorie dessert store and splurge. He'd said, "Let's go" like he had when it had been time to go to his mother's funeral.

"You're sure?" Uncle Marin said to his father. "There's no turning back."

His father's jaw muscles bulged, his lips pressed together, and his face contorted into what Zert called his *army look*. "You know when I say something I mean it."

Uncle Marin's foreboard flashed as he let out a whoop and began hopping around the room in a one-legged dance, his red robe flopping around him. "The greatest adventure ever," he called out. "No one will be able to top this."

"What's going on?" Zert said.

Chub pawed at his legs, asking to be picked up, but Zert ignored her.

His father glared at him, but then his blue eyes softened. "Forgive me, son. I promised your mother that I would do everything in my power to keep you safe."

"What's going on?" Zert's voice went shrill. "Tell me!"

"So, Marin, what's step one?" his father said, ignoring him.

Zert dropped to his knees next to Chub. He pulled his pet to him and hugged her so tightly that she howled.

7

A WRONG DESTINATION

Zert stroked Chub, who had curled into a ball next to him as he watched his favorite show on the holo-imagetube. Her upper lip trembled as she snored.

"But I was supposed to go to Up City Aspen," the contestant mumbled.

On the show, people traveling to luxury vacation resorts by 3-D Mag Lev, the fastest and most expensive way to travel, ended up in grim destinations instead.

Underneath his heavy alpaca coat, the super-rich contestant wore dark pants and a dark shirt. He scowled at the ocean, still brown and full of debris from the Nuclear Mistake. The man's brow hinted of a major temper tantrum, but on the island, with its ruined resort hotels, no one was around to yell at. Surrounding him were only the drooping palm trees.

With his free hand, Zert dipped into a bag of pickle/strawberry chips. He guessed, sour. Then, he bit into the chip and got his answer: the sweet taste of strawberry.

Cribbie liked Coca-Cola chips the best.

Cribbie! Not even his favorite show could take his mind off his best friend today. He had to find out how he was doing.

"Off," Zert said to the holo-imagetube. The light shriveled up, and the corner of the room where the contestant had stood was empty again.

His father must have hidden his I-ring in an old chest in the attic. Zert had already searched everywhere else.

He had set Chub down to go hunt upstairs for his I-ring when the door to their apartment opened.

As his father entered the room, he accidentally pinned Chub's tail with his foot.

Chub's growl was ferocious, not at all what someone would expect from a mini-wolf. His pet had no idea how small she was.

Zert picked her up and rubbed the spot between her ears. "Sorry, girl," he said. Her growl sputtered into a purr.

His father turned the desk chair around to face the couch and sat down. That morning he'd changed into a green Cage & Sons T-shirt, hung a "Closed" sign on the store, and left with Uncle Marin with hardly a good-bye and certainly no explanation. But now, his face bore that look, the one that said they needed to have a talk.

With the holo-imagetube now turned off, the squeaks of Okar's wheel, the thumps of Uncle Marin's footsteps in the attic, and the honks of the lifters on the street came through loud and clear.

But still his father stayed quiet.

A moving photo of his father and three of his army buddies hung on the wall behind him. When the photo had been newer, the men used to take off their coats, pick up axes, and hack at the ice. But now the picture was static, like an old-timey photo, and Jack and the others in the photo just gazed at Zert.

Their flat eyes seemed to say, "We're sorry. We're sorry for the Nuclear Mistake. We're sorry for all of it."

"Dad," Zert spoke up first. "I really need my I-ring. I need to call Cribbie. To find out how he is."

"You saw Cribbie, Zert. Pox can kill you," his father said

automatically, as if he were thinking about something else, something so bad that it drove every other thought out of his head.

"Cribbie's not dead," Zert said. "Roal had Superpox." He paused. "He lived." Roal, Cribbie's brother, was what people called a Superpox champ. Not everyone died.

His father nodded. "It's possible Cribbie's OK." He paused. "But have you thought about what it's going to be like after you're sentenced? How you're going to like serving time in Teen Jail?"

"That judge can't sentence me to twenty years for just one night," Zert said. "It's too unfair."

"Still, you might be locked up for a long time." His father sighed as he ran his fingers through his cropped brown hair. He was quiet a moment. "Your uncle's plan is weird and terrible. We don't have any choice but—"

"What plan?" Zert interrupted.

"We're moving." His father paused. "Well, it's more than just a move," he mumbled. "*Much* more."

"He should be here any minute," Uncle Marin called out from behind the door.

"Everything I do, I do because I love you," his father said.

Zert could read the doubt in his father's scrunched eyebrows, could hear the uncertain hitch in his voice. For once, Jack, the fierce soldier of the Antarctica Wars, nicknamed Jack the Giant Killer by his men, wasn't sure of the right thing to do.

The front door blared out its doorbell greeting.

"Who is it?" Zert demanded, his voice cracking. He led the way to the store.

Grayish light flowed in through the front window. Outside, it was pre-up, the time of day after the sun went down and before the artificial moon turned on. Until then, the only light on the street came from the Up City and the real moon.

Uncle Marin was standing in front of the counter, next to

the boxes of Roach Bait, Magnetized Dust, Xter Vacuums, and Rodent Rifles.

At first, Zert thought the familiar room was empty. But then, he noticed the stranger. The man sat very still at the end of the foldout table that his father sometimes used for meetings. He had jet-black hair and matching black eyes. The set of his jaw reminded Zert of his old Boy Scout master.

The stranger wore an old-fashioned communication device—a wide crystal bracelet—and he held it up to view the screen. His MedNow Coat was covered by neat rows of shiny buttons for blood pressure, oxygen level, temperature, and diagnosis code.

"Hello, Zert," said Uncle Marin. He walked over to the table and sat down. He was dressed in street clothes: a white long-sleeved shirt and white slacks. He motioned for Zert to sit down across from him.

"Let me put up Chub," Zert said.

At the sound of her name, Chub squirmed in his arms.

The stranger said to his communication device, "I'm on a house call now, sir. May I get back to you with those figures?"

The stranger was a doctor. Did his father think he was sick? Just to be sure, Zert glanced at his hands and arms again. No blisters. Besides, he felt fine.

Zert knelt next to Chub's cage and opened the latch. She thrust her soft black nose into his fingers. "That's my girl," he whispered. He gave her tummy a final tickle before putting her inside. The mini-wolf let out a howl of protest.

"I'll be back," Zert said and stuck his fingers through the door to pat her nose.

As Zert settled into the chair next to his father, the stranger clicked off his communication device and turned to face them. "Hello," he said. His gaze latched on to Zert, as if he were the most important person in the room. "My apologies, but that was Dr. Rosario himself."

The man said "Dr. Rosario" as if he were saying "Dr. God."

"Zert," Uncle Marin said, "this is Dr. Brown, a representative of Project Rosie—"

His father interrupted, "I didn't get a chance to tell him anything."

"Oh," Uncle Marin said, picking at a tattoo of a giant "NW" on the back of his thumb.

Underneath the stubble, his father's cheeks grew pink.

"That's fine. That's my job. But first, I have a few questions for Zert," said Dr. Brown, turning to Zert with a big smile.

Although Dr. Brown's features didn't look implanted, his smile resembled the "Manly Grin" style advertised by the implant doctors.

His father nodded. "Go ahead."

Zert braced for something terrible when Dr. Brown reached into his front breast pocket.

The doctor pulled out a notecard and held it up for Zert to look at. The piece of gray electronic paper was ordinary except for a blotch of black ink that swirled like a black tornado.

"What do you see?" the doctor asked.

Zert cocked his head and gazed at the messy blob. He imagined a boy about his age getting frustrated with the Quarantine and kicking over a can of black PeopleColor. "I see an accident. A mess," he said.

"Look closer." The doctor's voice was smooth, meant to be reassuring. But it was too smooth.

On the notecard, thousands of tiny wheels, like the insides of a miniature watch, emerged inside the black blob.

"What going on?" Zert muttered. Each circle revolved slowly, a wheel stuck in the ink, then started whirling faster and faster. The sight of all the activity made his head ache, and he looked down at the table.

Dr. Brown said firmly, "Keep your attention fixed on the page."

Zert struggled to follow the doctor's directions, but his eyes felt heavy. The wheels spun so quickly that they merged into a single black cloud that floated away.

〉〉〉

Zert opened his eyes and wiped the drool off his chin with the back of his hand.

Through the front window, he could see a passerby covering his head as the red, green, purple, and blue rain poured down. Low City rain passed through pollution clouds, causing it to shimmer with all the colors of Popsicles.

Dr. Brown, his father, and his uncle were heading back into the store from the apartment, talking among themselves as though nothing had happened.

Zert quickly closed his eyes and leaned back in his chair, pretending to be asleep.

"He's angry, of course," Dr. Brown said. "All adolescents are. And it's understandable that this generation is the angriest generation yet. But I didn't see anything so unusual in him as to bar entry."

"That's a relief," his father breathed. "It's hard to be a single dad. I've often wondered."

Often wondered what?

"Zert's going to do just great," his uncle said. "He takes after my side of the family—he's an adventurer at heart."

"Gentlemen," Dr. Brown said, "Zert still has to pass the physical in the morning. We can't approve your son if he has Superpox."

"Can't you examine him here?" his father said.

Zert fought the impulse to check his hands.

Dr. Brown shrugged. "You know Superpox is unpredictable. For most, it strikes twenty-four hours after exposure. But the symptoms have been known to show up later."

"I've got to make some plans," Uncle Marin said. "I need to know as soon as possible if Jack and Zert can go."

"I can't perform a definitive exam without my equipment," Dr. Brown said. "But while he's still out, I could perform a preliminary on him if you want."

At the thought of that stranger's fingers patting him down, Zert opened his eyes. "What's going on?" He tried to sound sleepy.

"Zert!" his father said. "Like I said, I'm . . . I'm sorry. I . . ." He wasn't looking at Zert but at the floor.

Dr. Brown ambled over. "We do owe you an explanation, don't we?"

"What did you do to me?" Zert demanded as Dr. Brown sat down.

"Spectrum hypnosis," Dr. Brown said. "You've heard of it?"

"The stuff the military uses to interrogate rebels and make them forget things." Zert glared at his father.

His father nodded as he sat back down at the table. "Sorry, Zert. You'll understand in a minute."

"Zert, there's always a cost to any adventure," Uncle Marin said as he pulled out a chair. "Always a price for glory."

"What's going on? Enough already!" Zert said. "Tell me!"

Dr. Brown smiled. "First, I must warn you that Dr. Rosario's project is top secret. It has to be. Unwelcome attention from the outside world would place the participants in great danger. If, for some reason, you don't qualify, you and your father will need to undergo spectrum hypnosis to ensure you forget this session."

This day was getting more and more bizarro. "OK."

"Do you like science, Zert?" Dr. Brown said.

Zert shook his head. "My favorite subject is English."

"Then I'll start with a simple explanation, and if you want more, I'll provide it to you," Dr. Brown said.

Zert nodded.

"Of course you know how 3-D Mag Levs work?" Dr. Brown said.

"Uh huh." He had learned in class that Mag Levs instantaneously transported solid objects in space-time through wormholes. Whatever that meant.

"All right then," Dr. Brown said. "A scientist named Dr. Apt Rosario invented a minimizer function on a 3-D Mag Lev. He has used it to successfully minimize volunteers. It's a way to build a sustainable world."

Zert tried to make sense of the man's words. "What does minimize mean?"

Dr. Brown held his gaze. "Shrink. It means shrink, Zert."

8

SCI-FI COMEDY

"You want me to *shrink*?" Zert asked, his voice rising to a squeak.

Dr. Brown's expression did not change, but Zert's father looked away with a pained expression on his face.

"Not just you," Dr. Brown said. "Your father and your uncle want to be Rosies too."

"Rosies?" Zert demanded. As he looked from his father to his uncle to Dr. Brown, he wiped his sweat-soaked hands on his jeans.

"The recruits are nicknamed Rosies," Dr. Brown said without a smile. "There are about fifty thousand of them now. We're—"

"How . . . How big will I be?" Zert interrupted. "I mean, how big would I be *if* I did this?"

Dr. Brown took a tape measure out of his pocket and put it on the table. "If I measured you, we could work out your height exactly."

Zert shook his head. *No. No. No.*

"About the size of your big thumb," Dr. Brown said. He used the same tone any doctor would use to say, "It's time for your checkup, young man," except this . . . this was not normal.

Zert stared at his right thumb.

"As I'm sure you're aware, the Superpox vaccine is prohibitively expensive," Dr. Brown said. Zert knew that the seaweed scientists needed to make the vaccine was nearly extinct. "However, just one dose of the vaccine can last Project Rosie indefinitely," Dr. Brown said, and he broke into a wide smile. "Once you shrink, you'll receive a vaccination. There's no Superpox there."

"Where's *there*?" Zert asked, even though under his breath, he said, "I'm not going."

"Remember the New World?" Dr. Brown answered. "Well, this is the Newest World."

Zert's mind was spinning too fast. This wasn't some sci-fi comic. This was a doctor talking.

"You would be making a contribution to mankind," Dr. Brown said.

Zert had read the word "mankind" in books. But he'd never heard a person say the word out loud before. "Could I talk to my father?" he asked.

Uncle Marin stared intently at him.

"Alone," he added.

The doctor frowned. "I need to go over a few practical details. Your father wants to leave tomorrow."

"I'm counting on you, nephew," Uncle Marin said.

Zert glared at him. "To become a thumb?"

"Now, Zert," his father said. He wiped the sweat off his forehead. "This is the best choice, given our messed-up situation." He paused. "The only choice," he muttered. "We need to do this."

Dr. Brown's mouth kept moving as Zert leaned back in his chair. He was suddenly conscious of his thumbs. All he had done was be a kid and enjoy one wild night. And now . . .

He gazed down at his thumbs, wiggling them. Life was twiddling him. Big time.

〉〉〉

A woman's giggle penetrated the thin door that separated their apartment from the store.

Zert tried to brush Chub's hair, but the wolf kept nibbling at the brush. He couldn't shrink. He wouldn't be able to brush Chub. He had enough trouble brushing her now. If he were thumb sized, it would be impossible.

His father faced him in the chair across from the couch. He was dressed as always in a T-shirt covered in the Cage & Sons logo and blue jeans. The T-shirt was tight around his middle, and one of his belt loops was broken and made a bump.

"I'm not going," Zert repeated.

Uncle Marin stuck his head inside the door. His broad shoulders almost blocked Zert's view of the young woman standing behind him. Her pink overalls matched her boots.

At first Zert didn't think he knew her. But as he watched her bright red lips pull back in a smile, he recognized Glade, his father's favorite server at the Old Timey Café. Before the Quarantine, he and his father had often gone there together.

Uncle Marin cast a worried look at Jack. His slicked-back blond hair was mussed. "I'll be at Gehozafat's Donut Bar," he said. "Let me know as soon as you can. I'm counting on you."

"I told you, Uncle Marin, I'm not going," Zert called after him.

"We're still talking this through," his father said to his uncle.

Zert glared at his dad. It was true that during the Antarctica Wars, his father had lived for three years in a tent. But ever since he had been born, ever since he had known him, Jack Cage had been a typical boring father. Not someone he would ever suspect of wanting to shrink.

Uncle Marin closed the door to the apartment.

"Uncle Marin loves his fans," Zert said as his uncle's footsteps died away. "He loves it when people pay attention to him. I think it's bizarro that he wants to leave"—he struggled to find the word—"civilization."

"He's an outdoors man like me," his father said.

"Really?" Zert said. On the *New Worlds* show, he'd seen his uncle step into a lion's den, ride a whale, and walk through a forest fire. The outdoors was supposed to be dirty. Yet Uncle Marin always looked like he had just stepped out of a CleanRoom, where he had spent a lot of time sprucing up in front of a mirror. Even the bathrobe he wore in their apartment looked pressed.

"I spent yesterday morning familiarizing myself with Dr. Rosario's outfit," his father said. "It's legitimate, all right. His nonprofit is dedicated to reducing overpopulation and saving the world."

"Dr. Rosario can save the world without me. I'm not going to become a thumb, Dad," Zert said as he twisted a pink ball on the couch's upholstery.

"Not a thumb. A *Rosie*," his father repeated impatiently. "You weren't even listening to the doctor. You're also forgetting that if we don't leave, you might have to go to jail for twenty years," he said, his voice rising. "This decision is vital to your life. You have no other options."

"Dad," Zert said, "after the doctor told me you wanted me to shrink, I couldn't think." He pressed his hands against his ears. "I couldn't hear."

His father moved the chair closer, but before he could speak, Zert began, "I didn't ruin the oceans, kill all the seaweed, and jack up the cost of the Superpox vaccine. Adults did that. All I did was make one mistake because it is so boring to be locked up inside this store 24/7. And now you want me to *shrink*?" Zert yanked one of the pink puffs off the couch and threw it at the trash can.

"I get it. This is a big change," his father said in the overly patient voice he used whenever he talked with the children of their customers. "But if you had been listening, you would have found what Dr. Brown had to say interesting."

Zert let out an extra-loud sigh.

"The Rosies are colonizing Rocky Mountain National Park," his father said. "The World Council's attempts to repopulate the national parks with wildlife have largely failed. Only some buffalo herds live there. Access is restricted, so very few people go. The mountains block the pollution clouds, and the air is still clean there."

His father's voice had changed as he said this. His tone was unfamiliar. He sounded . . . hopeful.

"The outdoors is dangerous," Zert said. He stared out the cracked back window, which his father had taped to keep out the bad air.

"It's dangerous here, Zert," his father said.

"We *know* the dangers here," Zert said. Superpox. The trampos who liked to catch kids doing wrong. The drug dealers who sometimes lasered passersby. "The outdoors is scary." He looked down at Chub. She was attacking a pink ball on the couch, and the ball was winning. "But say I went." He tousled the mini-wolf's head. "Could I take Chub?"

"No." His father shook his head.

"Please, Dad," he said. He turned to Chub, kneading her ears in the way that she liked.

"Only humans can go," his father said. "But I've worked out the details. Brew Mahouse will take care of Chub and Okar for us."

Brew Mahouse, the son of one of Jack's best Xterminators, had rescued a puppy from a broken g-pipe once. Zert trusted Brew, but still. "They're my pets. No one will take care of them better than I do." It was hard to breathe.

"Did you hear Dr. Brown say the Rosies have a good school?" his father asked.

Zert gazed down at his hands. He imagined rows and rows of thumbs sitting behind desks. "No," he said. "I'm not leaving."

His father let out a slow sigh. He cracked his knuckles. "It's your decision. I'm not going to make you go. But please. Think hard about this. Think about what this means."

Zert could see his father's worry in the slump of his shoulders. This was the kind of decision that changes everything. "Dad, I know you're doing this for me and I appreciate it . . . but I'd rather take my chances here," Zert said. "Could I . . . could I call Cribbie? Please, Dad."

His father closed his eyes, then slowly opened them again. "You can't tell anyone about Project Rosie," he said. "Remember: It's top secret."

Zert jerked upright. *Whoa!* His father hadn't refused him. "So if I promise not to tell Cribbie, you'll let me talk to—"

"I was protecting you, Zert," his father interrupted, standing up from the chair. "The news about Superpox victims is mostly bad. I didn't want you to have to see your friend . . ." His voice trailed off as he left the room.

Zert's heart thumped fast. He got up from the couch and went to stand at the door of the store. He saw his father head over to a stack of boxes. "Magnetized Dust. Made for use only with official Xter Vacuums," the sign read. His father opened the box on top and pulled out a crystal ring. Its screen drooped. It was Zert's battered I-ring.

For the second time in two days, his father had surprised him. Zert hadn't bothered to look in the boxes of unsold merchandise. That hiding place had seemed too obvious.

His father approached Zert and handed him the I-ring.

In his outstretched palm, it weighed next to nothing. But this I-ring was the way to reach Cribbie. It was his key to the whole world.

9

BLISTERS, WELTS, BOILS, PUS

Even before he sat all the way down on the couch, Zert spoke the command, "Messages." It had been a whole day since he last saw Cribbie. His friend *must* have called.

Sure enough, Cribbie's scratchy voice floated out from the blank plasma screen. "Don't believe everything you hear. I'm not doing so bad," his voice said.

Relief washed over Zert's body like a warm bath.

His I-ring was an inexpensive model without holo-image features, so callers remained flat images on his screen. But he should have been able to at least see Cribbie as his friend delivered the message. Zert pushed the imaging button again, but the small balloon-shaped screen remained transparent.

"I should be up and around in the next few days," Cribbie said.

Listening to a voice waft out of his I-ring without having a view of the person gave him an eerie feeling, as if he were talking to a ghost.

"Then we can track down Mr. Etc. and set up another trash

war," Cribbie said. He started coughing. When he could breathe again, he gasped out, "See ya."

Cribbie must have not turned his visual transmitter on when he left the message. Maybe his friend hadn't wanted Zert to see his boils. He scanned the date in the lower right corner of the empty screen. Two days ago. "Next," he said quickly.

When Zert hadn't called him back, Cribbie would have guessed that Jack had hidden Zert's I-ring. He would also have known that Zert would eventually talk his father into giving it back. His friend would have understood that Zert was worried, so Cribbie would have left another message . . . unless . . .

The head and shoulders of a man, a stranger, appeared on the screen next. He had eyebrows shaped like rainbows, only black. His implanted cheeks were only slightly rounder and fuller than his expensive chin. His tie, a blue bar of color above his collarbone, lit up his dark shirt.

Zert was glad this man was on a tele-screen. He wouldn't want to be in the same room with him.

"Bezert Cage. I'm Lawyer Freeze. Your court-appointed lawyer."

Oh no. "Save. Next," Zert said.

Roal Vimen, Cribbie's older brother, popped up on the screen. He had on a black T-shirt with the logo "Flade Street Holo-theater." Roal worked for Dan the Growl, the holo-theater's bouncer, as his assistant. Unlike Cribbie, who was broad and round, Roal had a slight build and a weasel-like face.

"You've probably heard," Roal said, talking fast. "Cribbie's in bad shape. We're at the Mobile Health Clinic—over on M street. I'll let ya know." The screen went black.

"Next," Zert said tersely.

Snow Blakely's photo pulsed. Her reddish-brown hair was clipped short and curled around her head. *I've missed you, Snow.*

Then a group message from Snow popped up.

Snow's mother taught at St. Lulu's, and earlier that year, Snow had taken it upon herself to send out a notice concerning the death of their classmate Jayle Papetus, a girl Zert barely knew.

Each square of the message board contained a photo of a kid in the seventh grade at St. Lulu's. Snow had marked Jayle's photo with an *X*.

Holding his breath, Zert scanned the squares to find Cribbie. His gaze swept the row of *V*s. He gasped when he spotted a black *X*. Oh no! It covered Cribbie's photo. Snow had to be wrong.

"Next."

Roal's narrow face appeared on the screen. A patch of wiry hair thatched his mouth. His eyes were swollen and red. "He didn't make it, Zert."

Zert dropped the I-ring on the couch. Cribbie, Mr. Fearless, the toughest guy in their whole class and his best friend, was dead. He felt the tears well up inside of him. He wouldn't cry. Thirteen-year-olds didn't cry. He was too tough to cry.

He had no idea how much time had passed when his father entered the room and bustled over to him. "Did you reach him?" He held out his hand to collect the I-ring.

Zert shook his head. He didn't trust himself to speak.

But his father seemed to take in the situation at a glance. "I was afraid of this," he said.

"You're not always right! You just *think* you are!" Zert shouted.

His father's face tightened. But when he spoke, his tone was mild. "I'm so sorry, son."

Zert looked away. Cribbie would never play zoink ball again; he'd never wage another trash war.

His father grabbed Zert's right hand. He squeezed it hard—too hard—as he stared down at it.

Zert followed his father's gaze. One of his freckles looked iffy. It was raised and too pink—a baby blister. "What is it?" he gasped.

This was probably how it had started for Cribbie. One blister, no bigger than an ant, and the next thing he knew, his body was covered in them, even his tongue. Then the blisters swelled up into welts, and when they erupted into boils, as quickly as that, his friend was dying. He felt small and helpless. It was so . . . unfair.

His father dropped his hand. His worried eyes searched Zert's. "The vaccine is effective even after exposure, so long as you don't have any bursting boils."

Zert would still have a chance if he got the vaccine before the disease progressed.

He looked down at the iffy freckle again. It could be a mosquito bite. But it could also be a blister. "OK, Dad. Let's go." He felt his throat catch. *Cribbie!*

His father nodded. "But I want to make sure you understand one more thing." Standing in the middle of the room with his hands loosely clenched, his father looked like he did when he had pushed his mother's ashes into the g-pipe, sending them to the sky cemetery upstairs.

"What's that?" Zert asked.

"This is permanent," his father said.

Like death.

10

A SAD WIND

Everything had to be just right: the store quiet and him standing in the middle of the room with Okar's cage on one side and Chub's on the other. He couldn't look directly at the counter but kind of sideways. He had to concentrate hard.

Then Zert could imagine that his mom had just stepped out of their apartment.

I'll be back soon, honey.

Flowers Cage was a wind that blew past and left him sad.

In the animated photo of his parents' wedding, she looked impossibly young. In the photo of his fourth birthday party, there was a shadow over half of her face. He could only see one green eye and the upward swing of her smile. It wasn't the way he wanted to remember her.

Now, when he tried to paint a picture of her in his mind, he could only see pieces. Her milky white teeth. Her skinny legs. The green fabric of her favorite shirt. Although he had given up trying to fit these bits into a full-sized image, tonight he could sense her presence. She was going to come through the door any minute. *What do you want for dinner?* She'd fix a hot meal. No chips for dinner like usual.

If he tuned everything else out, he could still hear the songs that she played on the Music Mixer while she worked behind the counter. "*If I get a vacation, I'll take it in my freezer. Do you want my love baked, boiled, or fried?*"

The feeling sat lightly on his shoulder. It was a warm, cold, happy, sad, silent feeling, and it smelled like flowers and pickles. But if he tried to hold on to it, it disappeared.

His father came in. "What are you doing standing in the dark, son?"

"Remembering," Zert said.

His father's face softened. "You need to get to bed. We have a big day tomorrow," he said after a few moments.

"Dad, are you sure this is the right thing to do?" Zert asked, still looking around. If they left the store, he'd have to leave the mom-feeling behind, too.

His father sighed. "Zert, you are more precious to me than life. This is the best idea that I have."

Chub began howling.

His father paused. "Can I see your right hand?" he asked.

Zert stared down at the iffy spot. He was pretty sure it hadn't grown. "It's OK, Dad."

"I tried, but they wouldn't let us leave tonight," his father said. "Hopefully . . ." He didn't finish his sentence.

> > >

Zert rolled over in bed. As he opened his eyes, he sensed that today was special—maybe a holiday even.

"Zert, are you awake?" his father's voice clipped his daydream short. "Let's get going. We have a lot to do."

Then it all came back to him. Today was the opposite of a

holiday. Today, he and his father had an appointment with . . . a doctor. *A shrink.* He couldn't even smile at his own joke.

He stared down at the iffy spot. Nothing had changed overnight. It had been a long night as he tossed and turned.

He pulled on his favorite jeans and then used *eenie, meenie, miney, mo, catch Chub by the toe* to pick a blue T-shirt, the T-shirt he would wear when he shrunk. When he was ready, he picked up his backpack and took one last look around his room before heading down the hall.

He found his father waiting in the living room. "Are you OK?" he asked Zert.

Zert looked down at both his hands again. "Yeah. Maybe the bump is an insect bite, Dad."

"We can't take any chances," his father said as he moved closer. He scanned Zert's hands and arms, then noticed Zert's backpack. "Dr. Brown said you can't bring anything," he said, but not in a sharp tone.

Zert dropped his backpack to the floor. Nothing he really cared about could fit in his backpack anyway. Chub. The holo-imagetube. The purple couch his mom bought. His whole room. Life as he knew it.

His father picked up his wedding day photo from the desk. "I'm going to keep him safe, Flowers," he said to the photo before slipping it into his front pocket.

Last night's bag of chips sat on the couch. Zert reached for the bag and pressed a handful in his mouth. Maybe they would be his last chips. But he had forgotten to seal the bag, and the chips were soft, not crunchy. *Yuck.*

"We're leaving in five minutes," his father said before walking out of the living room.

When Zert went into the store, he found Uncle Marin sitting at the table, talking into his I-ring.

He stuffed the bag of chips into his back pocket and headed over to Chub's cage.

Usually, Chub howled when she heard him coming and raked the bars with her tiny claws. But this morning, the cage was empty.

"Zert, stay away from Chub's cage!" his father called out suddenly. Zert could hear his father's footsteps hurrying toward the store.

"Where is she?" Zert demanded.

His father burst into the room, then stood there when he saw Zert. His eyes darted around the store. He was popping his knuckles. "Brew came for her and Okar early this morning," he said quietly.

"What?" Zert looked over at Okar's cage and found it empty too. "But you didn't even let me say good-bye." He stepped closer to Chub's empty cage. Her blue bowl and black blanket were the two loneliest-looking things on this planet.

"Stand back," his father said. "Someday you'll understand."

"I can't believe you didn't even let me say good-bye!" Zert cried.

"Jack, tell him about—" Uncle Marin said. He was standing near the door to the street, as if raring to go.

His father interrupted, "Let me handle this, Marin."

"OK. I'll meet you out front." Uncle Marin walked out the door, triggering the store's greeting. It was broken, and sometimes it rang not only when people came in but also when they walked out of the store. This was another thing Zert would miss.

"Tell me what?" Zert asked. Marin closed the front door behind him.

"Chub has Superpox," his father said to Zert, looking down.

"What!"

"This morning," his father said, swallowing slowly. "I found her sick. Her face was . . . covered in red boils."

"But how? The store has been closed."

"I know," his father said. But there was something he wasn't saying.

Zert's stomach tightened. He had opened the door. Chub had sniffed Cribbie's glow ball. He had exposed his pet to danger.

He had cradled Chub in his arms last night. It could already be too late for him. *Shrink or die.*

An itch arose in the center of his back. Superpox wasn't always predictable. He wanted to rip his T-shirt off and ask his dad to check. But what he didn't know couldn't hurt him. At least, not yet.

He rushed over to his father and folded his arms around him.

11

THE PUZZLE OF BRIGHT RED LIPS

Glade smiled with her red lips up at Uncle Marin, who was a head taller. "Promise me, Marin, that you'll stay safe." She brushed his bangs back from his forehead. She wasn't wearing an O-mask. Even though she was pretty young, she was one of the lucky vaccinated ones.

Uncle Marin and Glade were standing together underneath Roach Cowboy, the tall sign for Cage & Sons that his great-grandfather had installed decades ago. The roach's wings were raised as if it were about to fly off into the gray day. A red cowboy hat shaded its face, leaving the roach's mysterious smile barely visible. The enormous figure—designed to be seen from blocks away—had brought in many customers over the years. Low City DC was infested with roaches, and everybody—even drug dealers—hated them.

His father stood in the doorway. "Ready, Marin?" he called.

"Glade is going with us to the taxi-pad," Uncle Marin said.

Zert rolled his eyes at his father.

"Lead on," his father said, ignoring him.

Uncle Marin looped his arm in Glade's, and the pair stepped onto the moving sidewalk with their heads bent together, whispering.

Zert followed his father outside, breathing in the stinky, thick, beautiful air. Like Glade, he didn't wear an O-mask. He had convinced his father that a mask was pointless. If things went according to plan, he'd be vaccinated against Superpox in a few hours. If not, well, a mask was too little, too late.

The iffy-looking spot on his right hand hadn't changed. The bubble on top was still tiny. But his back itched furiously. The itch was in the dead center, and he couldn't get a good scratch. *Cribbie. Chub.* Zert's throat tightened.

Except for several dozen lifters rolling down the street toward the financial district and a few individuals wearing privacy hoods, Flade Street was deserted. The traffic flew overhead in the network of red, purple, green, and blue highways. And the gaseous tubes leading to and from the Up City were clogged with lifters transporting people to work.

No Superpox upstairs. Only the vaccinated lived and worked in the upper cities.

As they crossed the street, the beautiful green holostatues of liberty held up their torches like blazing suns. *Good-bye,* he mouthed to them as the moving sidewalk carried him past.

The giant poster for "Dream Hat," the latest blockbuster product from Far Out Toys, showed a hazy photograph of white clouds. "A camera for your dreams. Be the first one on your block to own one."

Zert wiped the sweat off his forehead. If only he *were* dreaming.

The sign for Eco-Hotel, the site of the lifter taxi stand, loomed in the distance. Each of the hotel's expensive rooms was based on a vanished ecosystem: a rain forest, a coral reef, a mountain valley, a redwood forest.

He pushed the cool button on his T-shirt to activate the

micro-fans in the fabric as he stepped off the sidewalk and joined his father in the short line for taxi-lifters.

The older model taxi-lifters with huge propellers and obvious air vents weren't used any longer to fly to the Up Cities but for across-town transport. Although the shiny faces of robots manned most, a few humans sat behind the automated dashboards, scowling over their com-devices or drinking their morning vita-coffees.

"Marin?" his father called over his shoulder as they moved up in the line.

A few yards away, tears rolled down Glade's cheeks, and probably not from the air pollution. Uncle Marin leaned over and whispered into her ear. She clapped her hand over her mouth and grinned.

Uncle Marin grinned back, and his foreboard lit up. That broken exclamation point at the end was embarrassing.

Uncle Marin hugged Glade, then ambled over to them.

"I'll talk to you soon," Glade shouted after him.

Uncle Marin waved but didn't answer.

Zert was confused. A thumb-sized Uncle Marin wouldn't be able to work an I-ring, even with his feet.

"Should we go robotic?" his father asked when Uncle Marin joined them.

"Sure," Uncle Marin said.

His father preferred human drivers. But robotic was probably safer for top-secret Mission Thumb.

His father climbed into the back seat of a beat-up old model, and Zert followed. He banged his ankles on the bicycle pedals crammed underneath his seat. Most lifters offered exercise equipment, and this economy model was no exception.

The taxi's weather system blew out freezing air, and he turned off the fans in his shirt. He was drenched with sweat, and not because of the heat.

Uncle Marin settled into the passenger's seat next to the driver. Like all service bots, the driver had a silly smile and wide, exaggerated eyes. His body, functional but not realistic, was a "Tin-Man" design with no faux clothing.

Uncle Marin recited the address and fed the dashboard with a credit chip.

The radiation meter on the control panel flashed yellow, indicating only a low level of threat today.

Churning dust, the lifter sucked up air to gather force for the takeoff. It began to rise, wobbling slightly.

Zert didn't get to travel in taxi-lifters often, and he wanted to enjoy himself. But he also knew this could be his last ever ride in a lifter. Worse, his back had started itching again. He had no way of checking to see whether it had erupted into a field of blisters. He didn't want to ask his father.

Blisters, then welts, then boils, then pus, then . . . He thought of Chub. He thought of Cribbie. He leaned his head against the window and sighed.

>>>

The taxi-lifter exited the blue high-highway and began circling. Once they got below the pollution clouds, an ordinary suburban neighborhood came into view, with g-pipe portals flashing in the sun and vivid green Instant Trees dotting the fake grass yards.

The lifter's wheels clanked as they lowered for landing in front of a midsized gray house with a darker gray roof. An oak tree with uplifted branches grew in the front yard. Its leaves were green and yellow, not like an Instant Tree, whose leaves were of identical size and color. A series of sprinklers sprayed water onto the trunk.

"This is it?" Zert said incredulously. "I thought we were going to an office building . . . a hospital . . ."

"A lab . . . with guards," his father said, looking around. "I did too. But think about it. What better disguise than an ordinary house? It makes sense."

"Thank you for riding with Auto-lift," said a voice from the screen. Magnets clicked. The doors slid open.

After the chill of the taxi, the outdoor air seemed to pant with heat. Zert followed his father and uncle out of the lifter into a neighborhood that was eerily still and quiet. They stepped onto the moving sidewalk to be transported to the front of the house.

As the taxi-lifter took off, tiny tornadoes of dust spun around Zert. When he opened his eyes, the lifter had nearly reached the blue high-highway in the sky.

Uncle Marin pointed at the back of the house as they drew near. "See that docked lifter attached to the back of the house? Project Rosie never stays in one place for long."

Zert rubbed his eyes to get rid of some of the dust. As he did, a roach scampered by. He tried to stomp the roach with his foot.

"Zert, stop playing around," his father called to him. He and Uncle Marin were already standing on the front porch.

Squish. Zert's shoe came down on the roach.

"Zert," his father scolded.

Zert jogged along the sidewalk, stumbled off the end, and took the final few steps on his own power to reach the ordinary-looking front door. The green grass mat on the porch read:

The smallest forge our future

Zert knew he had a future. He just didn't know what kind. He might have Superpox and die. Or he might live and shrink.

The front door sensors picked up their weight, and the door opened immediately. A figure in a white med-coat waved them in. Zert ground his heel into the word *future* before stepping inside.

12

A MYSTERIOUS STRANGER

Dr. Brown looked up and down the street before he shut the door behind them. "You left no clues as to your whereabouts?" Dr. Brown asked.

While Uncle Marin, his father, and Dr. Brown huddled together to discuss whether anyone could possibly have followed them, Zert studied the old-fashioned hallway. Pink roses dotted blue wallpaper. Roses. *Rosies!* Was this a joke?

Stairs, rather than a people mover, led to the next floor. Wood instead of that durable material, cybratom, covered the floors. Old photos lining the walls showed people doing the impossible things they did in the old days, like getting married in gardens, picnicking in fields of wildflowers, and fishing out of boats.

The house reminded him of visiting his Grandma Cage before she died.

But this house didn't feel safe and inviting in the same way that his grandma's home had. And he felt strangely itchy all over—not just on his back—but as if he were being watched. His eyes followed the wooden banister to the top of the stairs, where he caught a glimpse of a man with short-cropped reddish hair. The wild pattern of his retro-Hawaiian shirt swirled with greens, blues, and purples. The man stared at him, his eyes alive with curiosity. It was as if he was wondering, "Are you one of those weirdos who's getting shrunk?"

"Who's that?" Zert asked. But before he'd even finished the question, the man took a step back and disappeared into the shadows.

The adults looked in the direction of the empty stairwell.

Dr. Brown's eyes shifted uncomfortably. "Doctor Rosario's son, Benre, is here for a visit."

If shrinking was so great, why wasn't Dr. Rosario's son a thumb? Zert wanted to call out, "Hey Benre, you can take my place." But he remembered Chub's empty cage, and his stomach began to hurt.

Uncle Marin's gaze lingered on the spot where Benre had been standing.

"Where's Doctor Rosario? Aren't we going to get to meet him?" Jack asked.

"Unfortunately, Doctor Rosario was called away this morning. As you can imagine, maintaining Project Rosie is a major responsibility. He sends his regrets."

It was an excuse if he'd ever heard one. Dr. Rosario was probably off twiddling his thumbs in some beautiful place.

"Hmm," Jack mumbled. His dad always said you could tell a lot about an organization by its founder. Zert would have liked to have met the guy too. If he looked like a mad scientist, then he'd know for sure he was the subject of a crazy experiment.

"Come in. Come in," Dr. Brown said, motioning Zert into the office.

It looked normal, except for a screen that hung on the wall with thousands of tiny blinking lights clustered in one corner. And he couldn't ignore the tiny chairs on the doctor's desk. They were sling back and thatched with green and black cybratom, like the ones at the indoor beach inside Ocean Mall. The chairs were the perfect size for some little thumbs to sit back and relax in.

Zert sat down in a regular-sized chair and turned his head to face a line of tall metal boxes against the wall. He did not want to know what he was staring at.

His breakfast chips rose up in his throat. He took a deep breath to try to settle his stomach. There was so much wrong with this plan. What if the Mag-Lev machine killed him, his father, and his uncle instead of shrinking them? Even worse, what if it actually worked and he became the size of his thumb? He could end up in Rosie land, in Rocky Mountain National Park, miles away from everything he knew and loved, barred forever from modern life.

Zert began to squirm in the straight-backed chair he sat in. He rubbed his back against the chair, but the movement didn't quiet the itch. He tried not to think about the worst. Blisters, then welts, then boils, then pus, then . . .

If I make it, he vowed silently to himself, *I'll never risk my life for something stupid again.*

His father's face was bloodless. His fingers gripped the sides of his chair. Zert thought about how he'd brought his father into this too.

"We're excited to be here," Uncle Marin said, as if shrinking were as ordinary as foaming his teeth. Zert turned away before his uncle's stupid foreboard lit up.

"Let's get the exam over with," his father said.

"Good idea," Dr. Brown said. "Come with me, Zert."

The doctor took his identity wand out of his pocket. It was a standard model, the length and width of his ring finger. He waved it in front of a gleaming white door, and the side panels retracted.

As Zert followed him, he glanced over his shoulder at his father. His father stared straight ahead, his large hands clenching his knees.

The sharp itch kept biting into his back, no matter how hard he willed it to go away.

A narrow table took up most of the examination room, and complicated metal instruments lined the walls. As Zert hoisted himself onto the table, he tried to forget Cribbie's blistered face that night outside the store's front door . . . and Chub's empty cage . . . If only he hadn't opened the front door. But he hadn't meant any harm. He had only wanted to help his friend.

Sometimes, nothing made sense.

Like Project Rosie.

Dr. Brown waved his hand in the corner at his RASM portal, the newest model of computer, and said, "Begin calculations." He nodded at Zert. "The calculations have to be checked and rechecked, so we'll begin that process as I conduct the exam."

A screen on the wall lit up with his name, "Bezert Jackson Cage." Measurements lined up next to some pictures of odd shapes that he assumed had to be his organs.

He reached around and tried to scratch his back. But his arm wouldn't bend enough, and the itch raged worse than ever.

Dr. Brown walked over to the table and checked Zert's reflexes and his blood pressure. He listened to Zert's heart and lungs. In between, the doctor jotted down notes on his tablet. He met Zert's gaze.

"Strip off your shirt, please."

Zert peeled off his shirt one arm at a time. As long as he didn't know for sure, he could pretend he was healthy. He began shivering, and it wasn't because the room's weather system was set on blizzard. The dead center of his back itched uncontrollably.

Dr. Brown pressed a glow ball against his forehead, until the object ionized and stuck. Holding a magnifier in one hand, he began examining Zert's hands and arms. Then he turned to his back.

Zert held his breath. The blisters on his back had grown into welts. They were rising like fiery volcanoes from his skin. They'd joined up to form boils. They'd start popping soon, and he would feel the warm, wet pus gush out and drain down his back.

"See any signs of the pox?" his father's shout came through the open door.

"All I see . . . ," the doctor began. As the doctor straightened up to answer his father, the round light aimed straight into Zert's eyes. Behind the magnifying glass, the doctor's eye had grown to ten times bigger than normal. It didn't seem like a body part, but a weird, living creature. "Is a healthy crop of freckles," Dr. Brown called back.

He exhaled. *I'm going to live!*

Yes, he would need to live as a tiny person. But his feelings weren't tiny. They were BIG.

13

KILLER UNDERWEAR

Thousands of lights blinked on and off on the map. It hung on the wall behind the desk.

The map with the blinking lights reminded Zert of the trip he and his father had taken to the graveyard observatory. His mother's urn was marked, but his father had forgotten his skyoculars, and all they could see were millions of blinking lights.

"What's the story with that map?" Zert asked, nodding at the screen on the wall.

"The fifty thousand lights all represent Rosies," Dr. Brown said.

Zert gulped. Soon, he'd be light number 50,003.

"Once you're minimized, you'll head to a place called Ellis Log. It will be marked. That's where you'll get your vaccination pill."

"A pill?" his father said, scowling a bit. "You didn't mention that. I've never heard of a vaccination pill before."

"They're effective." Dr. Brown paused. "Think of the suspicion we'd arouse if we started making tiny syringes."

That reminded him. "Why is this top secret?" Zert asked.

Dr. Brown said, "Can you imagine what would happen if the

world found out about us? The reporters? The holo-imagetube cameras?"

Minimized *would be a really good reality show.*

Dr. Brown touched his wrist device, and a beam of light flowed out. "Zert, I recommended to your father and uncle that you all head for a settlement called Paradise, population 103." The beam from Dr. Brown's wrist device hit the map in the bottom right-hand corner. "Some of our settlements have grown so big that they risk discovery. Paradise still has lots of room to grow."

Paradise was a dot next to a square marked *parking lot.* "Why is the city close to a parking lot? It seems like Rosies would want to be as far away from . . ." He hesitated. Thank goodness Rosies were humans. *Not something even worse, like vampires.* "What do the little people call us?" he asked.

"The Rosies call us BIGS," Dr. Brown said.

"It seems like Rosies would want to be as far away from BIGS as possible," Zert said.

"I had the same thought, Zert," his father said.

"The lottery system enacted by the World Council to protect the parks ensures that almost no one uses them," Dr. Brown said. "However, you know human nature. Even a few people leave a lot of trash. The Rosies like to scavenge."

"So Rosies hunt for food?" Zert said.

"I suspect food is only part of their interest. Since all the Rosies kids were born in Paradise," Dr. Brown explained, "the BIG world fascinates them."

"*Born* in Paradise?" Low City DC had hololaser movie theaters, idearooms, anti-gravity fun houses, inside vacation spots that mimicked the lost outdoors, and a million other things that a kid wouldn't know about if he'd only vacationed in a parking lot.

Dr. Brown nodded. "Rosie kids have only ever known that world," he said.

Questions tumbled together inside Zert's head. *What kind of music do they listen to? Do they learn about BIGS in school? What do they do for fun?* He settled on: "How many kids live in Paradise?"

"We aren't in close communication, but I'd guess a dozen or so," Dr. Brown said.

"How old are they?"

"Paradise was founded fifteen years ago, so the oldest adolescents should be thirteen," Dr. Brown said.

"Their parents did this to them *before* the first Superpox epidemic?" Zert asked.

"Yes," Dr. Brown said. "They did. A lot of our clients were minimized after the Nuclear Mistake."

Clients? "Are we *paying* money to get shrunk?" Zert blurted out, turning to stare at his father.

His father's neck turned red. "We won't need money where we're going," he said.

"You're only paying your costs," Dr. Brown interrupted. "Even though a vaccination for a Rosie sells for a fraction of what it costs for a BIG, we still have to charge you." He paused. "And the ride in the 3-D Mag Lev is"—he rolled his eyes—"so expensive."

No one Zert knew had ever traveled by 3-D Mag Lev, and he had always wished that one day he would be able to. But he wasn't going to get to enter an ordinary 3-D Mag Lev. His would have a minimizer function.

"I told your father and uncle this, but I should warn you that after you're minimized, you'll briefly pass out," Dr. Brown said. "Upon awakening, some Rosies are disoriented. But everyone is usually fine within a few hours."

Usually fine? What happened when things went *un*usually? What happened if something went wrong? Would he be a dumb thumb? And what if the shrinking wasn't evenly done? Could he explode or end up in pieces? Would he become a huge arm with a tiny person attached to it?

His father and uncle just nodded. They had heard this all before. Zert took a deep breath and forced himself to listen.

"Our arrival booth," Dr. Brown was saying, "is located in the base of an ordinary light post next to the parking lot. That's where you'll wake up." He glanced at his wrist. "You have plenty of time to reach Paradise by nightfall. The parking lot will be to your east. Ellis Log will be to your west. You'll find clothes and backpacks, along with the vaccination pill, in Ellis Log." His gaze focused on Zert. "Remember to take your vaccination pill, Zert. We don't want to take any chances."

Dr. Brown stood up. "If there are no more questions, let's get busy." He pointed at the series of metal boxes that Zert had noticed earlier. "These are our 3-D Mag Levs," he said. "We have five of them."

Zert had more questions, but his father stood up with his gaze fixed on the 3-D Mag Levs.

Dr. Brown opened a drawer and held up some white gowns. "Please remove your clothes."

Just when Zert thought things couldn't get any weirder. "You mean I have to do this naked?" he asked.

"I have this for you." Dr. Brown handed them each a robe. "These disintegrate midflight." He paused. "Even your underwear could smother you on landing."

What a death. Zert took the robe and started to undress. He definitely did not want to be killed by his own underwear.

"Not only that; the Rosies don't want technology in the settlements. Rare goods cause trouble," Dr. Brown said. "You can be assured that all your valuables will be donated to Project Rosie."

Zert's Cool Man shirt with only one hundred mini-fans, his pants made from Breathe fabric, and his Wing sandals, "Faster than the fastest feet," already lay in a pile near his feet. "I don't have any rare goods," he said.

Dr. Brown gestured to the T-shirt on the floor. "Your T-shirt alone, Zert, would cause a sensation." He approached Zert, holding a straw basket. It looked like an offering basket for a church. He knew Dr. Brown was a doctor, but still, Zert felt embarrassed as he took off his underwear and dropped it into the basket. As fast as he could, he slipped his robe on.

His father took something out of the pocket of his shirt. It was the photo of Zert's mother on their wedding day. He held it up for Dr. Brown. "I already know the answer, but I have to ask anyway. May I keep my wife's photo?"

Dr. Brown shook his head. "I'm sorry. No exceptions. It's for your own safety."

Zert saw his father's eyes grow moist. His father kissed the picture, gazed at it one last time, then dropped it into the basket. Zert tried to catch a last glimpse of his mother in the basket also.

His father yanked his T-shirt over his head. He dropped his blue jeans on the floor, and they made the same sad shape as Chub's blanket in her empty cage earlier that day. The pocket of his father's jeans was torn. His father had worn them almost every day for the last month. Like Zert, his father was leaving the only home he'd ever had. But Zert had lived on Flade Street for only thirteen years; his father had been there for forty-eight.

Uncle Marin had stripped and changed into his robe. He was whistling as he dropped a handful of crypto credit coins into the basket, along with his I-ring and identity wand. He placed a sleek xiathium tube on top of the pile.

"Blood red," the label on the tube said. "One application, and you'll love your lips forever."

Glade's? Glade didn't need a tube of Permanent Lipstick. She already had permanently red lips.

"When I close the door after you enter, transmission will be instantaneous," Dr. Brown said, pointing toward the line of 3-D Mag Levs.

Eek! The moment had come. Barefoot and wearing only his robe, Zert found himself counting his steps as he walked toward the line of boxes. One. Two . . .

"This is an adventure of a lifetime, boys. Remember that. An adventure of a lifetime," Uncle Marin said. His forehead flashing, he hurried over to the wall.

Jack's jaw was set in a grim line.

Zert drew closer to the door. Three. Four. Five. He felt like a prisoner walking a gangplank.

Dr. Brown carefully opened the first door. "Zert," he said, "I wish you well."

Jack reached out and squeezed Zert's hand. "I love you," he said. He pulled Zert into a hug.

"Me too," Zert said. He did not want to, but after a moment, he let go of his father, and with his hands clenched into fists, he entered the box. He saw his father's knotted eyebrows as he looked back. His uncle wasn't smiling either. Would this be the last time he would see them? His feet felt like lead weights as all the blood in his body rushed to his head.

The box was smaller than a vertical people mover in an office building and barely bigger than a coffin. It had no windows. When the door closed, there would be no way he could escape. Zert tried to breathe evenly, but the metal room was stuffy. His breaths sounded outsized as they echoed off the walls.

Dr. Brown stepped up, and before Zert could even wave, he wrenched the door shut. Metal clanged, and the room went from dimly lit to pitch black.

A second clang sounded, and Zert heard the doctor shout, "What are you doing?"

Something had gone wrong. Were they going to die?

PART TWO

14

BETRAYAL COMES IN MANY SIZES

Zert couldn't tell if he was racing or if it was the walls of the metal box that were sliding past him, faster than the speed of light. Pink, purple, and blue beams of color pelted him on all sides until they began to blur together into a single, blinding white light. His body was a balloon, quickly losing air, and he was being sucked down a drain . . . or was it a dream . . . or a dream of a drain? As though a giant were sitting on his chest, his chest contracted. He felt as if his ribs were starting to crack, and the breath left his lungs. He smelled something strange, like cauliflower doused in chemicals. His last thought before he blacked out was: *This is worse than being crushed by an asteroid.*

Zert opened his eyes to see a room filled with green light. He was lying on a dirt floor, naked. His father wasn't there. The room was empty.

Across from him, an archway opened to the outside. Light poured in. Everything looked normal, except for the walls, which glowed green. As he crawled toward the white light, he tried to remember where the doctor said they would land.

Inside an ordinary light pole.

This place looked like a train station. The machine must not have worked. He looked at his arms, legs, and feet and decided that he was still his same size. He felt like a contestant on his favorite show, someone who had landed in an unexpected destination.

"Is that you, Zert?" his father called.

"Yes!" Zert yelled, relieved to hear his father's voice. He neared the opening.

"Come on out. It's safe!"

Zert crawled through the hole in the metal wall on his knees and struggled to stand.

The sun beamed down on him, but it wasn't the sun he was used to. This one was bright yellow, not yellow smudged with gray, and it stood out, huge and swollen, against the blue sky. The sun he knew was much smaller and was usually covered by pollution clouds. He reached out and touched the air. Only air. Not glass. This wasn't some virtual reality game, but something was warping his vision.

Zert's father wasn't there. He looked behind him to the train station, then he craned his neck to peer up and up and up at what appeared to be a green hat far above them. The lamp was so tall that Zert could barely see its top. He was standing in front of an ordinary light pole.

He had shrunk. His head throbbed with the craziness of what had happened to him. *I'm a Rosie now.*

He spotted his father's head moving through what appeared to be a tangled jungle of green fronds, ivy, roots, vines, and trees. It looked like the kind of lush jungle he'd learned about in school, one that covered the planet in the days when dinosaurs lived.

He could see glass beads clinging to a tall green stalk. One of the beads slid down the stalk and burst open when it hit the dirt ground. *A drop of dew on grass.*

A dog crossed the trail on its way to bury a bone. But its

movements were not wild and freewheeling like a dog's but stiffer and more controlled, like a robot's. Oh, and the beast had six legs. It wasn't a dog at all but an ant. It was plodding along with a piece of wood in its mouth, and its antennae were probing the air like a blind man feeling his way.

The trunk of a nearby tree looked taller than the tallest building he'd ever seen. It reached high into the cloudless sky, and he could barely make out its leafy green top. The trunk was covered in bark in irregular patches, not perfect squares. Even if he searched, he would never be able to locate any model numbers on its base. *This was a real tree.*

When his father came into view, Zert saw that he'd tied two short, narrow green leaves over his body with a length of vine. He dragged two more leaves. When he spotted Zert, he put his hand over his chest and then gestured to the forest around them. He approached Zert and held him. "This is the most beautiful place I've ever seen," he said.

He helped Zert cover up with the leaves and vine. "Let's get to Ellis Log and get some real clothes."

A blast of wind rushed past, and swirling brown leaves, each the size of a blanket, floated around them like magic carpets. The leaves smelled fresh and nutty with the baked scent of dried earth.

"It's . . . it's beautiful," Zert said. But that didn't seem to capture how small he felt compared to the forever blue sky, how colorless he felt compared to the green world around him, how clean it all was. The air tasted brand-new, not used by hundreds of people and companies and then spit out, like old chewing gum.

A deafening whir startled him. His father whipped around and stared in the opposite direction. When he followed his father's gaze, Zert gasped.

It was a parking lot. One for giants. A lifter was about to take off, and its headlights—planet-sized eyes—stared out at him. Its fender, a metal mouth, grimaced. Its roof was so high and its frame so wide that a whole city of Rosies could live on one of its front seats. The metal monster whined, then rose from the ground. Wind roared and spun around them like a tornado, a category 10 hurricane.

Zert was powerless against the wind. Dust stung his skin, face, and eyes. His hair whipped wildly. His feet were unable to keep a grip, and without doing anything, he bounced and floated above the dirt as if the earth had become a trampoline. His father shoved him back inside the light pole. As the wind gusted around them, Zert clung to the pole's frame to try to keep from being blown away. It was too slippery to hold on to, and he ended up just pressing his weight against the curved metal.

When the wind finally stopped wailing, Jack ventured back into the open, and Zert poked his head out.

The lifter rose up through the lacy green ceiling of leaves into the cloudless sky, toward the blue, green, red, and purple gaseous highways. It turned onto the blue highway and headed for somewhere he would never go again.

"Dad," Zert said, remembering Low City DC. "Where's Uncle Marin?"

"I don't think he made it," his father said. "I searched. The arrival booth is empty."

Zert stuck his head back inside the light pole. "Uncle Marin!" His voice rang uselessly around the circular space. Where was the man who'd come up with this idea in the first place? Where was the guy who'd wanted them to minimize?

It seemed like a lifetime ago that first one Mag Lev door, then a second one, had closed. Then, Dr. Brown had yelled, "What's going on?" Zert remembered smelling cauliflower and chemicals and then there was nothing.

But before that, there was plenty. His uncle's strange and excited behavior in the doctor's office and Glade's parting comment of "I'll see you soon" as Marin left for the taxi-lifter. And also . . .

"Dad, did you notice the tube of Permanent Lipstick that Uncle Marin dropped in the basket?" Zert asked.

His father nodded. "What about it, son?"

Once, Cribbie had dressed up as a Superpox victim for Halloween. He had drawn boils on his face with red marker, but when he sweated, the red dye had dripped onto his shirt. Permanent Lipstick never faded. "Do you think . . . Uncle Marin . . . could have drawn those boils on Chub? To make sure I didn't back out?"

"Don't be ridiculous," his father said. He began cracking his knuckles. "Dr. Brown was very clear with us. He told us there were risks. Maybe . . . Marin will still come through."

"Uncle Marin told Glade that he'd see her later," Zert said to his father.

His father closed his eyes slowly, then opened them again. "Maybe he just didn't want to tell her good-bye."

But Zert felt as if he knew better. Uncle Marin, the bold adventurer, had never intended to shrink.

His father shook his head even though Zert hadn't spoken his thought aloud. "He's your mother's brother," he said. "He wouldn't trick us."

Zert's ears grew hot. That third Mag Lev door hadn't closed. "I think he did," he said with a deep breath. "Dad, what about Chub? What if she doesn't have Superpox? Is she OK?"

"I suppose so. Brew came to pick her up. He wouldn't destroy her if he didn't think she was sick," his father said.

Zert felt his throat catch. How could this have happened?

"Why would Marin trick us?" his father asked. He was popping his knuckles.

"I don't know," Zert said. "But remember how he uses stunt doubles when a show is too dangerous? I can't help but feel like we're his doubles."

"We're not even on his show," his father muttered through gritted teeth.

"I get that, but . . . I don't know. It doesn't add up to me." Zert shook his head. "I'm thinking—"

His father interrupted, "Look, we have to make the best of this now." He scanned the forest, the parking lot, and the blue sky. When he spoke again, he sounded as if he had made up his mind. "We can't worry about Marin. He's not here, and we're small. We've got to concentrate on survival. Or . . ." His father's voice trailed off.

"Or else we're toast," Zert said, then added, "Mini-toast."

His father smiled a little. "Speaking of food . . ." He shifted his attention and stared down at the ground.

A shadow had detached itself from the dirt and was writhing.

It was a brown snake, some kind of python that wrapped around people's necks and squeezed them to death. Zert clutched his father's arm.

"Zert, it's just a worm," his father said.

The thought of having to kill their own food instead of buying it prepackaged was bad enough. "Are we going to eat worms?" he asked. When his father didn't answer, Zert felt his mouth go sour and practically shouted, "You're kidding, right?"

"Think about it," his father said as he grabbed the worm's tail. "Mankind has killed most of the mammals in the world, but there are quintillions of insects left." His father yanked on the worm's tail. Or was it the head? The two ends looked the same. But much to Zert's relief, his father's idea for dinner slipped away and dove back into the earth.

Yeah! His dinner had escaped. Zert knelt next to the hole. "I got here by traveling through one kind of wormhole." He peered into the deep hole and smelled only dirt. "If I crawled through this one, think I could go back?"

Jack put his hand on Zert's shoulder. "Good try," he said. "Let's go. We've got to get to Paradise before dark, or else."

Or else what?

15

HEALTHCARE UNDER A LOG

"Our entrance to a new world," his father said.

The log was crumbling around a door reinforced with wood that looked like Popsicle sticks. A sign embedded in the wood read:

Over 12 million people entered this continent through Ellis Island. Welcome to Ellis Log.

"A log," Zert muttered.

"A log," his father repeated in a respectful tone.

Inside, the walls of the unevenly shaped room glowed with the same eerie green light that he had noticed inside the light pole. There was no flooring, just dirt on the ground. Zert started to say, "On," for the laser lights, and then he remembered. *No laser technology. No wind or solar power. No bots. No RASM portals. No holo-imagetubes. No g-pipes.* Ugh. *Not even any electricity.*

Racks of clothes stretched across the room, but this didn't look like any clothing store he'd ever seen. It was too dark and jumbled inside the room. Backpacks were stacked on the floor. Boxes stood piled on a rough-hewn table.

"First things first. Let's get you vaccinated," his father said, smiling. He handed Zert a homemade box. The lettering on it—**"SuPeRPOX vaCCiNe. ONe taBLet CONFeRs iMMuNitY."**—was uneven, as if it had been written by a kindergartner.

The cough tablets at their old neighborhood drug kiosk were always triple-sealed in biodegradable wrappers, but here at Ellis Log, Zert was able to easily tear through the flimsy wrapping of the Superpox vaccine. A single blue tablet came out and rolled around on his palm. It looked a little dirty.

His father nudged him, and Zert put the tablet in his mouth. It sizzled on his tongue.

His father clapped him on his back and beamed. "Finally vaccinated," he declared.

Tears clogged Zert's throat. His father had given up so much for him to have this basic healthcare: his store, his customers, his home, his memories, everything. Unable to speak, Zert turned away and began flipping through some of the clothes on the rack.

Dr. Brown had said, "Your T-shirt alone, Zert, would cause a sensation." Now, as he chose a pair of blue pants and a blue shirt, both covered in pockets, he understood what the doctor meant. Even the cheap clothes he wore every day were much fancier than those he saw here. The stitches in the pants he held were uneven and far apart, as if sewn by a child. He imagined the Rosies wearing their simple, makeshift clothes as he tore off the leaves he had on and slipped into his new clothes. He'd read that old-fashioned cloth didn't heat or cool your body like clothes made from Breathe fabric. But his outfit of one hundred pockets wasn't completely uncomfortable.

He selected a backpack from the floor. Inside it were some tools: a knife, a cooking pan, a rope, and a hammer with a sharp blade. He held the hammer up for his father to see.

"'What's this?'"

"A hatchet," his father said.

In a side pocket of the backpack, Zert found a small container of water. He checked the backpack again. No food.

Shrinking made a person hungry. Dr. Brown had arranged for Zert and his dad to have water, but Dr. Brown should have given them something to eat, too. And worms didn't count.

He'd like to see his uncle eat a worm. Or wear these backward clothes. Or lose over six feet in height.

"Dr. Brown isn't in on whatever Uncle Marin's plan is," Zert told his father. The doctor had sounded surprised when Uncle Marin hadn't stepped into the Mag Lev.

"Zert, please stop talking about your uncle. He might be . . ." His father's voice trailed off. When Zert glanced over at him, he thought his father's blue pants and shirt looked depressingly like a prisoner's uniform. But on his head, his father wore a furry cap with a tail.

Zert had to laugh.

His father stroked the tail.

"What kind of fur is that?" Zert asked.

His father took off the cap and ran his fingers through the tail. "Rat," he said, putting it back on.

Zert shuddered. "Are we going to hunt rats?" he asked.

His father dodged Zert's gaze.

Jack, the rat killer. "You can hunt worms and rats, but I'm not going to," Zert said.

"Our first rule has to be survival," his father said.

Survival.

Zert's stomach rumbled. Had he escaped Superpox just to face starvation?

〉〉〉

A few hours later, it began to rain. From the trail where he and his father had been hiking, Zert saw lightning crack the sky open. It was the longest, thickest, and whitest lightning he had ever seen. And the thunder—deafening in volume—sounded like bones breaking. This was plain rain, not the modern colored rain that he was used to, and it beat the earth in a fury. It seemed as if the entire outdoors was creaking and groaning as the wind bent trees, bushes, and stalks of grass all around them.

Wearing the backpack he'd picked up in Ellis Log, his father darted toward the grass lining the path. "Follow me, Zert!" he yelled. "We need to find cover!" Another flash of lightning illuminated their path up the rise, and the hill took shape. They still had so far to go to reach the top.

In the BIG world, rain that came down this fast and furious fell in one thick sheet. Here, individual drops, the size of his shoes, fell with huge spaces in between them, but Zert couldn't tell where the drops would fall next. He managed to evade two drops, but he got splashed on the head as he joined his father at the edge of the path. His head rang as if he'd been hit in a boxing match by someone wearing a soft glove. *Two points for Zert; one for the sky.*

The cold rain drenched him as a gust of wind raced past.

"Hang on to the roots!" his father shouted over the roar of the storm. "So you won't get blown away!"

Zert dove for cover in the grassy jungle lining the path. The screeching wind tore through his clothes, but he steadied himself by staying close to the blades of grass, which formed a canopy over his head. The wind was picking up speed and growing stronger.

His father seized a stalk of grass. His clothes blowing sideways, Jack turned to say something else, but the wind seemed to tear the words out of his mouth.

Zert gripped the blade as if it were a rope, not letting go of one until he'd grasped another. He battled his way through the rain and mud for what felt like hours. All his effort and concentration were focused on following his father, not getting blown away, not slipping, not stepping on anything scary.

Every five or six steps, his father turned to check on him. Zert waved him on.

The rain slowed, but Zert didn't have time to feel relieved about this before water and mud torrented down the rise. He clung to the blade's roots and tried to get air as a thick soup of water and mud ran over and around him. He had been longing for a big breakfast, but now?

I'll settle for not drowning on my first afternoon in this new world.

16

THINK SMALL

"How m—u—c—h l—o—n—g—e—r?" Zert managed to ask. When his father turned to look back, Zert could see his face was ashen, his hair disheveled, his clothes soaked, and his breathing heavy.

The rain stopped as suddenly as it had begun. They hiked for a while, and now the sun beat down on them like an enemy. The grass provided little shade, and Zert's once-muddy clothes became dry and stiff.

"Just beyond that next rise," his father said after he had caught his breath. His T-shirt, which clung to his belly, was drenched, this time with sweat.

Zert wiped his forehead with the sleeve of his shirt. "You said that the last time."

"I know I did," Jack snapped. "But I hear a stream."

The sun must have gotten to his father. Streams didn't make noise. At least the one in Eco-Hotel didn't.

His father was sweating and breathing hard, but Zert knew he'd never admit he needed a break. "I need to stop, Dad," Zert said and plopped onto the ground, watching his father closely.

"OK," his father said. He stopped and, groaning softly, lowered himself to the ground. He folded his legs slowly.

Zert slipped off the backpack that he had picked up at Ellis Log. He still couldn't believe that neither Drs. Brown nor Rosario had provided any food. He'd had no breakfast, except for those soggy chips, and he'd barely touched the bag that he'd left in his jeans pocket. Zert took a swig from his water bottle. The water tasted so good. He wondered why he had never bothered to drink much of it before.

"How many meters have we walked?" Zert asked.

"Maybe a city block," his father said.

"For regular-sized people, right?" Zert said.

"Yeah. It's been so tough because we've been going uphill."

Zert tried to size the hill as he would have if he'd still been BIG Zert. It seemed only the height of Roach Cowboy, but it felt as high as Mount Everest.

"Ready?" Jack winced as he struggled to stand. "We should go now."

Even though Zert's legs felt better, he thought his father looked as if he needed to rest a bit longer. "Five more minutes?" he asked.

His father nodded and practically collapsed back down onto the ground.

"What do you think Paradise is going to look like, Dad?"

"I think we should just wait and see," his father answered.

Zert took another drink of water. "Did you watch that holomovie *Burning Guns*?"

"No," his father said.

"The good guy lived in this little town. The houses were made out of wood, not cybratom. Smoke came out of these little chimneys, and everyone rode horses."

His father gave a weak smile. "Well, we know Paradise won't be like a holomovie."

Zert shifted uncomfortably as something sharp pressed into his leg. He looked closer and saw a bone on the dirt in the middle of hundreds of footprints. He was sitting on an insect graveyard of broken bones and skulls.

"We should go," his father said, struggling to stand. "We need to get to Paradise by nightfall."

"Hey, Dad. Want me to carry your backpack for you?" Zert asked.

"No, thank you. I'm just a little out of shape. That's all."

Zert was about to insist when he heard a hissing sound. It was as though a kettle of chips were frying nearby, and when he looked up, he could see a pack of black birds coasting close to the ground. They were aimed right at him, their wings folded up so tightly against their sides that they looked like missiles swooping toward him.

"Duck!" his father shouted.

He was wrong. Those weren't ducks or even birds. In the second before Zert dove down to hug the ground, he found himself gazing into the milky white eyes of a gigantic insect, nearly his size. Its compound eyes bulged sightlessly at him. The insect had a small head; a long, flat body; and tattered wings. Zert saw that a large symbol was scrawled across the insect's chest in blue ink. It looked like a letter of the alphabet, a *B*. But . . . that was impossible.

Zert gasped, and gravel filled his mouth. The wind swept above his head as more insects flew past. His hands, pressed against the ground, were quivering as he waited for hairy claws to attack his back. He heard a final hiss, and then all was quiet.

"You OK?" Jack called, sitting up quickly to check on Zert.

"I thought we were dead," Zert said, his voice shaking.

"They weren't hunting us. I think they were fleeing something."

"What were those?" Zert asked, scanning the sky for another hoard.

"They were roaches," his father said quietly. "Giant roaches."

"I think maybe they were blind. Did you see their eyes?" Zert asked. "They were white."

"That might explain why they were flying so close to the ground," his father said, looking in the direction they'd disappeared.

"Did you see a blue *B* on their chests?"

His father laughed. "I don't think that's possible, Zert. What was it? *B* for *blind*?" He chuckled to himself.

"I wish you'd believe me more," Zert muttered.

"Hey, look at that sign." His father stood up to cup his hands over his brows. He squinted toward the rounded mound of the hill and pointed up at the top.

Zert scrambled up. "Where?" If there was a sign, that meant some kind of civilization, and that meant food.

"At the base of that tree," his father said.

There it was: "*Paradise*."

>>>

Zert hurried up the last hundred paces of a path strewn with slippery gravel. This close to the top of the hill, the jungle of grass lining the trail had disappeared, and he felt puny. The wind could blow him away, or he could get his head taken off by a herd of flying roaches.

The sun, nearing the horizon, beamed straight into his eyes. It was going to be dark soon, and Dr. Brown had said that they needed to reach Paradise before dark. Those flying roaches were spooky enough. He didn't want to face the *Or Else* of the night.

Zert put all his energy into a final push, and at last he reached the top of the rise. With his father still ten paces behind him, he scanned the valley below. A raging river raced between gigantic boulders next to two trees, one with dancing leaves and one with low-hanging branches.

But there were no people, wooden houses, or fast horses, like in the holomovie he'd seen.

He needed to think differently, to think *small*. *Houses for BIGS would stand out. But houses of Rosies would not.* He scanned the bases of the trees, beneath bushes, along rocks.

A thin trail of smoke wafted up from a flat rock that stuck out the side of a low hill.

His father reached him, breathing heavily. He sounded done for the day. Yet, that whisper of smoke was still so far away.

Paradise. Their future home didn't seem cute, orderly, or homey. It was a bit of gray smoke against a backdrop of gray rocks. *We hiked all that way for this? We left everything behind to come here? This is our new life?*

But then, Zert's eyes traveled to the mountain, a mountain so tall and proud that for just a minute, he forgot about his sore legs and hurting feet, he forgot about the speckled couch he'd left behind and the *Or Else* worry about his future, he forgot about what he was going to say to Uncle Marin if he ever saw him again, and he just gaped.

17

NO COMMUNITY WITHOUT A VOTE

The downward slope was steep and covered in tiny rocks that looked slippery.

Zert could get down, but navigating the path would be hard for his father.

Without saying anything, Zert's father dropped onto his bottom, the heels of his shoes pressed down for guidance, and started sliding down the gravel slope. He shouted over his shoulder, "In the army, we called this a two-cheek descent."

Zert squatted and started toward the fire on the rock below. Even though his butt was dragging, the bumpy ride was fun. But he kept alert in case another platoon of roaches blew in from nowhere.

He stayed focused on that swirl of smoke.

As they had traveled a thousand miles in a wormhole, could they also have traveled thousands of years back in time? What if only the new arrivals wore the clothes they received from Ellis Log but the Rosies in Paradise were more like cavemen wearing loincloths and sitting around a fire? His father's remark about eating worms had been his signal that everything going forward was going to be different. From now on, he needed to try his best to expect the worse, and then maybe he wouldn't be too disappointed.

Zert scuffed along on his bottom and occasionally set off a cascade of rocks rattling down the hillside. As he got closer, he could see a man tending a fire. The man stood on a large rock that jutted out over a cliff. Underneath an overhang in what appeared to be an outdoor kitchen, Zert spotted pots and pans. The man was wearing blue jeans—thank goodness, not a loin cloth—covered with pockets in weird places, similar to the outfit of one hundred pockets that Zert had on. The Rosie's hair was tied back in a ponytail, not tangled and wild. The man held a stick in his hand, not a spear, and his face was clean, not marked up with war paint.

Every once in a while, as they approached, the stranger glanced in their direction but didn't seem worried or surprised.

Jack reached the bottom of the hill first. He stood up slowly and brushed himself off, his eyes on the ponytailed man.

Zert was just a few seconds behind his father.

"Hallo, Rosies," the man hollered. A necklace of animal teeth hung around his neck. *Uh-oh—this guy is definitely a step away from normal.* The tooth in the center was stained pink.

His rat-skin cap crooked on his head, Jack walked over and shook the man's hand like men used to in the old days before the Epidemics.

"I'm Donjumpers Gibson. People call me Don G.," the Rosie said. "We all have simple names here."

"My name is Jack Cage," his father said. "I like your policy." He nodded at Zert. "This is my son, Bezert Cage. Everyone calls him Zert. He's named for Bezert Eberheart."

Bezert Eberheart had started Citizens Against Change, a movement to try to get people to live like they did in 2050. Zert had never liked his name, but now that he had shrunk, it seemed completely inappropriate.

Don G. turned to Zert. "How old are you, Zert?"

"Thirteen," Zert said.

"I've got a thirteen-year-old daughter. I'll introduce you in a bit," Don G. said. He was a little taller than Jack. Besides the lines etching his face, his most prominent feature was his mouth, small and sort of off center. He took on a firmer stance. "You aren't thinking of settling here in Paradise, are you?" His eyes locked with Zert's. Not giving him the time to answer, he asked them, "Where are you headed?"

Not exactly howdy and welcome, Zert thought. He shifted his weight a little. A caveman would be better than an unfriendly new neighbor who didn't want them.

His father turned pale under his sunburn. "Yes," he said, "we are. Is there a problem?"

"It depends," Don. G. said.

They couldn't get maximized. What were they supposed to do if Paradise wouldn't take them? Go back to the light pole and complain to customer service?

"Why don't you help me load up the fire?" Don G. paused. "We can talk as we work." He headed toward some chips piled in neat stacks alongside the hill.

"I can help," Zert said.

"No," his father waved him off. "Sit down, son." When Zert kept gazing at him, his father added, "I'm OK."

Zert plopped down while his father followed Don G. Better let his dad talk to Don G. for a minute. Show Don G. what a nice guy he was so the Rosie would let them stay.

And feed them dinner.

The fire smoldered in the middle of the rock. A pipe sticking out from the side of the hill dripped water. The water fell into a narrow tube and cascaded down the slope. He looked around for the outdoor kitchen he had spotted from afar.

A shelf neatly stacked with plates, bowls, pots, and pans was built into the rocky face of the cliff. But the pots and bowls were all empty.

On Flade Street, a new restaurant had opened a drive-through lane for Flairs—flying chairs. He didn't have to ask. There were no fly-throughs here.

His dad and Don G.—their arms full of blocks of something dark—were heading back toward the fire.

"It's a great community," Don G. was saying. "We all look out for each other. But not everybody fits in."

In the world he came from, you had to be wealthy to be able to live in an Up City; he and his dad had never fit in there, either. People who lived in Up Cities had access to vaccines and cleaner air and water. *Somebody* always got to decide who belonged or didn't belong. *Somebody* got to choose who to cut out. Zert glared at Don G. *And it was* never *the Somebody who got cut.*

Don G. held up a gray block. "Dried buffalo dung," he said as he tossed it onto the fire.

"Buffalo dung?" Zert sputtered.

Don G.'s eyes narrowed. "You weren't born here?"

"Nope. We just arrived," his father said.

The Rosie stared at Zert now, and his gaze seemed to size him up as thoroughly as an identity wand receiver, except instead of stats like DNA, fingerprints, and longevity, he sensed Don G. was registering softer stuff like his talent, energy level, and honesty.

Zert had never seen a gaze that asked so much. He rubbed his aching ankle, and Don G. turned back to the fire.

Don G. threw a chip on the fire and the flames rose up. "I'll tell you frankly, Jack. Minimized kids don't do well here. I'm the leader of our community, and if I had it my way, we'd ban them all." His voice trailed off.

Jack cleared his throat. "Don't tell me your community doesn't want to give all kids a chance?"

The smoke from the fire stung his eyes, and Zert felt a slight burning of tears. So Paradise was just like Low City DC, where they threw kids like him and Cribbie into Teen Jail.

"I don't want to get your hopes up," Don G. said. "We just finished dealing with a minimized kid. He never adjusted to living here, and we finally had to expel his family. He set a bad example for our other kids. For everyone."

"If you give us a chance, you'll want us to stay," his father said, smiling like he did at his reluctant customers.

But Don G. only looked at him and stroked his chin. His eyes turned to Zert, but he didn't say anything.

After a long pause, Jack turned to gaze at the fire. "If you don't mind my asking, why are you risking a fire so close to the parking lot?"

"We take precautions if there are campers in the area, but by and large, the people who visit this park never notice anything at all." Don G. shook his head. "I could be hanging out in my birth-day suit and they wouldn't notice me. We're almost invisible to them."

So no BIG would ever notice him again? And the Rosies didn't want him either? There wasn't a third choice for him. Where was he supposed to go? His stomach grumbled, and he scuffed his heel against the dirt to hide the sound of his hunger.

"We keep the fire going twenty-four hours a day," Don G. was saying.

Zert ducked his head and blinked to dry his eyes from the hot tears he felt coming on. They had made a mistake. The only ques-tion was just how bad his new life was going to be. And as his dad said: Would they survive?

The fire was the size of a haystack. In holomovies, fires were red. These flames were orange, black, and gray. The strands played around in the breeze, licking each other and drawing back.

"We require a vote before you can be allowed to settle here," Don G. said. His words hung in the silence between them. He turned to face Zert's father. "But we'll give you three weeks before we decide."

Three weeks! That was no time at all. But it didn't seem as if it would matter anyway. This man with the weird necklace had already decided.

"We'll give you some food and fur, but if we vote no, you'll need to leave the next day," Don G. said.

"And go where?" Zert asked, trying to control his voice so the others wouldn't hear the lump in his throat.

"There are more settlements. But your whereabouts are not our problem," Don G. said plainly. He stood with his arms crossed.

Zert saw that his father's shoulders were hunched.

"No matter where you end up, you'll have to find a trade. What did you say you did?" Don G. asked.

"Exterminator," his father said with a broad smile on his face. "I inherited my business from my father, who inherited it from his."

Don G. smirked. "The most useless profession in Paradise," he said.

"Before that I was in the army," Zert's father added quickly. "I was stationed—"

Don G. cut his father short. "Cobblers are in short supply here."

"A cobbler?" Zert asked.

"You know, a shoemaker," his father said.

"I know what a cobbler is, Dad," Zert said. His father had never made anything in his life, except for a few batches of inedible cookies. There was no way he was going to be able to make a shoe.

His father stared down at his bony hands. They would drop a needle.

"You asked me earlier what work you need to do if you want to support the community," Don G. said. "And I just told you."

Jack nodded.

Zert gritted his teeth. His father hadn't given any thought to how they were going to make their living here. This man didn't want them, and his father would never be able to learn how to make shoes.

Don G. said to Zert, "You'll probably want a look around while I gab with your dad." He stomped one foot on the dirt. "This is Pancake Rock." Then, he walked over to its edge and pointed toward the ground. "The school's underneath that bush there."

The school—the one that Zert probably wouldn't get to attend or graduate from.

Despite his aching feet, Zert wandered over to the edge of the rock. "I don't see it," he said.

"All right, I'll show you," Don G. said. Without waiting for a response, he started hiking down the stairs cut into the side of the hill. They looked like steps from ancient ruins.

"Our school's one of the safest buildings in the settlement," Don G. said. "We fused together bottles of PeopleColor to build it."

PeopleColor Middle School. If only Cribbie were with me and could hear this stuff.

Cribbie! Zert started walking faster to try to outrace the bad feeling that he felt in the pit of his stomach. He glanced down at his naked wrist; he couldn't even pull up a photo of his friend on his communicator.

"Where's the housing?" his father said.

"We have some nice caves left," Don G. said.

The World Council had built low-income housing on Flade Street known as "the caves" for their lack of windows. Cribbie had lived in one for a while. The house was clammy, dark, depressing, and it had had mold growing in the shower.

"We'll lend you one for now," Don G said.

Don G. sounded helpful and almost friendly now, except for his use of the word *lend*. They would have three weeks, but then what? "We'll go to the cave in a minute," he said. He pointed at a clearing near the base of the hill. "There's our playground."

Zert's old school didn't have an outdoor playground. He wouldn't mind playing outside, as kids did in the old days. But this playground, a jumble of cylinders, spools, and pipes, looked like an industrial site. When Zert adjusted for scale, though, trying to see everything through his old eyes, what he saw was a collection of trash: a tomato soup can, a spool without any thread, a plastic straw, a couple bars of soap, some eyeglass frames bent into some sort of a jungle gym, a stack of bottle caps, and half of a globe with nails stuck in its sides. It was a garbage playground.

As he stepped off the stairs and onto the hard ground, he again worked to keep his voice normal. "What's the tomato soup can for, Don G.?"

"The kids push each other down the hill," Don G. said. "They call it the Roll-er-ato. The inside of it is padded." He pointed at other items on the playground. "That globe there is a climbing wall, the kids use the bottle caps as sleds, and for art class, they sometimes carve soap sculptures. Let me call Beth. She can tell you the rest."

Don G. put his fingers in his mouth and whistled.

A girl popped out of a knothole in the base of a tall aspen tree. Zert couldn't see much of her, except that she had two arms, two legs, and a head. As she drew closer, he noticed that she was barefoot and had on overalls covered in pockets. She reminded him of farm kids he'd seen in Western holomovies, the kind that prompted him to change the channel in search of a good adventure program to watch.

Zert had never met a kid that didn't live in the city before. Whether he and his dad got to stay here or not, he felt as if he wouldn't find any friends. Certainly not as good as the ones he had lost. "Oh, Cribbie," he whispered under his breath.

18

THIS *IS* THE REAL WORLD

"This is my daughter, Zert. Beth will show you around," Don G. said.

The girl faced him. She looked familiar, but he couldn't have met her before. She was born here. *Wait a minute.* Trying not to stare, he realized that the girl resembled Isal Diyvik—his archenemy at St. Lulu's—the guy who once tried to dunk his head into a toilet before Cribbie rescued him.

Both Beth and Isal had bulging eyes. Bug eyes. And bulging biceps. And lank brown hair. His father had been wrong. *You couldn't escape from anything, ever.* The bad his father thought they'd be able to leave behind had followed them here, only the Rosie version seemed worse.

Beth held out her hand, even though kids never greeted each other like this, not even in the old days.

He gripped her hand. It was coarse, as if she wore a scratchy glove. "Hello," he said, careful to keep his voice even.

"Hi," Beth said.

He pulled his hand back and glanced down to see if her grip had dirtied his fingers.

Beth narrowed her eyes and looked at him closely.

His face grew hot.

"I'm going to go with Don G. to look at the cave, Zert," his father called.

As Don G. and his father walked away, Zert thought, *Don't leave me alone with her.*

As he heard the adults' footsteps set off, Zert took stock of this girl who was born here. Beth was about his height, maybe a little taller. She had a square jaw that made you not notice whether she was pretty or not. Her hair went every which way, like a mismatched pile of brown and gold socks. Outsized hands and knuckles dangled on the ends of her long arms. Her feet were bare and muddy.

She frowned a little at Zert, surveying him in much the same way. When she finished her once-over, she said, "So, what do you want to see?"

"Everything, I guess," he said. He wanted to know exactly how bad living here was going to be. At the same time, he wanted to dribble out the sights over the next twenty years so the shock wouldn't be so great as to leave him numb. *A numb thumb.* "I haven't seen very much yet."

"Where are you from?" she said.

"Low City DC," Zert said.

"You weren't born here?" Beth's voice rose. But Zert couldn't tell if she was excited or wary. "You're minimized?"

"Yeah," Zert said. He couldn't help feeling a tiny bit proud.

"We just had a kid like you," Beth said. "His name was Abbot."

"What happened to Abbot?" he asked.

Beth looked directly at Zert. "We got rid of him."

"Great," Zert said.

"Abbot was always bragging about things we don't know anything about, things we don't need to know about," Beth said.

Zert would give anything to get to meet this braggart. "Where is Abbot now?"

Beth shrugged and just kept looking at him. Zert waited for

her to say more. When she didn't, his mind began to race. Abbot and his dad could be lying dead in the wilderness somewhere. Beth didn't seem to care.

"I'll show you the trickle," she said suddenly.

"The trickle?"

"The first rule is that we call everything the same name as the BIGS do." Rule? There were rules? Before Zert could ask about the second or third rule, she started running. He had seen kids run before. Every once in a while, he ran himself. But he had never seen anyone who accelerated to a sprint as fast as this girl did. She'd have been in the Youth Olympics if she lived in the real world. He paused.

This is the real world. This world is as real as can be.

Beth tore down the path, hurdling over small boulders that Zert knew, in his former world, were mere pebbles. She raced down slopes without sliding or slipping, plunging though long patches of yellow grass, jumping over large, lacy ferns that sometimes blocked her path.

At first, Zert struggled to keep Beth in his sight. But it wasn't only the bottoms of his feet that hurt; every muscle in his whole body was sore. The effort burned his lungs, and his head ached from too much sun. When sweat poured down and stung his eyes, he gave up and began walking.

The roar of the water grew louder and louder, sounding like the inside of a lifter-bus terminal. His dad was right. Water was noisy.

Zert reached the bank. Beth had called this a trickle, but it looked like a raging stream. Green-and-white water splashed over rocks and crashed into boulders. Zert never knew how noisy water could be.

Fishing nets lined the sandy bank, and the place stunk. Beth wasn't there. He looked for her around some jumbled wooden boxes on the shore, but she wasn't anywhere.

He took a few more steps toward the water. He was parched but wasn't sure he could drink it. It couldn't be healthy, and he might die if he drank it. But maybe he could at least cool off by sticking his head in it.

Beth popped out from behind a nearby boulder. "Surprise!"

Zert jumped. "Why'd you do that?"

Beth shrugged and pointed at a swimming pool–sized body of still water close to shore. With her hands on her hips, she demanded, "What are those?" in a test-the-new-kid voice.

Zert looked down in the deep water and saw hundreds of shapes. "Fish."

"I already told you the first rule." Beth folded her arms across her chest. Pointing at the stream—wait, the "trickle"—she said, "Those are minnows."

The giant minnows darted around in the water. Zert could see their beady eyes, their mouths opening and closing. Minnows used to be just tiny squiggles to him. Now they looked substantial.

Beth gestured toward the nets. "We catch the minnows with those."

"You eat them?" Zert said.

"The water's not contaminated here," Beth said.

Zert pointed at the boxes lined up on the bank. The boxes were fashioned from twigs and mud and smelled like stinky cat food. "What are those?"

"Frog traps," Beth explained. "We eat frogs, and turtles, too." She paused. "We use the turtle shells for our baths. In the wet season, we flip a few of them and use them for hail shelters. In the dry season, they're barbecue pits."

Low City DC had only one season—it was hot year-round. Zert had never seen hail before. "Do you get lots of hail? Or snow?" he asked hopefully.

Beth squatted next to the trickle, poking a stick into the surging water. No, not a stick, Zert realized, a twig. She looked over her shoulder to grin at him. It was peculiar to see her with a smile on her face. "We get snow. But not as early as Third Halloween," she said.

"Halloween?" Zert asked. "It's Halloween here? But it's only September."

"We have the same holidays as the BIG world, but it's much better here because we celebrate them whenever we want. We might have another Halloween again in a week or month," Beth said. She scuffed her boot into the dirt. "What did you do for fun in that boring city you came from?"

Boring city? Zert felt a pang of homesickness as he answered, "Played zoink ball and stuff like that."

Beth threw her stick into the water. "Oh, yeah?" she said. "Tell me about that."

"OK," Zert said. "Uh, there's a pitcher who controls the jets of air and three batters who bat the balls." He took a swing at the air. "It's like 3-D Ping-Pong."

Beth shook her head, a blank expression on her face.

"It's hard to explain if you've never seen a game."

"If you!" Beth rolled her eyes. "Aaagh. That's what Abbot always said."

"What . . . ?"

"'*If you* haven't used the Internet, don't ask. I can't explain it to you.' '*If you* haven't seen a holomovie, don't ask. It's impossible to describe it.'" She shrugged. Beth moved so close to Zert that he could see her crooked bottom teeth. "We don't like it," she said with a glare.

Zert nodded.

"Have you ever ridden in a lifter?" Beth asked.

"Lots of times," Zert said. BIG Zert had dreamed about taking driver's ed and learning to drive.

"What's that like?" Beth asked.

Water raced past him in the stream. *No*, he corrected himself, *the trickle*. "Can you swim?" he asked Beth.

She nodded.

"Riding in a lifter is like floating in water," Zert said. "Only—"

"But you can't float in the air," Beth interrupted. "It's dry."

"I know, but—"

Beth flicked her unruly hair as she interrupted. "Been to an anti-gravity fun house?"

"A . . . A few times. A long time ago. A fun house once offered to buy my dad's store."

"You had a store?" Beth burst out. "What kind?"

"My dad's an exterminator."

"What's that?" Beth said.

Even Rosies ought to have exterminators. "He kills pests."

"Pests?"

"You know, roaches, ants, termites . . ."

Beth's mouth dropped open, and she gaped at him. "Roaches aren't pests."

"Yeah, they are. And my dad has this machine that vacuums them up and cuts them into little pieces," Zert said proudly. "It's called the Ultimate Xterminator."

"What does he do with the food?" Beth said.

"What are you talking about?" Zert asked.

"So, he's got this big machine and it catches roaches, and then who does he give the food to?" Beth said.

Zert shook his head. "What food?" he repeated.

"F-o-o-d," she spelled out, using a mocking voice.

"If you!" Zert said. That would teach her to treat him as if he were dumb.

Her eyes bulged as if they might pop out. Then she turned and started running away.

"Hey, wait up," Zert yelled as she disappeared underneath a bush.

In Low City DC, the streets were never empty. Some Flayhead who had drunk too much of the powerful drug was always sleeping on a moving sidewalk. Or a lifter was always revving for takeoff. Someone was always there.

But now that Beth had left, the bushes, rocks, and grass were his only company.

He felt all alone. In Paradise. In Rosieland. In Rocky Mountain National Park. On the North American continent. On Planet Earth. In the whole entire universe.

19

DOODLEBUG GOLF

Although Beth had disappeared, Zert knew he could find his way back. Pancake Rock stuck out from the landscape as much as the holostatues of liberty did in front of the souvenir shop.

"Hey, Zert."

Beth's voice came from the trail to his right. "Where are you?" he called out, looking into the thicket.

"Keep walking," Beth said. "You BIGS do know how to walk, don't you?"

Zert headed toward the sound of her voice. The trail dead-ended into a rickety twig hut. Magazine photos resembling store windows plastered the front. In one glamour shot, a woman with implanted cheekbones wore a long black dress. The script said, "Naturally beautiful."

Beth waited on the rickety front porch. "This is Shack Fifth Avenue."

At least Rosies had a sense of humor.

Zert stepped up onto the porch and examined the second photo. It was a silver-and-red tube with a string attached to it. On *New Worlds*, Uncle Marin had used a fly rod in an episode about fishing in Antarctica.

Uncle Marin. Zert flared his nostrils.

Beth turned and went inside. "Hello," she hollered.

No one answered.

Zert followed her into a room stuffed with goods. A lot of the stuff was labeled: *Ant Pudding, Rat Jerky, Honey, Ants' Eggs, Dried Minnows, Toasted Fleas,* and most awful of all, *Rat Brain Pickles.* All of the products were unpackaged and naked looking, as if they had forgotten to get dressed that morning.

"Everyone must be at Pancake Rock already," Beth said. "It's nearly time for dinner."

Zert walked up to the closest shelf. Buckets of crispy fried grasshopper and cricket legs were the only foods that looked even remotely tasty. Feathers stuck out of every available space.

"Come over here," Beth said. She stood next to the wall at the back of the store.

Zert wound around piles of black-and-gray furs to join her.

Squirrels. Rats. Maybe even some cuddly rabbits. He passed shelves holding acorn cups, twig hiking staffs, leaf tents, wasp nest paper, and mud skates. One area was crammed with weapons. The daggers, spears, and swords looked as if they had been carved out of teeth.

Eek! Zert felt the hairs on the back of his neck rise.

Beth stopped in front of a section labeled *Games.* She grabbed a stick and held it up. "What's this?" she asked.

Another test. Zert gazed down at the bin and read the label, "Putter for Doodlebug Golf."

"This game is the bee's knees," Beth said, smiling.

Zert stifled a giggle. *Bee's knees.* Did that mean *crunchy* in the Rosie world?

"It's a *lot* more fun than zoink ball," Beth bragged as she swung the stick. "And I'm good at it."

It was easy to imagine Beth smacking the doodlebug with a

stick and the gray bug sailing toward the sun. "Are the doodlebugs alive or dead during the game?" he asked.

She swung the stick at him. It barely missed his head.

"Hey, watch out," he said.

"Dead, of course." She pulled a jar from the shelf, but this time, she covered the label with her hand. "What about this?"

The jar was full of green powder. "I don't know."

"Firefly powder." She glanced at him with a gleam in her eye that said *you don't know everything, do you?* "We use it for light."

The light in the base of the light pole had been an eerie green. Same with the light in Ellis Log.

"What's this?" Beth held up a jar full of something that looked like ypersteroid pellets.

"I don't know," Zert snapped.

Beth smirked. "I wish I could explain it, but I can't. *If you!*" she taunted him.

Zert looked her in the eyes. "I get it," he said.

"Zert, Beth," Don G. called from a distance. "Time for dinner."

"I gotta go. I have to put on my costume." Beth turned toward the door.

"My dad said that you don't study Chinese here?" Zert said. Ever since the Chinese had won the Antarctica Wars, every student had had to study Chinese. It was part of the treaty.

"That's right," Beth said.

Hurrah. "What *do* you study?" She had her broad back to him, and he stared at her brown hair that trailed down like a shaggy horse's mane. He had never met a girl who didn't brush her hair before.

"Insects and society, insects and art, insects and history," Beth said.

"Insect history?" Zert interrupted. *Heroic mosquitoes and brave flies.* "What about George Washington, Abraham Lincoln, and stuff like that?"

"Yeah." Beth turned to face him. "Our teacher makes us study the BIG world, but I don't understand why. We'll never get to go there."

Never get to go there. Zert gasped, but Beth wasn't around to hear. She had already set off in a run.

He had been rude to stare at her hand to see if it was dirty. But she had been rude too, and *I'm a guest here.* He limped after her.

〉〉〉

As Zert approached Pancake Rock, he smelled a delicious smell, and his mouth began to water.

Above him, on the rock's shelf, Rosies stirred pots over fires. Two women had tied green-and-pink scarves around their heads. The BIG clothes discarded on the trail were made of the same material. One man wore a blue-jean apron.

Everyone in the entire village could dress themselves from just the jeans and clothes he and his father had dropped on the floor of Dr. Brown's office—and these clothes would probably last them for the rest of their lives.

Don G. stood on Pancake Rock near the buffalo chip pile.

"Don G.," Zert hollered up, "where's my dad?"

Don G. pointed down a trail that led toward a cliff. "Take a right turn at the Hat. And follow that trail until it dead-ends. You can't miss him."

"What kind of hat?" Zert yelled.

But Don G. had gone back to tending the fire and didn't answer.

Zert started down the dirt trail. It was lined with green stalks topped with see-through cotton balls. Soft white stars floated off the top of the plants and caressed his arms and chest—a nature tickle.

Ahead of him, a black, shiny rock rose out of the ground. It looked like a top hat with a wide brim, the kind a magician would wear. He took a right, and twenty or so paces away, the trail dead-ended into a structure, a sort of hut constructed between two moss-covered rocks that backed up to the cliff.

Crushed red-and-green cans tiled the twig hut's roof. The one round window was covered in blue cybratom with a *W* brand in the center.

W for *Weird*—whatever BIG had discarded that water bottle in the park had no idea that it would one day end up as a window for a species of little people.

Zert pushed on the purple cybratom door and stepped into an empty room. "Dad?" he called.

A retro-magazine photo hung on the far wall, showing some men in an old-timey car pointing their rifles at lions. He'd been surprised by so many odd things in Paradise, like doodlebug golf, that he hadn't stopped to think about all the things that he *hadn't* seen. Here, there were no laser pain rifles, no trampos, no zappers, no people so scared of getting shot that they wore privacy hoods so no one could ID them.

One wall was unpapered, exposing a wavy blue plastic that seemed vaguely familiar.

A hole the size of a door gaped in the back wall. He passed through it into a deep cave with glowing walls. With its eerie green light, the cave resembled a haunted house. The space felt cool, as if the temperature were controlled by a weather system, but the air tasted funny, as if he were licking metal.

He missed his couch, his I-ring, his holo-imagetube, his pet rat, Okar, but most of all, he missed Chub. If only he could hold Chub tight.

The miniature wolf had probably been destroyed. All because his father had let Uncle Marin trick him. Trick *them*.

"Zert."

Zert hurried out of the cave.

In the front room, his father held a twig broom so primitive it looked as if he had borrowed it from the holomovie set for *Cinderella*.

"Zert, isn't this great?" his father said as he started sweeping. "Someone moved away, and we can stay here for a while."

"Probably Abbot," Zert mumbled. "Before they murdered him."

"What did you say?" His father stopped working.

"I'm hungry," Zert said.

20

MANY HALLOWEENS BUT NONE SUIT

Zert stepped up onto Pancake Rock, which was now bustling with people and activity. One kid wore a T-shirt with a stinger protruding from the front, and around his neck was a sign: *Wasp-acula.* Another had a red cap on her head, twigs behind her ears, and the word "Fire" written on her forehead. Someone else wore overalls layered in tree bark.

The adults looked strange too. There was something about their patched- and pieced-together clothing that made them appear foreign. Or they could have been models for an old-fashioned sewing magazine that taught people how to make their own clothes. Or they could have been attendees at a convention of people who love pockets. He started counting all the pockets on people's clothes but lost track. There were too many to count.

A figure dressed in black and wearing a rat's head ran up to him, interrupting his thoughts. Glittering eyes gleamed out of the mask's eye holes, and its mouth, with its tiny teeth, was frozen open as if it were about to bite.

It was creepy. Whoever this was—was dressed like his pet, Okar.

The masked figure stepped closer, as did other Rosie kids in costumes.

Zert stood his ground as they all crowded around him.

The figure removed the mask.

"Everyone, this is Zert Cage. He's minimized," Beth called out. The kids seemed to move in even closer.

Beth began to tell Zert the names of the kids: Ivy Potts, who wore the fire costume, had acne. John Gibson, Beth's brother, was Wasp-acula. He had buck teeth. Rudolpho Orlando, who was dressed as a fall day with leaves all over his T-shirt, wore glasses. Except in historical holomovies, Zert had never seen anyone with buck teeth, acne, or glasses before. Everything in the BIG world was correctable.

The names and costumes began to blur together: Sylvester Martin, Dawn Nelson, Holly Cannon, and on and on. Just as Dr. Brown said, there weren't any older kids.

"Who did I forget?" Beth said. "Oh yeah." She pointed at a girl who looked a few years younger than Zert. The girl had been standing behind him.

A spider cap sat on top of black hair so straight it could have been used for a ruler. Lively green eyes peered out from underneath the girl's black bangs.

A few fly parts hung in the cobweb that spread across the front of her white T-shirt. On her chest, she had printed a sign that said "Spidergirl."

"Millicent Chang," the girl broke in before Beth could introduce her.

Millicent handed Zert a large bowl.

The surface of the bowl was brown and bumpy, and a stem stuck out from its base. It was the cap of an acorn. "Thanks," he said, looking at her green eyes.

"I'll take him through the line," Millicent said to Beth.

"OK," Beth said. "We're sitting over there." She pointed at a spot near the edge of the rock where some acorn bowls were resting on their stems.

The fur tail attached to Beth's overalls slapped Zert's legs as she turned away.

"They say a rat once carried away a Rosie kid at Knot Hole," Millicent whispered into his ear as she fell in beside him. "Her mother was doing laundry by the trickle. They say rats like to feast on Rosies' eyes."

He forced himself to look unconcerned. Surely, this was a tale meant to scare him for Halloween.

While he listened with one ear to Millicent's chatter, he surveyed Paradise from the vantage point of Pancake Rock. He had explored the part of the village built on the slope facing the stream, but even now that he knew that it existed, he couldn't pick out a single road, home, or store. *Camotown, USA.*

These Rosies were clever.

Millicent gave him a nudge, and suddenly, Zert stood at the head of the line. Soups bubbled in black pots on a series of grates over low fires.

He hadn't had hot food in . . . He couldn't remember when. Their Food Machine had broken down months ago, and his dad hadn't had the funds to get it fixed.

A Rosie woman stirring the first pot looked up at him. "Hello, Zert Cage," she said. "I'm Beth's mom—Cleama Gibson." She had a square jaw, but everything else about her was round, including her hair, which rose like a series of hills over her head and fell to her ears. Her stomach puffed out like a feather pillow, and her shoulders seemed padded. With a white apron tied around her waist, she resembled an old-fashioned cafeteria worker.

"Hi," Zert said.

Cleama Gibson pointed at the pot. "The first pot is roach stew."

"Roach stew?" Zert said, his mouth going stale.

Cleama Gibson frowned. "We boil the roaches to get rid of diseases."

In Low City DC, he had always hated those scuttling insects, with their hairy legs and dodgy antenna. And now in Rosieland he was supposed to *eat* them?

Millicent giggled. "It's really tasty."

The woman next to Cleama Gibson cleared her throat. She had parted her hair at her widow's peak and pulled it back with a cloth bow. "I knew tenderfeet would have a hard time eating roaches, so I made you some cricket soup in sunflower broth."

"Thank you," Zert said as he glanced over his shoulder. He looked around for his father—*the exterminator*—whose business had been to wipe out roaches. If his father was eating roach stew right now, he'd never let him forget it.

Jack stood in the center of a group of men, talking.

"It's in that second pot," the woman said, nodding to Zert.

Even as hungry as he was, he could not help but hesitate as he looked in the pot. Sticks—possibly antennae or legs—floated in a brown liquid. Just a few moments ago, he would never have believed that cricket soup would become his new normal.

"Go ahead. It's very nutritious," the woman said. "Dried crickets have a lot of protein."

Zert picked up the ladle and poured some of the cricket soup into his acorn bowl.

"We have lots of great food," Millicent was saying. "BeeLTs, snail sushi, cate-flowers, ant omelets, barbecue spider . . ."

"Th—Thank you," Zert said, and turned away.

"Wait for me, Zert," Millicent called. "Thank you for another great meal," she said to the women.

Red light stenciled Zert's hand as he waited for Millicent.

An advertisement for FastGrow in red lettering covered the face of the artificial moon. *One bottle, and you'll step on your hair.* The advertisers had written the text in six languages in order to reach the whole world.

A Rosie kid wearing a minnow's head bumped into him.

"Sorry," the minnow apologized.

"No problem," Zert answered. The kid stunk of rotten fish and sweat. *No deodorant here.*

He guessed that Rosies must use hatchets for razors because he could see that the men around him were mostly clean shaven. There was no ice in their drinks. There were no tasty bags of chips. There were no—

"Let's go, Zert," Millicent said, interrupting his dreary list. She was holding her bowl. It looked like—*yuck*—a pair of antenna was sticking out of the brown soup. "Halloweens are so much fun. In a few weeks, we hold the rodeo, and then there's Gulliver's Day."

Zert followed her as she walked toward a group of kids. Beth and her younger brother, John, had the same bug eyes. Sweat plastered Beth's hair to her head. The stinger in John's costume bobbed up and down as he ate. To join them, he stepped around the rat mask lying on the ground.

Beth took a sip of soup from the bowl. There was no silverware in Paradise.

Millicent settled next to Zert. "We skate here in the moonlight, square dance . . . ," she said.

Skate. Square dance. They probably made candles, too. This was stuff he'd read about in history books.

Zert held the bowl up to his mouth and took a careful sip. When he swallowed, he was pleasantly surprised. Although the cricket legs weren't hard-crunchy like chips, at least they were soft-crunchy like fried tofu. He wouldn't call the soup good exactly, but it tasted better than some of the stuff he'd eaten at the Mystery Meat diner on Flade Street.

"During the wet season, we eat frozen honey, we snowshoe, we . . . ," Millicent continued. She gazed up at the sky as she considered more things to tell him.

Zert followed her gaze. He had already noticed the FastGrow ad on the artificial moon, but the natural moon surprised him now. The moon and stars shone more brightly here than they did in Low City DC.

Millicent pointed at the real moon, not the artificial one. "Last night I dreamed I lived there." She grinned. "At least I *think* that's what I dreamed about. I'm not sure where I was."

"Someone just invented a camera that takes photos of your dreams," Zert said. "So you can remember them."

Millicent's eyes widened. "No way."

"Yeah," Zert said as he slurped down another bite of soup. "It's called Dream Hat. You can see your dreams in the morning. They're just flat pictures now, but I bet for Dream Hat 2, the images will be"—he tried to think of another word for the process but gave up— "holographic."

Beth's eyes bulged.

John's forced smile said, *You're a liar.*

Zert put down his bowl and balanced it on its stem. "I swear," he said to John.

John threw back his head and laughed.

"OK," Zert said. He could feel his face growing hot. "I'm here because twelve hours ago, I got minimized. If you can believe that, you should be able to believe anything."

"What's holo—gra—phic?" Millicent asked.

Zert tried to think of a way to explain it without using *"If you."*

John said to his sister. "He's just like the other guy. Abbot."

Abbot, who might be dead or dying somewhere in the vast wilderness.

Beth stood up. "Hey, Zert, you want to come trick-or-treating with me? You could say you're dressed as a BIG."

Zert looked down at his outfit of a hundred pockets. "*No* BIG would dress like me," he blurted out.

When Beth's brown eyes clouded, he realized how rude he'd sounded.

"Forget it, then," Beth said, turning her back on him. "Last one to Shack Fifth is a rat's butt!" she yelled before running over to the waterfall on the side of the rock to wash her bowl.

John followed his sister.

"Since you're new, I'll wash your dish for you," Millicent offered, taking Zert's bowl. "Thank you," he said as his stomach cramped. In the BIG world, people would sometimes say they had butterflies in their stomach. *I have actual crickets in mine.*

"Zert?" Millicent asked as she stood up.

"What?" Zert said.

"Is there really a camera for your dreams?"

"There really is," he told her. Millicent's parents had once been BIG. They should have kept her better informed. But to be fair, Dream Hat had just launched this month. The adults here wouldn't know that it even existed. There were no newspapers in Rosieland. No holo-imagetubes. Paradise—and everybody in it— was cut off from the rest of the world.

"You sure you don't want to come trick-or-treating? It's really fun," Millicent said, smiling down at him.

"I am so sure," Zert said.

Millicent waved. "Then I'll see you tomorrow at school."

"All right, Spidergirl," Zert said as she turned away.

Someday, he'd be sitting on this dusty rock, and a minimized kid, a tenderfoot, would arrive. The kid would tell him that five-headed aliens with dragon tails had invaded the earth. He wouldn't know whether that stranger was lying or telling the truth.

This was his future.

21

SECOND CHANCES

His father was still talking with a group of men. But when Zert started to stand, he groaned and fell back on the ground. His legs, his feet, and his ankles were so sore.

Besides, if he walked over, he'd have to meet all those adults.

He picked up a stick and began doodling in the dust. He drew his mom's purple couch. He sketched out a zoink ball. Then, he worked on a drawing of Chub, but the miniature wolf's ears came out lopsided. He looked at her funny ears and wished he could scratch them again.

As he doodled, he sang under his breath the new ad for Dream Hat he'd heard,

> *"Dreaming is one thing that all people do.*
> *Photographing your dreams is fun too.*
> *Dream on and on and on.*
> *Cuz that's what dreamers do."*

When Zert tried to correct Chub's ears, he made them too long, like rabbit's ears. He decided to work on Chub's nose, but his hand slipped and he wound up giving his pet a trunk. She looked like a wolf/rabbit/elephant blend. He'd like to see that. Too bad tri-species mergers were illegal under the anti-Frankenstein law passed by the World Council.

In the background, he could hear the fire sizzling, the adults' low voices, and something crackling. When he was a Boy Scout, they'd watched some nature shows, and he recognized the noise as the chirp of crickets. The crickets in his dinner hadn't been quite as chirpy.

He decided to lie down to rest—just for a second. The ground felt hard, like the bench at Teen Jail. *"My mother won't speak to me," the holobum called out. "My father died while I was in jail for the sixth time. Teens, you need to change. Change your lives before it's too late. This is your last chance."*

The next thing Zert knew, someone was shaking his shoulder. When he opened his eyes, he half-expected to see the holobum squatting in the corner of his cell. But it was a man wearing a gray fur hat. In another moment, he realized it was his father who was standing over him.

"You ready for bed, Zert?" he asked.

Zert rubbed his eyes and nodded.

"Let's go then."

As Zert worked to stand, his muscles felt like pulled licorice.

His father reached for Zert's hand and helped him up. "I brought you a piece of candy," he said.

Zert stood up, his legs still wobbly.

His father held out his hand. A green, unwrapped bar lay sideways on his palm.

Zert popped the candy in his mouth. "What's the flavor?"

His father's eyes narrowed, as they always did before he told a joke. "Grass," he said.

"Grass?" The candy was barely sweet, and it did taste like . . . grass. Zert sucked on it. "Ever see a cow grazing and wished that you could become one? Grass candy. You'll dine like your favorite cow," he said.

His father laughed. "That's my Zert."

Zert laughed with him, even though his stomach and chest muscles were sore. "I wondered what kind of candy people here gave out for trick-or-treat."

"Well, you just found out," his father said, smiling. "Let's get going. Tomorrow's your first day at your new school." He added, "I know you're going to really like it there."

School.

The laughter died in Zert's throat.

> > >

The eerie green light on the walls didn't reach the middle of the cave, where it was beyond dark, as if someone had colored a black painting with a black pen.

Don G. had warned them to sleep in the cave and not in the hut built in front. "In case of a sudden wind," he'd said.

Various community members had stuffed pillows and blankets into their hands as Zert and his father left Pancake Rock. One man with a fuzzy, uneven mustache had even told his father that he'd lend them a desk tomorrow. But now, all the hubbub had died down, and Zert was alone in the cave with his dad.

More light, Zert wanted to say to the faint green light on the walls. But firefly light wasn't interactive.

He rolled over. He was lying on a fur blanket, but a blanket could only do so much on a rock floor to make it comfy.

He imagined Uncle Marin sleeping in a soft bed with his head on stacks of pillows right now. Was his uncle sleeping with a clear conscience, or was he tossing and turning, worrying about them?

"Are you awake?" his father whispered.

"Yes," Zert said, and then blurted out, "It seems like we're all alone in the whole wide world."

His father sighed. "That's how I've felt since your mother died."

Zert felt rather than saw his father roll toward him.

"And I couldn't imagine my life getting any lonelier until I began worrying that I might lose you," his father said.

It was too dark to see the iffy spot on his hand. When Zert rubbed it, he couldn't even feel the bump anymore. It was nothing now, totally unimportant.

"This new life is going to be tough," his father said. "It's going to be the biggest challenge we've ever faced. But we've got each other. Remember that. We have our family."

"We've got *part* of our family. Uncle Marin is missing," Zert reminded him.

"Your mother and I had many conversations about her brother. She never thought much of him, but I always tried to believe in him." His father was cracking his knuckles. "She appreciated my confidence in him. When I think bad thoughts about your uncle, I feel like I'm letting your mother down," his father said.

"I don't like to be tricked," Zert said. That third door hadn't closed. He was sure of it. He could still hear Dr. Brown crying out, "What's going on?"

"Give him the benefit of the doubt," his father said. "That's what I'm doing." He rolled over onto his back. "Give him the same benefit of a doubt that you want Don G. to give to you." He paused. "To us."

"Why didn't you give Cribbie the benefit of a doubt then, Dad?" Zert said, surprised at his own anger. "Why do you get to give it to some people and not to others? Why do *you* get to decide?"

The greenish darkness seemed to warp the silence and make it deeper.

"I never told you this. I didn't want to upset you. But a year ago, I asked Glorybeth Vimen if Cribbie could come live with us," his father said. "I didn't have anything against your friend. It was just that without supervision, he was headed for trouble, and I didn't want him to take you down too."

Cribbie as a roommate. How crunchy would that have been? Cribbie could have been alive today. He could have slept beside him on this blanket. They could have woken up tomorrow morning and encountered all this bizarro stuff together.

"I was sorry when Glorybeth refused me," his father said.

"But you called him a juvenile delinquent," Zert said.

"That's where Cribbie was headed, son. But I know your friend wasn't a bad boy. It's just that no one can make it on their own without a family or a community. And in Low City DC, kids don't get a second chance."

"This new world is the same as the old," Zert said. "You heard Don G."

"I did. But I believe in second chances. That's just who I am," his father said.

"Cribbie didn't get a second chance," Zert said. "He didn't even get one chance."

"No, son, he didn't. And that wasn't fair. But you have one now, and your new life is going to be BIG," his father said.

His father was wrong about so much. The night before his mother died, Zert had begged his father to tell him how she was doing.

"She'll be fine, son. She's going to live."

His mother was killed by a fancy lifter on her way to pick up Zert from St. Lulu's. It was a hit-and-run. Bystanders reported that the fancy lifter that hit her had an Up City docking license.

"We're going to catch that driver and bring him to justice," his father had said to Uncle Marin after she died. He had said it to his customers. He had said it to Zert. He had said it to his net worth calculator. He had said it to his own reflection in the mirror. Zert had only been six years old at the time, but he knew they'd never find the person who had killed his mom.

His father had tried. The petitions. The lawyers. The trips to see the police. There was a time when his father was so busy that Zert barely got by. Zert didn't know how to wash up, get to school by himself, put a Band-Aid on a cut ... He'd lost a few toenails back then. Most days, he had chips for breakfast, for lunch, and for dinner.

His father had just been coming out of his fog when the Superpox Epidemic hit, and President Honestloyalkind had imposed a quarantine. His father had lost all his business almost overnight. His creditors wanted to take the store over. As his father explained their situation, "I borrowed to pay lawyers at the worst time."

Nothing came of all his dad's efforts. Whoever had been flying that lifter was still free today, living in Up City DC, breathing clean air, and feeling no fear of crime or of catching Superpox.

"How can you be sure that living here is going to work out, Dad?" Zert asked despite his doubts.

His father's snores filled the cabin, empty except for the uncanny green light.

22

PEOPLECOLOR SCHOOL

The next morning, Zert had already been up for hours when he stood with his body wedged flat against PeopleColor Schoolhouse and peered inside.

The kids and the teacher had their backs to him. The kids sat behind crude desks constructed out of cans. Some of the kids wrote on rough paper with feather pens. Others gazed at the front of the classroom at a stone blackboard. Although the setting was slapdash and primitive, without their weird costumes on, the kids themselves looked pretty normal.

While a few were darker or yellower than the rest, most kids had light brown skin, like Zert, his father, and the rest of people in Low City DC, who thought drinking PeopleColor to become blue, green, or whatever color they wanted was an expensive waste of time. But Zert could tell he would stick out in one way. He had a belly that protruded over the top of his pants. At St. Lulu's, the kids called these "chip bellies." Zert had gotten his from eating too many bags of chips.

The teacher was writing on the blackboard, "Math lesson."

Zert had had the bad luck to arrive just in time for math. But among this crew with their feather pens and stone blackboard, at least he was going to be the star pupil. He had to be a star pupil here because the kids in this class were so backward.

"Teacher, I see the new boy at the door," Beth called out.

Every single kid turned to look at him as though *he* was the freak.

The teacher stepped toward the round doorway. With brown hair and eyes, she wasn't pretty, ugly, young, or old; she was right in the middle of nearly any adjective Zert could think of. He thought of one adjective that fit, but he had never applied it to a person before; his new teacher looked peaceful. She had on a blue skirt and furry shoes and wore her hair in pigtails that touched her shoulders.

Smiling, the teacher motioned for him to enter. "Hi, Zert. I'm Mary Kay Casey. You can call me 'Casey' or 'Teacher.'"

Zert took his first step into the room. *Remember, you're smarter than these kids*, he told himself.

Someone had drawn a map of earth on the back of the *PeopleColor* label on the ceiling. The map looked to be about the size of an old-fashioned quarter. Zert guessed that the artist had done it from memory because he could see that the lower world bulged in funny places. He located the dot that represented Low City DC before he turned his attention to the class. Of course, they were craning their necks to stare at him, as the kids at St. Lulu's would be had he been new there.

"You may have met Zert Cage last night. Zert and his father are seeking permission to live in Paradise," Casey said.

His teacher turned to face him. The shimmering earrings dangling from her earlobes looked familiar, but he couldn't identify them. He studied them for a second longer. Insect wings—*the finest in fly jewelry.*

"Welcome," Casey said. "Are you excited to find out about your new school, Zert?"

"Yes," Zert said to be polite. All he really wanted was to find a Mag Lev with a 3-D maximizer button and blast back to St. Lulu's.

He wanted to be sitting behind his usual desk in English class (not math) with his RASM portal. He wanted to be looking forward to recess with Cribbie. He wanted to be gazing at Snow.

"Beth, why don't you show Zert how to use the abacus?" Casey said. She pointed at the rounded end of the room. "Take him to the study corner."

Zert followed Beth and watched her sit down cross-legged, as if she were doing a Yoga pose, next to an overflowing bucket full of balls. The round objects were insect eyes, not balls, covered with some kind of gloss, like nail polish. One black pupil, surrounded by gray, stared out at him and seemed to follow him, the minimized kid, around.

"You can calculate with this." Beth held the abacus out for his inspection. The device, if he could call it that, consisted of a bunch of twigs and dried berries. There was definitely no extended warranty for *this* machine.

The rock that Casey used for chalk screeched.

Zert was expecting to see *2 + 2 = 4* on the blackboard. But the teacher had instead written a word problem.

> *Artica Chang keeps 94 crickets in a pen. Each lays about ten eggs a day. How many baby crickets does Artica have at the end of 100 days? At the end of 200 days? At the end of 300 days?*

"Do you know the answer to that?" Beth asked. Although she hadn't bothered to brush her hair, she had tied it back with a bow.

Zert shook his head.

Beth quickly pushed the berries around on the abacus. "It's 9,400 eggs in a hundred days. You can probably do the first part in your head, but I'll show you how I did that." She leaned so close to Zert that he could hear her stomach rumble. "We start using abacuses in kindergarten. See, these are the tens . . ."

Beth's fingers moved too fast. Zert was a *C* math student at St. Lulu's, but he was going to be an *F* math student at PeopleColor School.

"So, do you understand?" he heard Beth ask.

"Who cares about this stuff anyway?" Zert said. His voice came out louder than he had intended.

The scratch of pens against paper stopped.

Zert felt a hot blush start at his feet and travel up to his face. Before he could stop himself, he shoved the abacus away.

"Oh no. Here we go again. Another Abbot," someone muttered.

"Minimized kids are jerks," another kid said.

"Something's wrong with him," a third voice spoke up.

"These abacuses are for cavemen," Zert said.

"If you don't like it here, you should leave," Beth hissed at him.

Casey cleared her throat. "Zert, you sound tired. You had a long walk here yesterday and probably haven't gotten enough rest. Why don't you go home for a bit and come back to school in an hour or so? We'll start over then."

Kicked out on the first day. Zert stood up and ran out the door of the schoolhouse.

23

TURTLE BATH

Once Zert had escaped, he glanced back at the schoolhouse. Through the walls of the bottle, all the kids looked warped, as if he were viewing them through a fun house mirror. Everyone was working on the math problem except Beth. She stared at Zert through the glass.

Bug eyes, he'd say to her if she gave him any more trouble. Only here, he was sure that was a compliment. To get to the rock formation that looked like a hat, he had to navigate around a pair of BIG blue jeans, a green-and-pink T-shirt, a pair of black Breathe shorts, a pair of ladies' underwear, and a trampo-shoe, without the springs, which blocked the path. It was like a Rosie mall.

Setting off down the path, he hiked past the houses where the Rosies lived. They weren't built of wood and enclosed with picket fences as he had imagined last night. Instead, they were boxes perched between intertwined tree trunks, FastGrow bottles wedged between boulders, a Bot's head hidden by a bush, a plant holder obscured by tall grasses, a crate for cloned dodo food covered with leaves, and even half of a discarded globe smeared with mud. To the eyes of a BIG Zert, the village would look like a jumble of trash.

Maybe he could escape this place and find Abbot and they could . . . That was the problem. There were no urban trash rifles, 3-D pool halls, or anti-gravity fun houses here. Even if he bolted, there was nothing he wanted to do. The Rocky Mountain park may have been wide open, but he felt as cramped as if he were locked up in a cell at Teen Jail.

At the Hat, he turned right and headed toward the cave.

A filthy Styrofoam doormat greeted him in front of their hut. *Correction.* Calling the place a hut made it sound grander than it actually was. It looked more like one of the shanties in Botland where the scavengers lived among the headless robots.

He pushed the door open. In first grade, he had had a lunchbox that looked like the blue-and-white cybratom that covered one wall.

I live at Number One Lunchbox Lane.

Only this shack wasn't funny. Their apartment in the back of their store hadn't been luxurious, but this Rosie house was one of the poorest he had ever seen. The magazine photos were torn and holey. The floor was packed dirt.

His father looked up. He was pushing a metal desk cut from a soda can against the wall. "Why are you home so early?"

"Their school is really stupid," Zert complained.

"So you already know everything that the Rosie kids are learning?" his father asked.

"They use abacuses and feather pens," Zert said.

"It's our new life," his father said, stroking his chin. "Let's try to make the best of it."

Zert looked around at the nearly empty shack. "We should have stayed home."

His father let out a sigh. "*This* is our home." He paused. "At least I hope it is."

"It may be your home." Zert remembered those berries stuck on sticks that Beth had called abacuses and how different it was from his sleek RASM portal back home. "But it'll never be mine!" he yelled.

His father glared at him. "Keep your voice down." He paused and then in a quiet voice added, "We've got to hope you're wrong. Because if you're not, things are going to get a lot worse."

Zert squeezed his head between his hands. Abbot and his family might have starved to death or been eaten by a ... what? He didn't even know all that could go wrong in this place.

He drew in a deep breath. "What will we do, Dad, if this doesn't work out?"

"Whatever we need to do. But let's try to avoid that predicament," his father said.

Zert sighed.

"This isn't easy for me either, Zert," his father said quietly. "I wish the Rosies understood how much you've been through in the last forty-eight hours and gave you a break. But I'm just afraid that their experience with this other family has prejudiced them into thinking we'll never succeed here." He paused. "And it's not true. We *will* succeed."

Zert started to shake his head.

"Look. You didn't even get a chance to clean up this morning. Why don't you take a bath? Then we'll talk," his father said.

"Where? There's no bathroom," Zert said. Last night, they had used the water remaining in their water bottles to wash off. "There's no toilet. There's no running water. We're on a camping trip that will never end—not *ever*."

His father smiled. "But you *can* take a bath. There's rainwater in a turtle shell nearby."

"The rainwater's clean here?" Zert asked.

"I told you. The Rocky Mountains block low-hanging pollution clouds. The park gets plain-rain. You saw the decontamination pills in our backpacks. Just to be sure, I've already treated the water. It's perfectly safe."

Zert grabbed his backpack. A tub with clean water. That was something.

"It's to the east of us," his father called as Zert hurried out the door.

Being a Rosie was permanent. But maybe he wouldn't have to live with that fishy smell he'd picked up yesterday for the rest of his small life.

〉〉〉

In Low City DC, the streets were labeled as east and west. Here, there was just vegetation, boulders, and a big open sky.

The sun set in the west. That's what his old scoutmaster had told him.

Zert turned his back on the rising sun to face a squat bush loaded with purple berries. Beyond that, he spotted the edge of an upturned shell.

He passed through a forest of weeds—some spiky and green, others with yellow pods, one with tiny red flowers popping out of its stem and smelling of garlic—as he hiked toward the shell.

A crude rock stairwell led from the ground to its curved rim. With the breastplate removed, the upturned shell resembled a large, funky swimming pool.

On Flade Street, if he had bathed naked in a giant turtle shell, he'd probably have gotten a month in Teen Jail. Or a year in the Teen Insane Ward. But bathing in turtle shells was on the low end of the new Rosie Bizarro Spectrum.

After he stripped down, he climbed up the rock stairwell and dipped his body into the water. It was cool, not freezing. The dirt from his hike clouded the water around him. He pressed his back against the hard, bumpy surface of the shell.

Overhead, the artificial moon was there as always, but there were no lifters, there were no cloudscrapers, there was no Up City.

He could barely make out the gaseous high-highways through the branches that curled and twisted to form a green roof above him. His bath was almost as refreshing as a dip in the hot tub at the Blue Line Health Club, built in the old subway system.

A hundred years ago, people had burrowed into the earth to build underground stores and trains. Then, after it grew so hot and the radiation level on earth became too high, people constructed whole cities in the skies—the Up Cities—so they could start over again.

Now the Rosies were building in plain sight. In the wild.

He surveyed the trees and bushes and saw them graying as a cloud passed over the sun. He had no idea who or what lived in those shadows.

As he struggled to stand, he gazed down at the water's mirror.

The dirt had settled, and his reflection glittered back at him. He looked exactly the same: too much brown hair, too many freckles, light brown skin, and brown eyes. The world was completely different and exactly the same. Cribbie would have said, "Too much philosophy, Old Man."

Only he never got a chance to grow up to be an old man.

And I might not either.

> > >

Shivering, he hurried down the steps of the turtle bath. At the Blue Line Club, an attendant rented towels. Of course, in this background country there was nothing to dry off with except . . . leaves.

Zert "leafed" off. As he pulled his dirty boxers back on, he wished that he had thought to pack an extra pair. He had no comb either, he realized, as he ran his fingers through his wet hair.

He was pulling on his outfit of a hundred pockets when the ground started shaking. He heard the sound of a tank.

The shaking ground made him feel as if he were in the middle of a war, standing in the path of an army. Something crashed toward him, something that would have been huge even if he had still been BIG. He froze, too scared to move.

The animal's head burst out of the bushes first. It was as tall as a skyscraper. Its neck was thicker than a hyperloop, its coat shaggy, its horns spiked and powerful. The animal's face was too far away for him to even see it.

For an instant, the buffalo stood still in the yellow light.

Zert's heart was pounding. The animal could grind him into the dirt. It could gore him with one flick of its horns. But he was so small, and the buffalo was so big. He and that buffalo lived in two different worlds. He withdrew underneath the shelter of the turtle shell and watched.

The buffalo trotted toward him. This animal wasn't some designer animal, despite its strange-looking lumpy head and the saddlebags of fur on its sides. There used to be millions and millions of buffaloes all over this country, and then the cowboys killed them all. Now, he was in one of the few places where they had returned and were allowed to roam free.

The buffalo paused close to his hiding place. Its deep-black hoof was several times his height. Thick black hair covered its ankle.

Zert sucked in a deep breath to stifle a laugh. The animal smelled like leather shoes. The hoof raised up. If it were to drop down on the turtle shell where he hid, it would crush him.

Suddenly, Zert was engulfed in a horrible smell, and he staggered backward. Plump brown bullets splatted onto the ground outside the shell.

Smell warfare.

Zert could hear the buffalo trotting away. Holding his nose and covering his mouth, he ran out from under the shell to try to catch one last glimpse of the animal. At the edge of the clearing, the creature stopped and tossed its big head. Its eyes—two brown moons—turned to stare right at him.

Zert started to use his communicator to take a photo of the animal, and then he remembered. The buffalo snorted, as if he and Zert shared the joke. Then it galloped into the bushes and its furry tail disappeared.

I'm an explorer of this New World, Zert thought. *And I've seen my first buffalo. But it means nothing if there's no one I can tell.*

He squeezed his naked wrist where his communicator used to be and stared at the steam rising from the pile of buffalo poop.

24

MUNGO JUMBO

Once upon a time in a far-off land, Chinese had been his worst subject in school. *If only my life were a fairy tale*, Zert thought. *Fairy tales have happy endings.* But his face stared back at him from the shiny top of his can-desk at PeopleColor Schoolhouse. He could see his feather pen and his blackberry inkwell. This was not some bizarro dream.

Even though he'd washed in the turtle bath that morning, his outfit smelled like campfire smoke. The smoke had overtaken the scent of miniature wolf. *Chub, I hope you're alive.*

"Before we continue our unit on insect agriculture, I'd like someone to tell Zert about our first settler," Casey said. Her gaze landed on Beth. "Beth, why don't you?"

Millicent broke in, protesting, "I'm sure Zert's heard about Millard R. Dix." As usual, her cheeks looked flushed and her green eyes flashed with excitement.

Of course. Cribbie and he had often talked about Millard R. Dix. The Rosie hero *was* as famous as George Washington or President Honestloyalkind. *NOT.*

Millicent turned to Zert. He was sitting between Beth and

Millicent in the second row. "Millard R. Dix is my namesake," she said.

"You're named after Millard Dix. He's not named after you," John protested.

The kid needed braces. What would the Rosies use to make them? A soda can?

"Zert, you know who Millard R. Dix is, don't you?" Beth asked in a you've-got-to-be-kidding tone.

Zert considered lying for a moment. But then he admitted, "No."

The class tittered.

"Millard R. Dix . . . ," Beth began. Her tone was flat, bored, as if she were talking to a kindergartner. "We call him MD . . . was the first person to volunteer to test the minimizer function. His wife, Ethel, wanted to try it too. MD shrank first. As an experiment, he was minimized in Doctor Rosario's office. When Ethel Dix saw how small her husband was, she refused to shrink."

Uncle Marin hadn't just lost his nerve. He had never planned to leave his new girlfriend. He was probably kissing Glade's red, red lips right now. But why? His dad was right. You needed your family. Why would Uncle Marin betray them?

"Can I tell him the rest of the story, Beth?" When Beth shrugged, Millicent jumped in. "Doctor Rosario didn't want MD to travel to the park alone, you see, Zert, but MD wanted to make sure that if another war or Nuclear Mistake happened, people had a new way to live and another place to go. Neither Doctor Rosario nor Ethel Dix could talk him out of it."

Milliard R. Dix needed to see a shrink! Stifling a laugh, Zert looked around at the faces of his classmates: Beth's bored eyes, Millicent's eager expression. He had a great joke, and not a single kid would get it.

"Doctor Rosario took him to Rocky Mountain National Park,"

Millicent explained. "He made arrangements to meet MD in the parking lot in two months' time. But from the beginning, MD had bad luck. The weather was unusually cold, and it rained a lot. And on one particularly wet day, he slipped on the banks of the stream and lost his backpack. After that, all he had to eat was a stick of jerky. The history books tell us that MD scoured the parking lot for food, but he found only a few crumbs of mongo."

Casey interrupted, "Millicent, tell Zert what 'mongo' is."

"I don't remember exactly, Casey," Millicent said. "I think MD found a few crumbs of pickle chips and Choco Bombs."

Smiling, Casey said, "I mean the definition."

"Oh. It's salvageable trash," Millicent said to Zert.

Zert nodded. The fact that the Rosies had a special word for garbage made sense. Almost everything in Paradise was made from trash.

Casey nodded at Millicent. "Go on."

"Since snow covered the ground at the time," Millicent said, "MD holed up under a log. He was starving. He didn't know if he would survive long enough to be able to meet Doctor Rosario later on. MD was afraid that if he died, the doctor would call off the whole project.

"One day, as MD was staring at the frozen ground, hungry for a meal, he noticed that the snow-covered log he used for shelter was infested with roaches. He caught a roach and cooked it for dinner." Millicent paused for a breath, then finished with, "The rest is history."

Instead of pilgrims eating the first turkey with the Native Americans, Zert imagined shrinkmeister MD biting into a roasted roach, stuffed with soy oyster dressing, a tiny apple in its mouth. This version of the classic tale was so bizarro that it was interesting.

"Roaches are an excellent source of protein," Millicent said.

Zert swallowed his smile.

"Zert," Casey said, "before he died of old age a few years ago, Millard R. Dix wrote a book. It's called *A Second Chance*. It lays out our mission."

Mission Thumb. Zert couldn't keep his smile away this time. Dr. Brown. Then Don G. Now Mary Kay Casey. These Rosies took themselves seriously.

Casey frowned at him as if she guessed his thoughts. "Zert, the BIG world has many problems. We are trying to create a self-sustaining world to show them the way, if things were to fall apart."

But BIGS would never shrink.

Or would they?

He and his father did.

"Now, class," Casey said, "get out your tablets. You have a test on Friday on the advantages of micro livestock. Dawn, how many cubic feet of land space do insects need to produce a pound of food for BIGS?"

"Only two cubic feet," Dawn said. With short, light-brown hair and dark eyes, her oval face reminded him of an acorn.

An acorn. What was happening to him? BIG Zert wouldn't have had this thought.

"Compare that with cows, John," Casey said.

"Cows need two acres of land to produce one pound of beef," John said.

"If we contrast the life cycle of a grasshopper with the life cycle of a cow?" Casey went on.

Geez. A grasshopper's lifestyle.

Zert dipped his pen in the inkwell in the corner of the desk and dragged his pen across the page of recycled paper. A quill pen wasn't easy to write with. His handwriting came out bumpy and uneven on the rough paper. He wrote: "Bugs stink."

He lifted the quill pen off the page, noticing that something was causing his hand to shake. His feet were quivering. The bottle was jiggling.

Beth and Millicent dropped onto their knees on the floor. Dawn crawled underneath her desk. The entire room seemed to be shaking.

Zert wobbled up. "What is it? A bomb?" he yelled to his teacher, noticing the beginning of a loud noise.

Mary Kay Casey's mouth was opening and closing, but he couldn't hear her words. A roar was building in the background.

Casey motioned for him to lie down on the floor.

Zert shook his head. If terrorists were dropping bombs, this PeopleColor schoolhouse with its plastic walls was the last place he wanted to be. He began crawling toward the lip of the bottle as the noise grew louder and louder. It was slow going as he slid from side to side in the room. Finally, he managed to pull himself out of the lip and gazed upward.

A lifter was overhead, flying low, right above the tree line. It was gray, and Zert had never seen the model before. There was an advertisement written on its belly between its retractable wheels: "The First Lifter Microscope."

Zert gasped. Already there were developments in the BIG world that he knew nothing about.

The lifter passed overhead, and he clutched a thick vine to keep from being carried away by the wind. It was so intense, he struggled to hold on. And if the vine gave way, he was lost.

Until this moment, he had never thought he would owe his life to a vine.

When the wind finally died down, he looked up to see his teacher's worried face peering at him from the lip of the school-house.

Zert released the trailing plant and started for the door.

"Zert, it doesn't happen often, but every once in a while, a lifter will pass overhead," Casey said. "The school is staked into the ground to withstand the high winds. It's the safest place you can possibly be."

"I thought it was . . ."

"I don't care what you thought," Casey interrupted. "In the future, you will obey me. With that high wind, you could have been"—she put her hands on her hips and glared at him—"in Timbuktu by now."

"Yes, Casey," Zert promised, his hands still white from clutching the vine.

"There are many dangers here that you can't even appreciate yet," Casey said. She leaned in closer to him until her pigtails brushed his shoulders. "You *must* listen to me. Do you hear me?"

"Yes," Zert said again. Through the plastic walls, he could see Beth mouthing at him, "Coward." His new teacher already hated him too.

What happened next was so unexpected that, for an instant, he forgot the cold feeling of loneliness that had filled his stomach ever since he had seen those Mag Lev machines lining Dr. Brown's walls.

His teacher reached for him and hugged him.

As she held him tight, he started shaking.

"I know," Casey whispered. "I know."

25

A CAMEL COMES A' CALLING

"Race you to the community center." "What's your chore today?" "Are you ready for the rodeo?" the kids were calling to each other as Zert turned to find the Hat.

He and Cribbie used to give directions like: "It's on the same side of the street as the water factory." Or "It's a block from the tele-school broadcasting station." Now he lived in a place where the landmarks were *rocks*.

When he rounded the bend, he found Millicent squatting in the middle of the path. She held a cricket, about her size, on a rope. No, a string.

The insect's long body rested on powerful-looking hinged legs and arms skinny to the point of looking malnourished. When BIG Zert had looked at a bug, he had only seen an impression of colors and a blur of wings, but here in Rosieland, he was able to see this insect's face. The cricket had coffee-colored eyes that hung like jewels above its trapdoor mouth. With its green-and-yellow cheeks flanking a flat, noseless face, the cricket was so homely that it looked sweet.

Millicent stood up. Bits of string bulged out of a front pocket of her overalls, a couple of hooks poked out of another, and a third was stuffed with bark. "I was waiting for you. How was your first day of school?" she asked.

"A little tough," Zert said.

Millicent turned red slightly, then said, "I can imagine." His bad day hadn't been her fault.

"What are you doing with the cricket?" he asked.

"We raise them," Millicent said. "My dad has the biggest bug ranch in the valley."

He was reaching for the cricket to pet it when a "halla-halla hoop" pierced his ears. Then, everything was still.

"What was that?" Zert asked.

"It's a gifting," Millicent said. She tied the cricket to a shrub. "Come on." She ducked into the shrubbery. He tried to follow but lost her in a tangle of leaves, underbrush, and roots.

"Millicent!" Zert called. Smiling, she popped out from nowhere. "What's going on?" he asked as he bumped into her.

"They're divvying up a rat," Millicent said. "Hurry!"

"Why are you running?" Zert asked as he started jogging after her.

Millicent called over her shoulder, "This is exciting news. Rats are great."

"Because?" Zert said.

"The meat, of course," Millicent said as they passed by a yellow sunflower on a hairy stem as tall as a holostatue of liberty. It was surrounded by jagged green stalks that ended in spears. "And it's my mom's turn for a rat drumstick. She uses the bones to make dishes."

Rat fat could be used to make candles. Rats' teeth were for . . . well, knives. Zert was surprised to realize the possibilities.

He ran hard into something and fell backward, as if he had been shoved. He tried to get up, but something that seemed like an older lady's white hair net held him back. It stuck to his skin and clothes. He fought and struggled to pull free, but it was useless.

"Millicent, help!" he shouted after her. She was too far ahead, and his words were carried away on a gust of wind.

He was trapped, food for some spider . . . if they ate meat. He couldn't remember what they ate. Would they eat his eyes first? No, that's what Millicent said about the rats.

Don't panic.

Zert was getting more entangled and knew he needed to force himself to stop thrashing around. He had to get out of here. He gathered his strength and gave one last mighty yank to free himself.

Millicent popped out of a green hedge, her eyes huge. "Stay still!" she shouted as she ran over.

Zert froze. Was there a spider? He bet he was about to get bitten.

"My dad will kill you if you bust a hole in his pen." Millicent began plucking at the string and pulling it off his shoes. "You've collided with the fence for one of his spare corrals. In the spring, this corral is loaded with hoppers and crickets."

She unwound a string from Zert's hand. "It took about twenty spiders to make this much webbing."

The spiders would have been as big as he was. "Wh—Where are they?" he asked, looking around.

"You mean the wild spiders? We don't have to worry too much about them." She lowered her voice and added, "Except at night."

Zert shuddered. Spiders could be the *Or Else* of this place. What if he and his father wandered into a hoard of spiders when they had to leave? The insects would catch them in their webs and eat them for dinner.

"There. You're free," Millicent said. "I forgot you don't know anything." She pointed at the ground. "Now, stay on the snail-slime trail so you don't ruin another corral."

A shimmering path cut through the weeds. It was silver,

studded with shining specs of pink. "You get snails to mark your trails for you?" Zert asked.

But Millicent was already running again.

Zert jogged after her, dodging a caravan of doodlebugs and stumbling on the uneven ground. He was out of breath by the time he reached a clearing full of Rosies. Round baskets that looked like wasp nests lined the space. Wormy things poked their heads out of the baskets. *Bug babies.*

"A fine rat," Zert heard someone say.

"To help during the wet season," another person chimed in.

"And we can make our gift to the tenderfeet," someone else added.

An old shoebox with a sign that said "Butcher Shop" stood in the center of the clearing. The shoebox was shellacked with a shiny paint. Some carcasses—skinned caterpillars?—dangled from the ceiling of the front porch.

The dead rat was propped up on a stick in front of the hut. A man, maybe the butcher, stood next to the rat. Dried blood covered him from his bald head to his feet, except for his white teeth, which flashed as he grinned.

A few Rosies lined up in front of the rat. Don G. was first in line. Millicent took a place at the end. Even his father was there, talking to one of the Rosies in the line.

The butcher handed Don G. a purple triangle, almost too big for him to hold in both hands.

"Thanks, Bear. I'm going to take this back to the rock," Don G. said. "It'll make a great soup for tonight's dinner."

The heart, Zert guessed. Breathing in the smell of blood and death, his own heart felt shaky, as if it, too, had come loose in his chest.

Beth emerged from one of the snail trails and jogged by, smiling. "You feeling sick?" She didn't wait for a response but hurried over to claim a place in line.

The butcher handed out claws, teeth, and body parts to the waiting Rosies.

Jack walked over to him. He had a string tied around his neck with a Rosie-sized needle dangling from it, like a real cobbler might wear. "Guess what? The villagers have given us the rat coat," he said. His grin was huge and fake. "Which means we help skin the animal."

"Dad, really?" Zert said.

"You may not be aware of this," his father whispered, "but the entire village is watching us right now, trying to decide whether to let us stay." He looked over his shoulder.

Zert tracked his father's gaze. The few men and women left in the clearing were staring at him. Their expressions said, *Yep—we'd be fine if you two starved in the wilderness.*

"This is going to make a great rope," Beth said as she walked by, holding a furry whip—the rat's tail.

His father clapped Zert on the back as if they were the best of buddies.

A few days ago, he didn't believe things could possibly get any worse than the Quarantine. But look where he was now. Living with a group of bug-loving, rat-killing thumbs.

He took a deep breath.

His father was smiling at him in an annoyed way, as if he were a customer but one whom his father didn't like.

Zert managed to smile back.

"Why are they giving us the coat, Dad?" Zert said.

"It's a Paradise tradition," his father said. Then, in a lower voice, he added, "If they were to turn us away, this gift would help us survive." He paused. "For a while."

"So," Zert said, eyeing the rat, "what are we supposed to do?" He had no idea how to skin anything, let alone a rat.

"We'll do whatever Bear Nelson says," his father told him. "Come on." He started toward the rat.

The rat's paws were curled into tight balls. Its chest was sliced wide open.

"I left a saw up on the ground for the head, Jack. Want to help me over here, Zert?" a spooky-sounding voice called out from inside the rat.

Zert wanted to puke. He glared at his father, but his father refused to meet his gaze.

"I've got an idea. Bear, don't you need someone to wash off these entrails in the trickle?" Jack pointed at the tubes piled on the ground.

"Good idea," Bear Nelson said. He emerged from the rat's body.

Bear Nelson's head was big for his body, as if Dr. Brown had gotten his proportions wrong in his machine. Bear's eyes were the only thing that weren't covered in blood. Even his vest was brownish red. "Hello, Zert. Good to meet you," he said, holding out his hand.

"Hi," Zert said, staring at Bear's bloody hand.

"Zert, your dad has a good idea. Why don't you carry the guts to the trickle?" Bear said, taking his hand back. "You can wash them off. Then, wrap them in leaves and take them to the smokehouse."

"W—Wrap . . . l—l—leaves?" Zert stuttered.

"There's some string on the porch of the butcher shop," Bear Nelson said, nodding toward the shoebox.

"Where's the smokehouse?" Zert asked.

"It's behind Raul Orlando's furniture store," Bear said. "You know where that is, don't you?"

Zert nodded. On his way home from the trickle yesterday, he had passed the storefront littered with cans. Raul Orlando, the furniture maker, was the one who had lent a desk to his father for their hut.

His father was standing on the porch of the butcher shop examining a shelf full of tools. He grabbed a ball of string the size of his fist and tossed it to Zert.

Zert stuffed the ball in a pocket and then leaned over the pile of stinky entrails, summoning his courage. He decided that the gooey purple object lying on the ground could be . . . a zoink ball. He picked it up and jammed it under his arm. The guts could be . . . rope. He draped one rope over each shoulder. He picked up a floppy thing that felt sticky . . . a pancake with syrup . . . and tucked it under his other arm. He smelled as if he had been rolling in dead meat.

And to think he used to complain when his father made him sweep the store.

His father was examining a saw constructed from an animal bone.

As Zert passed by the shop, he hissed, "Dad, this is repulsive."

His father looked at him. His blue eyes were icy. "This food is the difference between life and death to all the villagers."

"I understand, but . . ."

"I don't think you *do* understand," his father said under his breath. "Now go."

> > >

Zert knelt by the river—*no*, he corrected himself, *by the* stream, *no*, *by the* trickle—and pulled the last organ out of the freezing water. His hands were bright red, and he blew on his fingers to warm them up.

He dropped a gooey intestine on a green leaf, rolled it up, and tied it with a piece of string. *Rat organ sushi.*

Right now, BIG Zert would have been at home sitting on his purple couch. Maybe he would have been watching his favorite show or a holomovie. Chub would have been cuddled next to him.

If only his uncle Marin had never come for a visit. If only his father had never agreed to go. If only he had refused to go along with this crazy plan.

His tears came suddenly, and he pressed his face into his hands. He had shrunked, or was shrunken. Whatever the right word was, he'd never be a regular kid again. He cried for Chub and for Okar. For Cribbie. For his mom. For his friends at St. Lulu's. For Snow Blakely. For his apartment on Flade Street. For his communicator. But most of all, for himself. Zert Cage, glum thumb.

He didn't know how long he had been lying there when he heard his father call his name.

His father, now next to him, stooped to pick up a rat organ roll. The saw was looped over his shoulder, and his blue shirt was stained red. "Let's go find that smokehouse before it gets dark." He nodded toward the trail.

Zert picked up the other two rolls. He felt like a pack horse for body parts and guts.

"Dad, about Uncle Marin . . . ," he said as he hiked after his father.

His father shook his head. "Zert, we have enough to worry about . . ." His voice trailed off. "We only have nineteen days until that vote."

"If I ever catch him . . . ," Zert threatened.

"You'll do what? Bite his toe?" His father laughed.

Zert couldn't help himself. He started to laugh.

26

WHO DESERVES A WELCOME?

A few days later at school, Casey stood at the blackboard. In her leather pants and shirt, she might have looked like a frontier schoolteacher, if it weren't for her rat-skin vest.

A torn postcard leaned against the stone blackboard. It was much taller than anyone in the room, and the words on it were the size of zoink balls.

Zert had to look away from the photo on the postcard. It was of the dear old Statue of Liberty.

"In 1884, the people of France gave the Statue of Liberty to the people of the United States District to symbolize America's freedom from foreign powers," Casey read from the enormous words on the postcard. She paused and turned to gaze at Zert. "The card doesn't say who the artist was. Zert, you don't happen to know, do you?"

Zert shook his head. He could barely remember his own middle name.

"All of you, ask your parents, will you?" Casey said to the class before turning back to the postcard and reading again. "The Statue of Liberty has seven spikes on her crown. Can any of you tell me what the spikes stand for?"

"The spikes stand for the seven seas and the seven continents," Rudolpho said. Like the rest of the boys, he had on an outfit with a hundred pockets. But he stood out not only for his black-frame glasses but for the necklace of dried berries he wore over his shirt.

"Our statue should have one more spike," Beth called out. During art for the last week, the class had been carving a Statue of Liberty out of a bar of green soap.

Beth's bare and dirty toes wiggled underneath the desk they shared. Her brown hair drooped down over her shoulders and onto her red T-shirt, which looked smudged.

"Yeah," Millicent said. Her cheeks, pink as if she had just finished scrubbing them, clashed with her fuzzy purple shirt. She wore overalls, and her pockets bulged with trash. "The eighth can represent the Newest World."

"Good idea," Casey said. "Zert, you're working on the crown, aren't you?"

Zert nodded.

"Remember to carve an extra spike." His teacher smiled at him. Today, her earrings hung low and ended in dragonfly wings.

"Zert, did you ever see the Statue of Liberty?" Casey said.

"Not the real one," Zert said.

That terrible night when Cribbie had stood at the door of the store, holding his glow light, his friend had looked like a damaged Statue of Liberty. Zert had cracked the door, Chub had poked her nose out, and everything had ended so badly, despite what he had intended that day. He pressed his fist against his chest to drive away the memory.

When Casey kept her gaze fixed on him, he added, "But I saw her every day anyway. A store across the street from my house sold Lady Liberties made out of light." He remembered the shining statues. With their green trunks and golden torches, the Lady Liberties were beautiful.

Millicent burst out. "*Light* statues?"

"Oh, Millicent," John said in an impatient tone. "You know he's just going to say, *If you!*"

"It's hard. But can you try to explain light statues to the class, Zert?" Casey asked.

This was the first time Casey had encouraged him to talk about his old life. She must have guessed how much he missed Flade Street, his home. Somebody cared about him. Somebody wanted to hear about something that *he* cared about.

"Holostatues look solid," Zert began carefully. "But they're made of millions of points of light. When you stand inside them, you feel like a star has exploded in your head."

The faces around the room remained blank, as if Zert were speaking to them in Chinese.

These kids had never even flipped on a light switch, so how could he possibly explain dense light? *Think of something in nature.* "Holostatues are people made out of moonlight."

Beth shook her head. She tapped her dirty foot against the dirt floor. "You can't trap moonlight. I've tried."

Zert sighed.

"Good effort, Zert," Casey said. "I know it's difficult to explain these things." She turned toward the students. "Class, I wanted to show you that Zert has a lot of good information. You should feel free to ask Zert questions. He's an expert on the BIG world."

Zert smiled a little. *I've got a PhD in trash wars, rats, and mini-wolves, for sure.*

"Can any of you guess why I chose the Statue of Liberty as our class gift to Ellis Log this year? What is its meaning for the Newest World?" Casey said.

Beth raised her hand. Her red cotton shirt was rolled up past her elbows, and her arms were rounded like a weight lifter's. "We came here to be free. Free of war, pollution, crime, and disease . . . millions of stupid things like holostatues"—her tone became angrier—"and FastGrow and PeopleColor and all the other products that BIGS think are so important."

"You don't know what you're talking about. I think products like FastGrow are stupid too," Zert said. "And my dad and I *never* drank PeopleColor."

"Beth." Casey smiled at Beth. "You say the statue stands for personal freedom. It's true that here in Paradise, we've succeeded in creating a beautiful, clean, self-sustaining world and that our class is carving a great statue." At the mention of the statue, along with the rest of the class, Zert looked through the wall of the schoolhouse. The funky object that the class planned to donate to Ellis Log stood just outside. "But I was actually thinking of another meaning of the Statue of Liberty. One that applies to our classroom. Can anyone guess what it is?" Casey asked.

"The poem we studied," Dawn said. She wore her sandy-colored hair parted on one side and pulled back in a knot. Probably the latest in Rosie fashion. But with her rough blue outfit, she looked like a pilgrim who had traveled to the United States District a long time ago.

"Good." Casey nodded approvingly. "What does the poem say?"

Millicent raised her hand but spoke out before Casey called on her. "Something about poor and huddled people."

"And who are those poor, huddled people?" Casey said.

If only Zert had Abbot or some other minimized kid to huddle with.

"The immigrants," Dawn called out.

"That's right," Casey said.

Casey looked pointedly at Beth. "What do you think the statue said to the millions of immigrants who came to America?"

Beth rolled her broad shoulders in an exaggerated shrug.

Casey said, "Beth Gibson, you can do better than that."

Beth scowled. "Hello, and glad to see you."

"Exactly," Casey said. "Paradise is a town of newcomers. It's the job of every Rosie to say, 'Hello, and welcome.' That's what the Statue of Liberty symbolizes for us Rosies."

Beth muttered, "Hello and good-bye." She paused. "That's what my dad wants us to say to all the minimized newcomers. And that's what I want to say to Zert Cage."

Casey's neck flushed. "Beth Gibson." Her earrings swung as she hurried over to the girl. "You need to be civil to Zert. If not, I'm going to talk to the village council. Not all of us agree with your father, and until the vote, Zert and his father have every right to be in our community." She wagged her finger in Beth's face. "You understand?"

Beth looked down at her desk. "Yes, Teacher."

When Casey turned back to the postcard, Beth glared at Zert, her eyes bulging with dislike.

〉〉〉

If he were standing in front of his old school, Zert would never have noticed the mass of purple clouds blocking the sun or felt the breeze rushing past. All he ever paid attention to in the city as he stood on the concrete in front of St. Lulu's were the passersby, many of them strange looking.

As he carved the crown of the statue, shavings piled up at his feet, and Zert breathed in the smell of soap. If he closed his eyes, he could imagine himself back at St. Lulu's in the CleanRoom, where Isal had pushed his head into the toilet and Zert had almost drowned.

He wouldn't let himself think about the way Cribbie had busted into the stall and saved him.

The crown of the soap statue was crooked. He was filing its eighth point, but it looked lopsided.

Millicent sanded Lady Liberty's long robe, which was supposed to fold and flow, only it didn't. It hung straight like a farmer's dress.

John worked on the tablet, which Lady Liberty held in her left arm and which bore the date of the Declaration of Independence. Beth chipped at the middle of the statue's face to make her nose. There was supposed to be a chain at the statue's feet, but that was too hard. Raul and Ivy were instead fashioning a rope. Dawn and the rest of the class chiseled the poem inscribed on the plaque.

Beth stepped back to admire her work. The knees of her pants were stained green from the grass. "Do you think the nose should be longer or shorter?"

"It looks good," Millicent said, squinting at the statue.

"Fine," John agreed without looking up.

Zert could feel Beth's gaze burning into his back.

"What do you think, Zert?" Beth said.

The real Lady Liberty looked brave, happy, and hopeful. With her fish lips and humped nose, Soap Liberty was an abomination. "It doesn't matter." He kept his back toward Beth as he put his knife to the crown and peeled off a layer of soap.

"What do you mean, it doesn't matter?" Beth asked.

"This doesn't look a bit like the Statue of Liberty anyway," Zert said, turning to face her.

Beth, who had been kneeling on the other side of Lady Liberty, said, "Say that again." She dropped her knife and took a step toward him.

"I said," Zert repeated loudly, "that it doesn't ma—"

Beth's muscles bulged as she rushed toward Zert, her hands in fists and her hair swinging wildly around her face. His whole body stiffened as he readied to face her. But she came to a screeching halt, her eyes flared wide.

Casey screamed, "NO!"

Zert looked down. He had been holding the knife to carve the crown. It felt cold and hard in his hand now. He hadn't meant to threaten her with it. When he dropped it near his feet, it hit the ground with a thud.

Beth took a sharp intake of breath. Her face was blood red, and her eyes bulged more than usual.

Behind her, John gaped as if Zert were an axe murderer.

Casey hurried toward them. "This is absolutely unacceptable!" She grabbed Zert by the arm, then Beth by the back of the neck. "You will both stay after school today." She held out her hand. "Now, Zert, give me that knife."

Zert picked up the knife and handed it to his teacher.

"We don't threaten each other with weapons here," Casey said sharply. "Violence goes against everything we believe in. You understand?"

Zert nodded. *I forgot I was holding it*, he wanted to tell her.

"And Beth, I'm even *more* disappointed in you because you know better. We came here to create a better world. This is truly your last chance. I understand your father's views, but that's no excuse. Now, apologize and shake," Casey ordered.

Beth stuck out her hand. "I'm sorry."

Zert shook her hand, which was wet with sweat. Despite her tan, Beth's face had now turned pale. She had truly believed that he was going to stab her, a defenseless kid.

Millicent's mouth hung open. She was wiping a tear from her cheek. What she thought he'd done, threatening another kid with a knife, was probably the worst thing she'd ever seen in her life.

"Apologize!" Casey instructed Zert.

"I'm sorry," Zert said.

"You'd better mean it," Casey said. She shook her finger at first Beth, then Zert. "If I ever catch you two fighting again, the consequences are going to be much stiffer."

Beth was bigger and stronger than Zert, and this world that they lived in was full of nooks and crannies. Zert knew that Beth didn't need to jump him at school; she could ambush him from anywhere. But Beth's head hung down, as if Zert had beaten her. She looked as if she didn't want to have anything to do with him ever again.

He had been wrong about her. About all of them.

Beth wasn't a violent girl, after all. She was like Lily Bridges at St. Lulu's, whose parents had never let her watch a zombie flick or even one with any blood in it. Beth didn't even know what violence was.

"You'll both stay after school today," Casey said again. She nodded her head so hard that her dragonfly earrings were in danger of falling off.

"Yes, Casey," Beth and Zert said in unison.

"Zert, you just made things much more difficult for yourself here," Casey told him. "And it's too bad."

But it was her unspoken words that stung. *You've wrecked things. Not just for yourself but for your father too.*

27

SACRED TRASH

Zert plopped down on the rise above the playground. The shadows of aspen trees fluttered above them. Their leaves rustled in the wind.

"I'm sorry you don't like it here," Millicent said, squatting next to him. Despite her outlandish outfit—her fuzzy purple shirt looked too fancy for her trash-overstuffed overalls—she reminded him of Melving Laird at St. Lulu's, who had talked to everyone. Especially the kids whom nobody liked.

"What did Abbot do that got him kicked out?" Zert blurted out.

Millicent sighed, and her green eyes darkened. "It was during dinner. Abbot stood on the ledge over Pancake Rock one night. He yelled 'Trash War' and threw mongo at all of us."

Trash wars were the thing kids his age did to get respect.

Millicent shrugged. "He ruined some good trash."

Here, throwing trash was like throwing gold and jewels.

"Mary Kay Casey and my parents wanted him to be able to stay, but Don G. and some others got his family kicked out," Millicent said.

"So you don't know where Abbot went?" Zert asked.

She shook her head and looked into the distance. "I feel a little bad." Then, she shook her head again and gazed down at her hands. Unlike Beth, she brushed her hair, but even her fingernails were black lines of dirt.

"What, Millicent? Tell me," Zert said. He sensed that she wasn't telling him something important.

"Zert's a loser!" he heard. The words had boomed out from the playground below them.

Zert gazed down the slope. Beth stood at one end of the plastic straw and Ivy at the other.

"You're a loser!" Ivy shouted back into the plastic straw before breaking down into giggles.

"Beth hates me," Zert said to Millicent.

"It's just that . . . you've seen so many things we haven't," Millicent said. She plucked a piece of grass and started tearing it into smaller pieces.

"When I first met her, Beth asked me a lot of questions," Zert said. "I tried to explain. It's just hard."

"Beth's in a tough spot." Millicent paused. "Of course, she's curious. Everyone is." She paused again. "But her father thinks that learning about the BIG world will make us sad and jealous about stuff we'll never have and that we'll lose interest in the mission."

John Gibson tore up the hill toward them, as though it were a fancy running track and not a trail lined with pebbles. He was barefoot. "I'll race you up a tree, Zert. How about it?"

John couldn't be feeling friendly. Not after what had just happened in art class. "Why are you asking me?" Zert said.

Millicent interrupted, "Not yet, John. He might hurt himself. It's only his first week here." She turned to Zert. "We scale the knots in aspen trees and see who can climb the highest."

"It's easy!" John said. His buck teeth poked out of his mouth when he smiled. It was a smile that meant its opposite. "Besides, you need to get ready for the rodeo"—he scowled at Zert—"unless you want me to beat you at *everything*." He spat on the ground. "Don't you dare ever threaten *my* sister again," he muttered. "Loser."

Before Zert could think of what to say, John ran off without a backward glance, yelling, "I challenge everyone to a tree race."

"What rodeo?" Zert broke the awkward silence.

Millicent replied, "It's after school next week. There are lots of contests: Worm Fishing, Archery, Fire Starting, the Catch-a-Greased-Roach Contest, Beetle Armor Fighting . . . But the hardest event is the Aspen Tree Race." She laughed. "I've been climbing all my life, and my fingers start shaking after a minute. Aspens go straight up."

First, the primitive abacus. Then, bloody rat skinning. Then, Zert had brought Paradise its first almost-stabbing. And now, greased roach contests and aspen-tree climbing. In Low City DC, at least, he had been good at zoink ball. In the Newest World, he'd never manage to even be average at anything.

Holly Cannon stepped on the clothespin to release the tomato soup can. As the can rolled down the rise, laughter floated out from inside the can.

At the bottom of the hill, Rudolpho tumbled out, wearing brown overalls that looked as if they had been made from drapes. He laughed as he tottered dizzily around. His glasses fell off. "Oh no," he said as he knelt and began searching for them.

Rain Martin hooted and did a cartwheel. She wore a red cape that looked suspiciously like the corner of a pocket handkerchief. Or maybe a napkin.

Next to him, Millicent tore another blade of grass into smaller and smaller pieces.

"You don't have to stay with me. Why don't you go play with the others?" Zert said.

"I don't mind," Millicent said. She looked off into the distance, as if searching for the best way to explain something. "Beth and

John lost their three older sisters because of the Nuclear Mistake," she said after a few moments.

On Flade Street, the owner of Roadkill Restaurant, Majong Pyler, had lost his wife in the nuclear blaze. But he didn't know anyone who had lost three family members.

"They died before Beth's and John's parents became Rosies . . . before Beth and John were even born. But the Gibsons really like Paradise." Millicent shot Zert a long look before she stood up. "All Beth and John and the rest of them really want is for you to like it here too."

He could work hard and try to control his temper, but if liking this place was what it took for him and his dad to be able to stay, well: *Impossible.*

> > >

"The early pioneers saw the settlement of the West as a divine mission. We are more like them than not."
—Millard R. Dix, *A Second Chance*

After school, Zert wiped Millard R. Dix's silly quote from the rock that served as a blackboard and wrote: "I will not harm another Rosie."

"Write it twenty times, please," Mary Kay Casey said. If he closed his eyes, it could have also been the voice of his old St. Lulu's teacher telling him to do something he didn't want to do. Teachers everywhere had the same teacher voice.

His mother used to be a teacher before she married his father.

This whole upside-down world would make more sense if she were here. She knew how to make things better. She used to put a cold rag on his head when he had a fever. She tweezed splinters that he couldn't even see out of his throbbing feet. She made sure the customers paid them today, not tomorrow. She could see through her brother.

She was not like his dad, who tried so hard but who burned dinner in the Food Machine, even though that was supposed to be impossible. His dad, who let Uncle Marin trick them. His dad, who now believed that the Rosies were going to let them stay in Paradise when they weren't.

Beth wrote on her side of the blackboard: "The BIG world is not all bad."

She may have written the words, but she didn't mean them. There was no way a girl who had never even seen one of the old flat movies would be able to appreciate the experience of watching a holomovie. No way a kid who grew up eating roach stew would understand how tasty meatloaf chips were. No way someone who had only lived in Paradise would ever be able to imagine Low City DC, alive with thousands of places to explore and be curious about. Beth didn't understand one thing about the BIG world.

Zert finished his fifteenth line. Adults were always talking about how confusing it was to be a teenager because your body was growing and changing. Well, it was confusing to have your body shrink. Besides wanting to go back to Low City DC, the only thing he wanted now was to be left alone.

Through the clear walls of PeopleColor Schoolhouse, he could see Soap Liberty lying faceup on the ground. She looked as plain and homemade as ever. He squinted to see her better. Maybe it was just the angle of the sun, but the chunky thing that was supposed to be a torch looked like, well . . . a roach.

Mary Kay Casey had remembered the name of the artist who had designed the Statue of Liberty. His name was Frédéric Auguste Bartholdi.

You see, Mr. Bartholdi, there's a group of tiny people, and we copied your work, but Lady Liberty is holding a roach. Do you mind?

Heck, yes, I mind, Mr. Bartholdi would say.

Zert wrote his last line and put the chalk down. *I don't blame you, Mr. Bartholdi.* "Can I leave now?" he asked Casey.

"I want you kids to be friends. That's got to be the plan. Understand?" Although Casey smiled, neither she nor the dragonfly wings dangling from the ends of her earrings looked happy.

Zert nodded.

"Yes, Teacher," Beth said. For the past hour, she hadn't met Zert's gaze, not even once.

He was Abbot the Second. And that was fine with him. Not for the first time, he wished that his father wasn't burdened with him. His father would fit in fine here.

If only he didn't have a loser for a son.

28

A HIPPO SUNBATHING

The flimsy front door of their hut stood open. On Flade Street, they'd had a double lock. Here, they had double protection too. *No burglars, and nothing to steal.*

Dropping his backpack on the floor, Zert slipped off his shoes and dug his toes into the scratchy rug that he and his father had made from rat hide.

His father sat on the floor unlacing a boot, or a thing that was supposed to be a boot. It looked more like one of the misshapen cookies that his father used to bake.

There was this beetle on the trail. It was enormous, and it was just sitting there. If it's still there when I return, I think I can catch it, Zert wanted to tell his father. He waited for his father to call out, *How was school?* Or *Made any friends today?* Or to ask him any of the other predictable questions that he asked at the end of the school day, even though Zert usually ignored him.

Zert walked over to him. "Are you OK, Dad?"

His father lifted his head. He wore his dark hair slicked back as always, but he hadn't shaved for a few days and black stubble covered the lower half of his face. His father's eyes looked moist.

"The boot I made is lousy," his father said. He had on the

convict outfit that he had picked up at Ellis Log, but it was covered in rat hairs.

Zert sat down on the fur carpet next to him.

"See?" His father held up the pile of leather. "I wore this around the cabin, and it's already ripped."

Zert took a deep breath. "Sorry, Dad."

The boot collapsed into scraps when his father dropped it. "This village needs a cobbler. I suppose I could try something else, but if I can't figure out just *any* work to do, the Rosies will think we're useless and we'll be voted out." He fingered a scrap of boot.

"Why didn't you think about this *before* we got here?" Zert asked.

Without looking up, his father mumbled, "I needed to get you away quickly."

Zert started to argue, "You're wrong," but the sight of his father's hands stopped him. His father's fingers were fumbling to fit the pieces of leather together, as if they were a puzzle that was too hard for him. Blood clotted on his thumb where the needle had pricked him. He looked beat-up and pathetic, but he wasn't giving up on his boots.

His father hadn't given up on him, either.

His father hadn't given up even in front of that holojudge. That judge had no mercy. If his father hadn't acted, Zert might be locked up in Teen Jail right now, listening to that holobum whine.

His father collected the scraps of leather, stood up, and walked over to the open door. He held the pieces up to the light, studying them. "I need to figure out how to make the seams stronger."

At this rate, there was no way his father was going to be able to make a pair of sturdy boots in time. In the end, his father's extermination business had been a failure too. If they were going to succeed in the Newest World, it was up to Zert. But first, his dad needed bucking up. *A* for *effort* and all that.

"Dad, I want a pair of boots."

His father smiled. "I've got an idea," he said. "This has got to work." He headed back toward the desk. "The string is fine. I just need to double it," he said to himself.

"Dad," Zert said, "I saw a beetle on the trail. I'm going to go catch it." He picked up a ball of string from the desk.

"Really?" his father said absentmindedly.

The string wouldn't fit in Zert's front pockets. Too many fish-hooks. He found some space in one of his back pockets. "If I catch it," he said, "would you help me build a corral?"

His father didn't look up from his wannabe boot. "Sure."

Zert couldn't open a bug pet store. People around here grew bugs to eat, not to play with. "Cage & Father Ranchers. Established 2083?" He grinned.

"It's a deal," his father said.

Zert stepped outside. The temperature had dropped, and the tip of Zert's nose was soon cool to the touch. As he tiptoed down the path toward the beetle, he realized that the snow, ice, and freezing cold of the wet season were right around the corner.

〉〉〉

Zert snuck around the bend and came face-to-face with the beetle in the middle of the trail. The bug would look like a baby hippo sunbathing, except that its shell, glowing blackish green, was shiny like the hood of the newest lifter, not rough like animal skin. Its legs were bent in funny places and covered in brown hair. Its flat brown face was earless and noseless, and the color of its beady eyes matched its enormous shell.

It must have heard him coming because the beetle, which was larger than Zert's head, fluttered its dark wings and took a step forward.

The beetle's eyes, which didn't seem to be able to move in their sockets, only stared straight ahead as Zert rushed over, slipped the noose around its head, and pulled it tight.

Batting its wings, the beetle took off and hovered above him like an insect version of a lifter. Zert tugged on the string, and the beetle landed in front of him. "Let's go," he said to the beetle.

Cribbie had once called him "a beetle brain." This must have been just some empty BIG saying though, because there was nothing beetle-brained about this bug; the insect knew that it had been captured. As Zert headed back toward his cave, the beetle followed his lead and lumbered after him slowly and deliberately, as if its shell were made of iron.

With each step, the insect squeaked, a sound so soft that BIG Zert would have missed it. Was it complaining or talking to him? Or were its legs just rubbing against its sides as it moved? In a few weeks, he promised himself he'd find out the answer to these questions and more.

Zert's Bug Ranch. The finest stock of Brahman Beetles in the land.

In one of her lessons, Casey had said that a beetle mother chewed up food and fed it to her children for thirty beetle years. But what did beetles eat? For all he knew, it could be something incredibly common, like dirt.

Ahead of him, Millicent turned onto the path from a side lane. She was running. Unlike Beth, who ran like an athlete, Millicent ran like a kid on an errand.

"Millicent!" he called out to her.

Millicent stopped and faced him. She had a white apron on over her overalls and was carrying a bucket labeled "Hopper Feed."

When she saw the beetle, she set the bucket down and came toward him. She patted the beetle on its curved back. "Nice one."

The beetle's eyes weren't warm like a mini-wolf's, but that was OK, because this beetle was going to be his supper someday. "Where should I put him?"

"My father can help you build a corral," Millicent said.

"Really?" Zert asked. He yanked on the beetle's leash in excitement.

"I'm sure he will. But you can ask him yourself," Millicent said, stooping to collect her bucket. "He's going to the giving circle to check the snare."

"I'll go find him after I show this beetle to my dad," Zert said.

"I've got to go to the community center. To finish my chores," Millicent said. "But I'll come help you after I'm done," she promised as she hurried off.

The kids all talked about the community center, but newcomers weren't even allowed to know where it was.

"Thanks," Zert called after her.

Flapping its layered wings, the beetle halted, like Chub used to do before Zert trained her.

Zert tugged on the string. "Come on, beetle. We've got a lot to do. Let's go get started."

29

WHERE THE ROACH AND THE CATERPILLAR ROAM

At the giving circle, the leaves had all been pushed aside. Deep scratches gored the earth. A gray rat, the size of a horse, lay by itself on the ground, its feet kicking and twitching.

The animal looked more like a Halloween demon than Okar. Froth foamed from its mouth, and its dark eyes sought out Zert's. Something stretched between the animal's neck and a thick wooden stake in the ground. It was a black wire.

Zert's father used to kill rats too. But although his father had lots of faults, he wasn't a rat torturer.

Zert bashed a pebble against the stake. After a few hard knocks, the stake toppled over.

The rat stared into his eyes for a long second. Then, it shook its large head and stumbled off into the weeds with the wire still circling its neck.

Voices approached, and he ducked into a nearby thicket.

"What the . . . ?" he heard Don G. say.

He peeked out from behind a cluster of ferns.

Don G. was staring at the hole in the ground where the stake had been. He wore a necklace of wire around his neck in addition to the rat teeth necklace he always wore.

Millicent's father emerged from a wall of weeds and joined him. Artica Chang was as tall as three bottle caps standing on their sides. He had a hooked nose and crinkly eyes. The hair on his head was sprinkled with white, unlike his jet-black mustache. Like Don G. and most of the adults, he wore a pair of pants of a hundred pockets, but his purple vest was cut from the same soft, fuzzy cloth as the shirt Millicent wore. Zert tried to remember where he had seen this fabric in the BIG world and decided that he had seen it in church.

"What happened?" Artica Chang asked.

"I don't know," Don G. said. "I've never see a rat pull out a stake before."

Artica Chang knelt next to the hole. "The wood must have been rotten."

"Maybe," Don G. said. He cupped his hand above his eyes and stared into the bushes, as if looking for the culprit.

A leaf tickled Zert's nose, and he sneezed. He took a deep breath and slid out from the bushes. He tried to look as innocent as a caterpillar.

"Mr. Chang," Zert said quickly. "I've caught a beetle, and Millicent told me that you'd help me build a corral."

Don G. glared at him. "If I find out you let that rat go . . ."

"What are you talking about, Don G.?" Artica interrupted.

"Did you know that boy threatened my daughter with a knife?" Don G. said, scowling.

"But . . . ," Zert started to defend himself. Then, he thought about what Millicent had told him. Don G. had lost children in the Nuclear Mistake. He didn't blame the man for being furious with anyone who threatened his daughter. He'd never be able to listen to Zert's side of the story.

"I heard that tale," Artica said. "But Millicent said Zert didn't even know he had the knife in his hand."

Zert nodded. "It's true."

"Say whatever you want, Artica," Don G. said, his voice rising. "But the new boy is never going to make it here." He stomped off.

Artica Chang turned and gazed patiently at Zert.

Zert remembered why he had come. His beetle needed a place to sleep tonight. He explained the situation to Artica. "I'd really appreciate your help," he said.

"I tell you what," Artica said, smiling. "Let me pick up some webbing, and I'll meet you by the school in an hour."

> > >

The slope was so tightly grassed over that it seemed to be painted green, except for the brown trail that zigzagged from PeopleColor Schoolhouse to the banks of the trickle.

Artica Chang hiked toward Zert, carrying a bundle on each shoulder as the sun played hide-and-go-seek behind some gray clouds.

Zert waited next to a homemade cart constructed from a can and four spools. The class's deformed Statue of Liberty lay on its side inside the cart, ready for a volunteer to haul it to Ellis Log.

"Let's go be bug cowboys," Artica Chang called out when he drew near.

Zert smiled. If he could trap enough bugs, he wouldn't have to get along with the other kids. And his dad could forget about trying to make boots. He and his father could just leave. Insects roamed in every corner of this giant park. He could hunt them and enlarge his herd. But first, he would need to learn how to take care of them.

"My dad has already started building our corral," Zert told Artica as they set off together on the trail up the slope to the caves. They had chosen a clearing just a pebble's throw away from their hut as the site to grow their herd.

"Millicent told me that you have hundreds of hoppers and crickets each spring. How do you keep that many penned?"

"Our spiderweb netting is strong," Artica said.

"I remember," he said softly. That day he'd gotten trapped in one of Artica's spare corrals seemed so long ago now. Yet they had been in Paradise for less than two weeks.

"Of course, we lose a few sometimes," Artica was saying. "But in six months, you wouldn't believe how many insects we have here." He shook his head. "Our crickets and hoppers are even more plentiful than the buffalo were when the first BIG settlers arrived in the west."

"Where do you find the webs?" Zert ask him.

"We have a spider farm," Artica said.

Whoa! Zert pictured a line of spiders with chairs underneath them and farmers milking them for silk.

"Someday," Artica said, "this whole valley will be full of insect ranches. We're developing the most varied and sophisticated techniques for growing and harvesting insects that the world has ever known."

"What do I feed my beetle, Artica? How often do I water him? What's that squeaky sound they make? And when do they mate?" Questions started tumbling out of Zert's mouth.

"Hold on!" Artica Chang said, smiling. "One at a time."

But they had already reached the dead end in the trail.

Zert heard the sound of chopping as they approached the cave.

"Dad, it's us," Zert called.

"I've got a good start on our corral," his father called back.

The beetle stood in the middle of a clearing, tethered to a stake while his father chopped wood. The plan was to build the corral around him.

Artica crossed the clearing. "Your beetle's huge," he said. "Where did you find it?"

"On the way home from school," Zert said.

"Zert roped it and brought it here," his father said.

Zert walked up to the beetle and petted its shiny wings. His own reflection shone back at him. His brown hair had grown shaggy, and his face looked darker than it had when he had arrived.

"When I was growing up in Antarctica, we had fat stock shows. This one would win a blue ribbon," Artica said.

"I guessed that's where you got your nickname," Jack said. He had tied a bandana around his forehead to keep the sweat from dripping into his eyes.

"Antarctica was the last frontier." Artica chuckled. "Until now."

Jack stood up straighter. *Oh no.* He was about to launch into one of his stories about the Antarctica Wars.

"Will I be able to find any crickets or grasshoppers this late in the year?" Zert interrupted.

"Not likely," Artica shook his head. "You'll have to look to roaches to fill out your herd."

Zert grimaced.

His father cracked his knuckles. He had to be thinking about all the years when roaches were the most disgusting of all bugs.

Zert was about to remind his father of the crummiest motel on Flade Street, where all the drug dealers hung out. It was called "Roach Motel." But Artica interrupted.

"I know. I know," he said, pulling on his mustache. "It's strange. Like you, I used to hate roaches. Now I grow them. My wife has at least fifty roach recipes." He shrugged. "We laugh about it all the time."

Millicent skidded into the clearing on sandals tied to her feet with bark. She stopped so fast that a bag labeled "fleas" tumbled out of her front pocket.

"How'd you find us?" Artica asked.

"Heard your voices," Millicent said.

"Well," Artica said, "let's get started, Jack. Where are your twigs?"

"Over here." His father pointed at a pile of wood.

"We'll be finished in no time." Artica started whistling. "And then, Zert, you and I can have a little talk about micro-ranching."

Millicent dragged a twig to the corner where Zert's father had dug a hole.

Zert set the twig upright while Millicent shoveled dirt around it. It was his first insect corral and his best moment in Paradise so far.

"Home, home on the range," Artica sang.

"Where the deer and the antel—" Zert started to sing along, but stopped.

"Where the roach and the caterpillar play," Artica and Millicent crooned.

A bug rancher. There were worse things to be. *Maybe.*

30

BEING BAD AT
STUFF IS HARD

Saturday afternoon, Zert stepped up to a peg in the ground with his bow while the whole village of Paradise watched from the sidelines.

His father wouldn't let him sit out of the Rosie rodeo. "Don't let them think you're a quitter," he'd told Zert.

The archery target was a piece of a BIG blue T-shirt stuffed with pine needles. Only part of the original slogan was visible. It read: "HONK IF."

Honk if you're living a thumb-sized nightmare.

The string from the bow cut into his fingers. If only it was a zoink toggle instead. Then, he might have a chance to hit a bull's-eye. He might even have a chance to hit the target.

He hitched up his baggy pants and recalibrated his aim. As he got ready to release, he heard his father whisper from behind him, "You can do it, Zert. You can do anything."

Even as he fired, his fingertips told him that the arrow was going to miss the target. The arrow whizzed past "HONK IF" and lodged in the dirt with a thud. Before his father could say anything encouraging, Zert lowered his bow and hurried away.

He spotted Millicent's dark, straight hair in the crowd. When he slipped in beside her, she smiled at him. The ends of her mouth crinkled, and her eyes lit up. Her smile would win her friends in the BIG world. It was a smile that said she knew him and liked him anyway. "Don't worry," she said softly. "We've been doing this all our lives." If he'd lived here all his life, he still wouldn't be able to shoot like these kids. Millicent had missed the bull's-eye by only a minnow's scale.

When he didn't respond, she added, "You've only just been here for two weeks." All of the Rosies had dressed up for the rodeo, and Millicent's pink T-shirt was decorated with bits and pieces of pebbles that glinted in the sun.

"Good job, son." His father had found him and clapped him on the back.

"Sure, Dad," Zert mumbled. He'd never been athletic. But here, he felt downright uncoordinated. He was a loser, as John and Beth had said.

"I'm going back to work," his father said. He wasn't wearing a cowboy hat, like many of the Rosies—he didn't own one—but he had worn a rat-skin belt in honor of rodeo day. "My boots are really getting good."

"See you," Zert said. His father was obsessed with finishing those boots. He had stuck around only to support Zert's rodeo efforts. *A lot of good* that *did*.

Wearing blue-jean shorts and a blue T-shirt, Beth stepped up to the line next. She wore a Rosie version of a cowboy hat on her head and had pulled her messy hair back with a furry ribbon. In one motion, she put the arrow in place and stood taller as she drew back the bowstring. It twanged, and the arrow hissed as it raced toward the target.

Thud. A bull's-eye.

Millicent cheered along with the rest of the crowd. Zert gave a few claps.

Dawn Nelson approached the start peg to compete next. From the neck up, she could have been any ten-year-old girl anywhere. But her cowboy hat fashioned from moss and her blue cotton overalls with bulging pockets were unique to Rosieland. She took a pair of fur gloves out of one of them and slipped them on.

Dawn didn't hit a bulls-eye, but *thud*, she hit the target, right in the middle of the "IF."

Fifteen minutes later, it was clear that Zert was the only kid whose arrow had missed the target entirely.

Artica grabbed Beth's hand and raised it upward. His cowboy shirt looked as if it had previously been a garbage bag. He had drawn white circles on the black plastic where buttons should be. "We have a winner in Archery!" he shouted. "For the eighth year in a row, Beth Gibson." Beth leaned forward. When she straightened up, another silver medallion hung from her neck. This one said, "Grand Champion." Beth beamed at the crowd.

Zert had come in ninth in Fire Starting and last in the Doodlebug Roping Contest. He wasn't able to get off the ground in the Aspen Tree Race. Even Holly, Dawn, and the other little kids . . . er . . . and even littler kids . . . had earned more points than he had.

But the Rosie rodeo didn't matter. Not really. His beetle was thriving on the chopped-up plants he fed it and with water from the trickle. He'd learn as much as he could about bug ranching. Then, he'd escape with his dad and never have to see Beth Gibson or her dad again.

"Our next event, the Catch-a-Greased-Roach Contest, is about to begin," Casey shouted. Her pigtails fell down over a long-sleeved shirt with real, not painted-on, buttons. As Zert was trying to figure out what kind of insects the buttons were made out of, he heard a scream. "Aahh!" Casey's mouth hung open as she pointed toward a tattered forest of thistles, ragweed, and grass.

Zert looked where she had aimed her finger. For an instant, a rat stared right at him. A necklace of skin circled the rat's neck where the wire had cut through the fur.

Zert nodded at the rat before its tail whipped the air, and the animal disappeared into the quaking vegetation. He wouldn't swear that they were friends or anything, but that rat had gazed at him as if he knew that Zert had been the guy who had saved his life.

Cleama Gibson, Bear Nelson, and Harriet Chang rushed up to Mary Kay Casey. "What's wrong?" "What did you see?" "Are you all right?"

"A rat!" Casey said, her face drained of color, as if she'd come face-to-face with the fiend on that show *World's Scariest Faces*. "It was over there, staring at all of us," she said in a shaky voice.

Millicent clutched Zert's arm. "That must have been some rat. Casey doesn't usually get upset."

The thistles were still wobbling where the rat had escaped.

"How big was it?" "How close was it?" "Do you want to sit down?" the women asked Casey in panicked voices.

Don G. and Beth had already picked up their bows. The father-daughter team was headed off-trail into the wilderness to chase their quarry.

Millicent and John walked up. Millicent took his arm. With her pebble-decorated shirt and his mossy cowboy hat, they made quite a pair. John had on a cowboy vest of polka-dotted cotton that Zert guessed was once men's underwear.

"Don't be scared," Millicent said.

John gazed at him, and for once, Zert was surprised to see concern in John's eyes. "My father and sister will find that animal."

Rats weren't dangerous to humans. Even small humans. He was sure of that. One-thousand-percent sure. But the way John and Millicent were looking at him made his stomach ache. "I used to have a rat as a pet," Zert told them.

Millicent mouthed the word *no*.

"Yeah," Zert bragged, his voice growing louder. "Okar lived in a cage with a house and a fire pole. I played with him every day."

John gawked at him. "We have this game." He glanced at Millicent. "It's called Rat Attack."

"John," Millicent said, pushing her bangs out of her eyes. "No. Not that."

John grinned, showing his buck teeth. "Someone keeps the fire going. The rats come out and investigate the smoke. Then we yell 'Rat Attack' and shoot the rat." He smirked. "You should come play with us."

"I don't want to hunt rats." Zert turned his back on them. He wanted to go home. Since he couldn't go back to Flade Street, the cave would have to do.

"Zert, wait," Millicent said.

"Aww," John said, "if he wants to doodle out, let him."

"The next game is really fun. The winner is crowned as 'Roach Cowboy,'" Millicent called after him.

"We let the biggest loser in the rodeo win the title. It's usually a little kid, but this year . . ." John's voice trailed off.

Zert pushed past a low-hanging vine. He set off in a jog down the snail trail in the direction of the Hat. The rock formation looked so much like a hat that it could have been a man-made statue.

The statue of a roach in front of his father's shop had worn a red cowboy hat, which had cast a shadow over the lower half of its face.

The roach cowboy's lips had been twisted into a mysterious smile, as if the statue knew a secret, and it was terrible.

31

A DOUBLE DOG DARE

Zert set his bow by the door of the hut.

"How was the Catch-a-Greased-Roach Contest?" his father asked without looking up from his workbench.

"Didn't go." Zert joined him at the red-and-silver table, originally a Vita juice can, that his father had bartered for a piece of rat hide.

"Why didn't you stay for the game?" his father asked.

"Didn't want to," Zert said. Before his father could scold him, he added, "On the way home, I trapped a roach." It was a baby, and it had made an awful hiss as he had roped him.

His father looked up from a pair of gray boots that he was working on. "Did you put him in the corral?"

"Yeah," Zert said. "Dad, those boots look better." No one would ever want to wear them, but at least they looked like boots now rather than melted chocolate chip cookies.

His father beamed. "The problem was the string. I doubled it, and it works much better."

"That's great, Dad. Are those mine?"

"You bet!" His father met his gaze. "The sun's still out. Why don't you go outside and play with the other kids?"

"I'll just stay here," Zert said. But when he looked around the small space, he realized that there was nothing to do except play a rousing game of tic-tac-toe on the dirt floor. Against himself.

"Part of your problem, Zert," his father said, "is that you hold yourself apart. If you tried harder to be part of the group, you wouldn't be so unhappy."

Zert sighed. "You used to get mad at me for being a follower. I can't do anything right."

His father began cracking his knuckles. "I'm sorry. I know it's hard for you here. It's just that the village votes on us on next Saturday. That's only a week from now, and I'm worried."

"I know, I know," Zert said. He gazed out the door of the hut. The setting sun lit the mountain's peak into a reddish flame. The sky was the color of strong lemonade. Or here, in a land with no lemons, it was the color of . . . well, itself.

"If we mind our manners, act enthusiastic, and do everything we can, we'll convince them to let us stay in Paradise," his father said.

Zert sighed. "I'm going to the trickle, Dad."

"Think about what I said," his father called after him.

His father might be able to be hopeful. But Zert couldn't be. They were going to get kicked out soon, and they wouldn't be able to eat his father's misshapen boots.

Zert hiked to a sandy spot next to the trickle. He spotted Beth, John, Millicent, and Rudolpho sitting on the overturned turtle shell under the lily pad.

Turtle Shell Resort.

John held part of a half-eaten cricket leg to his mouth.

Millicent held up a cookie. "Hi, Zert, come on up."

"Nah, I'll stay down here," Zert said. He tried to skip a pebble over the trickle, but it sank midway. *Can't even skip a pebble.* But none of the kids seemed to notice.

Beth popped a cookie into her mouth. Her mother made delicious cricket cookies.

"Zert told me that he used to keep a pet rat," John said.

Beth frowned. Her hair was pressed to her head where her cowboy hat had been, and the sun glinted off the medals hanging around her neck. "He's a liar. No one would want a rat for a pet."

"I'm not scared of rats," Zert said firmly. There was so much he couldn't do and didn't know. But here in Rosieland, he was *the* rat expert.

Beth cast a sideways glance at John before facing Zert. "My dad and I found the rats' nest. It's by the abandoned cabin. Who wants to play Rat Attack after dinner tonight?"

"I don't like that game, Beth," Millicent said.

"I double dog dare you. Come with us, Zert," John said.

That's how Cribbie had caught Superpox. Eckle had dared Cribbie and him to wage a trash war. He should say no. It was stupid to take a dare.

"Are you in or are you a scaredy dog?" Beth asked Zert.

He winced at the mangled BIG-world phrase. "I'm in," he heard himself promise.

"You're bait," Beth said.

"Are you sure, Zert? I don't think . . . ," Millicent said. She gazed at him, her green eyes round.

Maybe he *didn't* want to do this. But it was too late.

"We'll set up camp by their nest," Beth interrupted. "While Zert keeps the fire going, the rest of us will hide behind the rock. When they come out of the nest, we'll yell, 'Rat Attack.'" She nodded at Zert. "You run away, and we'll . . ." To demonstrate, she picked up her bow, aimed an arrow at a gnat buzzing by a nearby twig, and let the arrow fly. The arrow grazed the gnat's delicate wings.

Zert wiped the sweat off his brow. What had he gotten himself into?

〉〉〉

Next to the fire, Zert couldn't see the rats' nest, but he sensed an animal's presence. Beth had said that the nest was behind a ramshackle cabin about a meter from him. Its bark roof was collapsed in places, and it looked so flimsy that a hard wind could blow it away.

"Start the fire. The rats will come out and investigate the smoke. But don't worry. They won't bother you so long as the fire's going," Beth had said when the kids left.

A raindrop fatter than his toe splashed the fire, and the flames sizzled and smoked. He hunched over the small flames to protect them.

That afternoon, when the sun still blazed on the horizon, Beth's game had seemed troubling but sane. The darkness had changed everything. Now, the moons' rays—the pearly color of Okar's teeth—shone down on him.

Okar was usually friendly and playful. He used to hang by his tail to impress Zert, and some days the rat would run to greet him.

But the next-to-the-last day at his home, his pet hadn't given any warning. The rat had just opened his mouth and bitten him. As the sharp pain had run up Zert's hand, Okar had shot him a cold-blooded stare.

Zert drew his rat cloak tighter around his shoulders and threw his last twig on the dying fire. He had burned through his supply of wood. Yet still, the rats hadn't come.

There were no watches in this backward world, but he was certain that at least thirty minutes had passed.

A sudden shower doused the remaining flames.

Zert fanned the coals but only managed to create a cloud of smoke. He needed more twigs, but if he left the fire untended, the kids might conclude he had "doodled out."

He couldn't stay here without a fire.

Unless he wanted to put up with some "scaredy dog" jeers, he would have to try to retrieve some more wood.

No need to carry his bow and quiver. In case the rats charged, he'd shout *stop*. No matter his size, he was the human here. *They're only rats. Only some Okars.* Besides, these weren't even ypersteroid rats like Okar had been. Normal rats were more timid, weren't they?

A breeze blew and engulfed him in smoke. His eyes stung, and he coughed. *Act now before the fire goes out.*

Instead of his bow, he picked up a smoking twig. It had grown chilly since the sun had gone down, and the air turned even colder as he moved away from the coals. He was creeping toward the abandoned cabin when a gray shape emerged from the night.

A rat, more than twice his height, stood before him, motionless except for its writhing tail and quivering whiskers. Its eyes were backlit, as Zert's communicator had been. They were a supernatural red.

This rat was sizing up its prey. *This rat wants to kill me.* He tried to scream, "Stop, you rat! I'm the human here!" But only air came out.

Zert hurled his torch at the rat's face and ran toward the trail. He smelled burnt fur and heard the rattle of claws and the slap of a tail on the rocks as the animal fell back in confusion.

For the moment.

I'd rather be a coward than a snack for a rat. He raced past the smoldering campfire and the abandoned cabin and had crested the rise when he heard voices.

"I told you," Beth said. "He's bolted." The voice came from behind a rock on the far side of the abandoned cabin.

"How long?" John asked.

"He made it for thirty-five minutes," someone answered.

They tricked me. Beth and the others had never intended to attack the rats. This was just another test.

"You won, Millicent," Beth said. "You got the closest. You said thirty-eight minutes."

Millicent had been in on the trick too.

"Thirty-five minutes is a lot, Beth," Millicent said. "I'd like to see *you* sit by that fire for thirty-five minutes in the dark, thinking a rat might attack you. He doesn't know there are no rats around here."

This was just another stupid test, not meant to be dangerous. But he had seen a rat. A granddaddy of a rat.

Zert reached the rock the kids were using for a hiding place. "A rat *did* try to attack me," he yelled.

Beth's head popped out. Moonlight flowed down on the rat mask that she was holding. No doubt she had planned to scare him with it. "Sure it did. In your mind," she said. "The nest my dad and I tracked was on the other side of the trickle."

"This rat was real!" Zert yelled.

"Zert's not a liar," Millicent said to Beth.

"He *is* a liar. He said he had a rat for a pet," Beth said.

"I'm not lying. I could have been killed!" Zert yelled as he hurried past, not waiting for a reply.

"Zert's going home to play with his pet rat," a voice he recognized as Rudolpho's said in a sing-song voice. Rudolpho just wanted to impress John and Beth, but still the boy's taunt stung.

"Zert, it was just a game," Millicent called after him.

"A game?" Zert said, turning around to face these heartless kids. He'd never play with them again. Not even Millicent. He hated everyone. Including himself. Hadn't he promised himself after he escaped Superpox that he'd never risk his life for something stupid again?

"Abbot didn't like it either," Beth said. She was standing on the moonlit trail with the bow slung over her shoulder. She held the rat mask in her hands. Despite the cold, she wasn't wearing any shoes, but she did have a muffler wrapped around her neck.

Zert stopped walking. "So you tricked Abbot with this phony game too?"

Millicent stuck her hands into her fur pants pockets and looked down at the ground. "He bombarded us with trash the next night," she said.

"My dad didn't like him anyway," Beth said.

Zert decided that when they got kicked out, he and his dad would go look for Abbot. They'd form a colony of minimized people with whoever else wanted to join. They'd all get along. It would be a true Paradise, not like this sucky one.

"It's not OK to try to kill people just because you don't like them," Zert yelled back to them as the wind kicked up suddenly.

A roar was drawing closer.

He looked up at the sky glittering with stars and spotted a lifter flying low. He dove for a rock to hide behind.

The lifter was the same kind he had seen before. "The First Lifter Microscope" was written on its glass belly. But at night, its interior was all lit up, and he could see faces pressed against the glass floor.

Wide lips and tall foreheads. Noses as big as zoink pins. And something else so disturbing he just gawked. A bright red "NW" shone on the side of the lifter.

NW—the logo for his uncle's adventure show.

32

SNUG AS A BUG ON A RAT-FUR RUG

Zert made a beeline over to the fire to warm his cold face and hands as the twig door swung closed behind him.

In the candlelight, his father was sewing rat fur onto a pair of boots.

His father looked up at him and grinned. "You'll be snug as a bug when you wear these."

As snug as a bug. Please. The boots looked as if they might hold up for a day or two on the trail. But it didn't matter whether his father figured out how to make boots or not. They were going to get kicked out. And if the Rosie kids kept it up, Zert might not survive till Decision Day anyway.

His father eyed Zert's bow. "Shoot anything?"

He had told his father that he was going to practice moonlight archery. "Are you kidding? I couldn't hit the side of an AR theater," he said, but his stomach felt tight. "Dad, I saw something really strange. A lifter flying really low."

"Yeah, I heard they occasionally do that," his father said.

"Ouch!" He stuck his finger in his mouth before picking up the needle again.

"I saw the same kind once before. It's a tour advertised as 'The First Lifter Microscope,'" Zert said as he continued to try to warm himself by the fire. He'd sleep with his cloak on tonight.

"Hmmm," his father said. "You told me about that."

"This time, I spotted a *New Worlds* logo on the side of the lifter." His chest and knees had warmed a bit, but his back still felt frozen.

His father lifted his head and stared at him. His blue eyes looked black in the dimly lit hut.

"Don't you get it, Dad? Uncle Marin's show. Don't you think that's strange?"

His father put his needle down. "No," he said. "Uncle Marin told me that he had arranged for the producers of *New Worlds* to rescue us if there was a problem. All we had to do was to spell out 'Help' in mongo at the parking lot." He paused. "I bet this lifter's the signal for us to call for help if we need it."

"Why didn't you tell me?" Zert demanded.

"Lots of reasons." His father paused. "I didn't want you to think that things might not work out. When Uncle Marin didn't make it," his father said, staring off into space, "I didn't know whether his producers would care about us." He sighed. "Also, once I got here, I realized that there's nothing anyone can do to help us anyway."

"So what should we do?" Zert said.

"Ignore the lifters," his father said, returning his attention to the worktable. "They'll go away eventually."

"Dad, you stepped into that Mag Lev after me. Tell me the truth. Did you hear a third door close?" Zert said.

His father cracked his knuckles.

"You didn't hear it, did you?" Zert said.

His father shook his head. "But as I've been saying all along, we could be having bad thoughts about a dead man."

When Zert didn't respond, his father picked up his needle and started sewing again. "I brought you back a wormdog. It's on the desk."

The wormdog, on an acorn-bread bun with leaf relish, waited on the desk next to Zert's short story, "The Adventures of Henry Popter." Zert had written the story for school on recycled paper with a down-feather pen and blackberry ink. The assignment was due on Monday morning.

"No thanks," Zert said.

"I thought you liked wormdogs," his father said.

"I'm not hungry." As he stared at the fire—the closest thing to a holo-imagetube in Rosieland—he listened to the chorus of insects. After only a couple of weeks here, he was able to make out the crackle of the crickets, the buzz of the mosquitoes, and the hum of the gnats.

The sounds at home hadn't fit together as well: Their greeting for the door was a recording of the yelp of a woman surprised by a roach, the squeak of an ypersteroid rat, and the whoosh of a g-pipe vacuum.

He could also remember the blare of the radiation meter when the radiation grew dangerously high. The plop of a Wing sandal when it hit a moving sidewalk. The sizzle of a zoink ball when it passed through the hoop.

The sound of that Mag Lev door closing. Once. Then twice. But not a third time.

〉〉〉

The next morning, a worm slid into its muddy hole on the bank of the trickle. He needed to catch a slew of these if they were going to have enough to eat on the trail.

"No, you don't," Zert warned the worm, although he wasn't sure whether worms had ears.

He grabbed its tail with both hands and yanked with all his might—worm fishing, the Rosies called this activity.

His father had tried to keep a worm from diving into its hole on their first day, but that worm had slithered away. This worm twisted and writhed at his feet. It might have been just a weak worm, but for the moment, he felt like a strong Rosie.

Zert knelt over the worm and sliced its body into bite-sized bits with his knife. But then the pieces started wriggling away on the sandy bank, and he had to chase after them. When he collected them, he stuffed the slices into his pockets. He'd smoke some to make wormdogs, then he'd grind the rest into bug mash.

Zert removed the shoulder strap for his acorn canteen and knelt next to the trickle. As he submerged the acorn and waited for it to fill, he stared down at the baby minnows playing hide-and-go-seek in the rocks.

If only his herd wasn't waiting for water, he'd try to catch a few. His beetles only ate plants, but the roach that he caught yesterday would eat anything.

As he waited for the canteen, he stared down at ants the size of his feet marching along the banks. The ants had huge butts and antennae that looked as though two arms were sticking out of their dinosaur-shaped heads. One ant was eating, and its big jaw slid sideways. Black goo foamed out of its mouth and dripped to the ground, since the insect had no chin.

"You've got the worst table manners I've ever seen," Zert said to the ant.

A group of gnats with black heads, shiny green bodies, and see-through wings swarmed around an abandoned snail shell. Dining on escargot?

Nearby, a sandy-colored flea with a nose so long that it almost touched the ground hopped along on a mission. Flea-geolocating? Or could he be moving to a new flea city? Or searching for a girl flea to love?

A fly with four red eyes landed on a log. The bug started beating its wings, which looked the color of plain rain and the shape of the stained-glass windows he'd seen in church. He had just compared fly wings to stained-glass windows. Was he losing his mind?

At his feet, he noticed the poop of an animal. The droppings looked like black peanuts. Probably a rat's.

Rat Attack. He was lucky to be alive.

No wonder Abbot had retaliated the next night and doused those Rosie kids in trash. They deserved it.

Zert capped the acorn canteen and stood up. He had already caused enough trouble for his father with one trash war. He wasn't going to start another one here. Besides, if he had learned anything, it was that breaking rules wasn't a good way to earn respect.

A centipede trudged by. Two black eyes stared out from underneath what looked like the horns of a longhorn cow. Were these antennae? Mary Kay Casey used a dried baby centipede for a comb. It made sense, since a centipede had so many feet. But how many was it? Thirty? Twenty-five? He bet even little Dawn Nelson knew the answer.

Zert took off the rope that he used to hold up his pants. He looped the end and threw it. When he caught the centipede, he rolled the insect onto its back. Its orange feet pedaled the air, as if the bug didn't know that it had stopped walking.

He started counting the centipede's legs. One, he didn't need Millicent's help. Two, not Beth's, either. Three, not John's. Four, not even Artica's. Five, certainly not Uncle Marin's. He'd never spell out "Help" in garbage on the parking lot.

He never wanted to see that broken exclamation point ever again.

〉〉〉

"Come with me to church?" his father asked. He had bartered a square of rat fur for a new tan shirt, sewn from a BIG sock. When he first brought it home that afternoon, he had pulled a toenail clipping half the length of his forearm out of it. "Don G. is giving the sermon."

"Probably about why newcomers should go home," Zert said. *Only we can't.*

"I admit Don G. isn't as friendly as everyone else, but I think he's going to change his mind once he sees my boots," his father said. "You sure?"

"Yeah." Zert shrugged. "I'll stay here."

"You like your teacher. She's coming," his father said. He had a goofy smile on his face.

Mary Kay Casey had given the class homework over the weekend. Going back to school tomorrow morning with those kids was going to be miserable enough. He didn't want Casey to be angry with him too. "I should finish my short story," Zert said.

He picked up "The Adventures of Henry Popter" from the desk. "Leave the door open, will you?" he called to his father. If the world's weather was controlled by a thermostat, this morning he wouldn't adjust it even a degree.

"I'll see you after church," his father called as he headed off down the trail.

Zert lay down on the floor next to the open door and listened to his father whistling and the leaves of a nearby aspen tree fluttering in the breeze.

He reread the beginning of the first sentence on the paper in front of him: "When I undocked from the floating garage in Shanghai . . ." His story was about a lifter racer who flew around the world.

A black thing with hairy legs scuttled by him and then ducked underneath the wall—a roach. Another bug for his herd. Roaches lived year-round. Although toasted fleas and fried minnows tasted better, with the wet season coming, he was going to have to get used to roach soup.

He picked up a string from the table and twirled it overhead—like a roach cowboy.

As he headed to the door, he spied a flash of purple through a chink in the hut.

Millicent burst in the door. Her hair was tousled and her purple shirt muddy.

"Zert! It's Beth Gibson!" Millicent cried out. Tears flowed down her cheeks. "By the trickle!"

"What's wrong?" Zert asked.

"A monster's got her."

33

A QUARKING JOKE

As Zert raced down the trail after Millicent, he heard her screaming for Don G.

Rudolpho, Carlos, and John stood along the bank of the trickle next to Cleama Gibson. They looked as if they had been on their way to church, because all of them wore their hair slicked back and their T-shirts tucked into their pants. John was shaking a stick at the monster, and Carlos was aiming a doodlebug at it.

The giant winged animal stood in the middle of the trickle. It had its back to the crowd and was wagging its tail. These basset hound–duck blends—designed by some prankster scientist—were featured in the windows at Frank's Pet Store. With its warm eyes, dangling ears, sausage body, and stunted white wings, the bassetduck was a quarking—barking, quacking—joke. But he could see how the Rosies would mistake the animal for a monster.

The bassetduck stood in the shallow part of the trickle between two rocks. "Hi, girl," Zert said as he rushed forward. Then, the bassetduck turned to face him.

Beth's head and neck hung out of the animal's half-open mouth. Her brown hair spiked downward.

The bassetduck tilted her chin back as if she were going to toss Beth into the air.

Beth let out a bloodcurdling scream as she clung to the animal's front tooth.

The bassetduck began looking around for the terrible sound. Its ribs stood out like a basket underneath her lackluster coat and tattered wings. No collar circled her brown-and-white spotted neck. She must have been a stray.

He looked around for his father and Don G., but Cleama Gibson was the only adult on the bank. Moaning, she drew her cloak around her and bent over toward the ground.

Zert waded slowly toward the bassetduck. If he startled the animal, it might swallow Beth, and she would slide down the creature's esophagus and end up in the dark ocean of its stomach. But if he waited, the animal might hiccup and . . . same slimy fate.

Above its saggy lids, the bassetduck's eyes were warm and mischievous, like Chub's. But he'd already made one mistake with that rat. He needed to be careful not to overestimate his abilities again. Not with someone's life at stake.

As Zert drew closer, his nose filled with the familiar odor of wet fur.

Chub had smelled this way after a bath.

Zert stopped walking when he reached the bassetduck's shadow. Feeling lucky that the bassetduck's body was so low to the ground, he took a deep breath and yelled, "Keep quiet, Beth."

He stroked the bassetduck's oversized leg. "Hey, girl," he said. "That's a girl." Her long ears grazed the surface of the water. He took a deep breath. "You're a good girl. Yes, you are. Anybody can see that. I'm sorry that you're lost. We'll try to get you a little meat later. But first you've got to help us. That's a girl. Good dog." He took a breath. "SIT!" he shouted.

The bassetduck swished its tail and raised its stubby wings that stuck out of its sides.

"SIT!" Zert repeated as a twig floated by. The bassetduck ignored him.

Chub had loved to chase anything. He grabbed the twig and hiked away so the animal could see him.

"Wait, Zert, your father's here," Cleama Gibson called from the bank.

But Zert had already heaved the twig with all his strength. "FETCH!" he yelled.

The bassetduck slowly opened her mouth.

As Beth tumbled out, Cleama Gibson let loose a long, jagged scream.

The dog bounded down the trickle as Beth splashed into the water.

The animal grabbed a branch, not the twig that Zert had thrown, with her huge teeth. The teeth that could have torn Beth in two.

Zert sloshed toward Beth. His father was running toward her too, his sock shirt flapping in the wind.

When Zert helped her stand, Beth spit out a mouthload of water. His father grabbed Beth's other arm.

"You hurt?" his father asked Beth.

She shook her head, and her long hair sprayed them with water. "It was just a dumb game—a dare," she gasped.

A dumb dare like the rat attack.

"I touched its leg," Beth said. She bent over and gagged. More water flowed out of her mouth. She wiped her lips with the back of her hand and looked up. "That animal's tongue was quick. It surprised me." So the animal had licked her up. *Yuck.*

"I'm glad you're OK," Zert said.

Beth pushed her hair out of her eyes. She turned toward Zert. "You saved my life," she said.

Zert flushed.

"Cleama," Jack called, "your daughter is as good as new." He turned to Beth. "Now, run over and give your mom a hug."

Keeping an eye on the bassetduck, Beth headed slowly toward shore.

"Good job, son." Zert's father clapped him on the back.

Cleama Gibson's fur cape came untied as she ran toward Beth. The Rosies never wasted anything, yet Beth's mother didn't stop running when the cape fell into the water and drifted away.

"Good job, Zert," Millicent yelled from the bank. She had on her purple shirt and matching purple shoes that were fashioned out of . . . bubble gum?

A few meters away, the bassetduck held the branch in her mouth. The animal stared at Zert as if to say, "What do you want to play now?"

"Millicent, get me a big hunk of squirrel meat or jerky," Zert's father called.

"OK." Millicent rushed away to perform the errand.

"I'm fine," Beth said as she pushed her mother away, but freckles that he had never noticed before stood out against her bloodless face. They were the spread-apart kind, like his own.

Beth had been inside that animal's mouth. Lying on its bumpy tongue. Basting in dog spit. *Ugh.*

The bassetduck bounded toward them, flapping its stunted wings and wagging its long tail. The animal was just playing, but Zert stepped backward anyway as waves doused him. He struggled to stay upright but lost his balance. The bassetduck was wagging its tail, creating a powerful current that jostled him and caused him to topple over. As he started swimming, waves flooded the banks.

Holly Cannon screamed.

"Everybody! Stand back!" Jack shouted, his head barely above water.

The crowd stepped back from the trickle in unison.

"Zert and I are going to lead the animal away from the village," Jack called to the Rosies standing along the bank.

Zert struggled to stand as the waves died down. The bassetduck rolled its head, flapped its wings, and shook its coat, slinging pellets of water in all directions.

Artica Chang had appeared, along with Don G. and a few of the other villagers. They all wore dark clothes, probably Rosie church-wear.

"Did Zert dare you to touch that animal?" Don G. shouted into Beth's face.

"No, Dad," Beth said.

"But I bet he told you it was safe," Don G. muttered. He had on a bumpy black shirt that was made from some kind of . . . cushion?

"No, Dad," Beth repeated.

"Then why would you be stupid enough to pet that animal?" Don G. thundered. His hair, pulled back with a leather tie, stuck out like a horse's tail.

"Dad! Zert had nothing to do with this. He wasn't even here!" Beth said.

Artica waded out, holding two huge hunks of rat meat.

Jack took the pieces of meat. "I've got some more rat meat in the smokehouse. You can have some of ours," he offered.

"I'm not worried about that, Jack. Your son just averted a tragedy," Artica said. "Good job, Zert." He started back toward the bank, not seeming to care that his black pants were getting drenched.

"Thanks," Zert said, taking one piece of meat from his father.

Millicent waved. "Yeah, Zert."

Zert wiped off his face and patted the bassetduck's leg.

The silly animal still held the branch in its mouth.

Zert and his father began wading through the trickle toward the parking lot. "Here, girl," his father shouted.

The bassetduck trotted toward them.

The Rosies on the bank all clapped and cheered.

Don G. had his arm around his daughter and wife.

Cleama Gibson was crying.

Beth was staring at him. "Thank you, Zert," she mouthed.

No problem, you ol' scaredy dog.

>>>

"I wish we could keep the bassetduck," Zert said to his father. He and his dad had passed the outermost boundary of Paradise, and Rosie nets and buckets no longer lined the banks. "She seems sweet. Maybe we could use her for our getaway next Sunday."

"Zert," his father laughed. "How would we feed her?"

"It's just for a week. Then, after we get kicked out, we could climb up the bassetduck's long ears and get onto its back." He'd hold onto its wings as they loped across the meadow to their next home. "Think about how far away she could take us."

"So long as the dog doesn't mistake one of us for a mouse."

Zert shuddered. He had to face facts. Now that he was thumb sized, animals that he used to think of as pets would never be entirely safe for him again. He must take new care around them.

That would be a lost dream except that he had discovered insects. There were so many kinds of bugs, and they could do so many crunchy things: spin webs, walk on water, walk up trees, and build houses underground.

"Besides, Zert, what you did was a game changer," his father interrupted his thoughts. "Those kids will never call you a coward again."

His father had never mentioned the kids' taunts before, but then again, his father never told Zert all he knew. "It looks like we still have a problem with Don G, though."

"Did you hear what he said to Beth?" Zert said. "And I wasn't even *there* when the bassetduck licked her."

"Don G. has got it into his head that you won't succeed here," his father said. Jack's reflection sparkled in the trickle. He was staring off into the distance. "Did you try to attack Beth with a knife?"

"I was carving the stupid soap statue for art class," Zert said. "I wasn't attacking her."

"That's what Mary Kay Casey said." His father sighed. "Well, we'll find out next weekend."

"Dad," Zert said, "where will we go when we get kicked out?"

"Mary Kay Casey says we've got good reason to be optimistic," his father said. "I like her. Don't you?"

"I think we should just follow the trickle." Zert wondered why his father never answered his questions about their future plans.

Without warning, the bassetduck stopped in its tracks. It started flapping its wings and bark-quacking.

"What's going on?" Zert said.

His father threw back his head and laughed.

The bassetduck was staring at its ridiculous reflection in the water and quarking at her bizarre white wings sticking out of her furry back, her own long snout, and her droopy eyes.

Zert started laughing. He hadn't laughed so hard since he and Cribbie had slid down the side of the old concrete dam on cardboard boxes. Chub had waited on top, howling in excitement.

Before the Quarantine. Before Teen Jail. Before he lost Chub.

Before . . . He couldn't see it yet, but if his past was any guide, the next catastrophe had to be right around the corner.

34

A COUCH WITH A NEW KIND OF SPRING

There was a knock on the door a few hours later.

Beth stood in front of Zert's hut in the fading light. Her long, stringy hair fell unbrushed from under a cap woven from pine needles. Her knees, knobbed from crawling around on all fours, poked out of her holey overalls. Tiny red wildflowers peeked out of her front pockets.

"Can I come in?" Beth asked.

Zert swung the door open.

"Where's your dad?" she asked as she followed Zert inside. Her bare feet padded soundlessly on the dirt floor.

"Bath," Zert said simply. His father had gone to the turtle bath to wash off the smell of wet bassetduck, but Zert didn't want to remind Beth of her awful experience.

As he walked over to the couch, Zert saw the room through Beth's eyes.

The rat-skin rug on the floor gave the hut a homey, lived-in look. His father had removed the magazine photos from the walls, exposing the cheerful blue cybratom, and had built a series of shelves for his work tools and unfinished boots, and a bench.

Zert's new gray boots sat in the center of the table. They were sturdy and comfortable. Once his father figured out how to make laces, they'd be perfect for the frigid, wet weather that the villagers had warned was coming.

His short story, "The Adventures of Henry Popter," lay open on his desk, surrounded by his growing collection of objects: a snail shell, the stalk of a bird feather, a piece of frog skin, a baby pine cone. And his prize finds: four pairs of waterbug feet that felt like wax paper. He was studying these to try to learn how to walk on water.

Zert sank into the couch stuffed with dandelions that his father had rented in exchange for a patch of rat hide. He used to think his old purple couch was the most comfortable in the world, but he knew better now. This new couch was not only softer but smelled of spring—the season, not the metal springs that had popped out of his old couch's upholstery.

Beth, who was still standing there, cleared her throat. "I feel bad about the rat attack game."

You should.

Beth looked into Zert's eyes. "Did you really see a rat last night?"

Zert nodded. "I did."

"I didn't know we were putting you in any danger," Beth said, sitting down next to him. He was about to say, "That was stupid," when he remembered that he hadn't thought he was putting Cribbie in any danger on the night they'd snuck out to fight that trash war. He could have stopped Cribbie. Or maybe he could have gotten Cribbie to promise to keep his mask on. He would never know.

He had been stupid that night. And death was permanent. He knew now that you didn't get any do-overs.

Beth kicked her feet against the side of the couch. "You were great with that animal." She stood up and began pacing the room. "We're not allowed to fight here, because of the mission and everything." She passed by the couch without looking at him. "I'm trying to say that I won't hold things against you anymore."

"What things?" Zert asked as his past nasty comments ran through his mind: "These abacuses are for cavemen"; "No BIG I know would dress like me"; and "This doesn't look a bit like a Statue of Liberty."

Before Beth could answer, he spoke up, "I know I haven't been easy to get along with either."

"It's not all your fault," Beth said. She cocked her head curiously at him. "Have you slit someone's throat before?"

"What? No!"

"But isn't it much more violent where you lived?" Beth said.

"Yeah. It was." Zert nodded. Not just on the holo-imagetube. When he was just a little kid, he had seen some trampos pain-laser a drug dealer known as the Umpkin, right in front of the store. Lying in bed at night, he often heard the blasts and screams of gang fights.

Beth looked out the door. "How many different kinds of designer animals are there?"

"I don't know." Zert shrugged. "Ten thousand, maybe."

"Wow." Beth's eyes lit up. "Do you have plans next weekend? On Saturday morning?"

Zert shook his head. Saturday was their big day, the day they were going to get kicked out. But the vote wouldn't be until after dinner on Pancake Rock.

"After I finish my chores, will you go with me to the parking lot?" Beth said as she started pacing again. "I'd like to spend some time with you in case . . ." Her face grew red. "I don't mean to hurt your feelings. I just mean . . ." She looked down at her bony hands. "It's the adults' decision. If it were up to me, you'd be staying. I'd—"

"OK," Zert interrupted. "I'll go." He had been thinking that if he could find a water bottle at the parking lot, he and his father could float down the trickle with their herd. They still had some details to work out, like how to get out before they drowned, but they had the beginning of a plan.

"We can look for some magazines. I'd like to see some photos of designer animals. What did you call the one that had me?"

"A bassetduck," Zert said.

Beth had stopped pacing next to his desk and was gazing down at his paper. "Are you finished with your short story?"

Henry Popter. The fastest lifter racer in the land. Garage. Shanghai. Casey had warned the class that students would have to read their story out loud.

If I read that out loud, Beth will think I'm showing off. Zert shook his head. "Nah. It needs a lot of work."

Beth turned to leave. "I better go home and write mine." At the doorway, she slowly pulled her hand out of her pocket to shake Zert's hand.

Zert shook her hand. Strange. Her skin no longer felt rough.

As Beth scampered away, he examined his own hand and counted three calluses. He turned it over and saw the same old patches of freckles on the backs of his hands. Some looked like couples hugging. Others like colonies of ants. One bloated one resembled a clover leaf.

A month ago, shrinking had felt like the most radical change possible. But not anymore.

Walking over to the desk, he noticed a bunch of tiny red wildflowers tied with a leather bow. It smelled like licorice.

He turned over his short story and started writing on the back of the rough paper.

Once upon a time . . .

35

A ROACH'S KISS

The next morning as Zert walked to school, hurried footsteps pounded the trail behind him. He broke into a jog down the path to get away.

"I'm sorry," Millicent called out.

Zert stopped and faced her. She stood in the middle of the trail. Her hair hung straight to her shoulders, and bags of seeds and insect parts hung out of her pockets. She wore a green T-shirt under her overalls that made her eyes seem greener.

"Why'd you go along with those other kids?" Zert asked. "I thought you were my friend."

"After you scared Beth with the knife, she was always calling you a coward." Millicent paused. "I knew you weren't."

"You could have warned me," Zert charged.

Millicent's pink cheeks flushed red. "We don't tattle on each other here. Besides, you did show Beth. And then you saved her. You're brave, Zert."

"Yeah, well," he said. "Thanks." He tried to keep his pleasure from leaking into his voice.

"I told my father about what we did to you and to Abbot," Millicent continued. "And he says that I was wrong to go along with the game." She paused. "I mean, I had no idea that a real rat would be around. But still . . ."

"It was worse than a game," Zert insisted.

"I made a mistake," Millicent said, looking at her sandaled feet. "Not just with you but with Abbot."

"I can't speak for Abbot," Zert said. "But everything's OK with me."

As Millicent's face broke into a smile, he felt as if he had stepped inside a 3-D Mag Lev with a maximizer button and grown BIG again.

›››

"Today, we are going to start our unit on short stories," Mary Kay Casey said. With a black skirt, a red T-shirt, and a red-and-black pin, she looked like a . . . ladybug. "Zert, will you be the first to read to the class?"

Zert pulled his paper out of his backpack. Last night, he had written a new story on the back pages of his first draft.

"Stand up, please," Casey said.

Zert hitched up his pants and cleared his throat. He worked to keep his hands from trembling as he began.

> Once upon a time, there was a mother witch who had two witch daughters named Prunella and Crunella. The mother witch had a hump in her nose that the other witches thought was attractive, but she had a cruel temper, and for that reason, her friends nicknamed her Red. One day, Prunella and Crunella were supposed to be cleaning their broomsticks. Instead, they were staring into a mirror, combing their coarse hair and arguing about who was the most beautiful.
>
> Their mother, Red, flew into a rage and yelled, "May you both turn into roaches until someone kisses your ugly lips!"

Just as the sisters felt their thin witches' arms, legs, and face dry up into hard shells, a horrible wind blasted through their yard, and they were blown away.

Poor Red! Their mother immediately regretted her harsh words. She ran out into her front yard and down the street, searching frantically for her daughters. Neighbors stared as she got down on her hands and knees and kissed every roach she saw. She was trying to break the spell, but none of the kissed roaches turned into her daughters.

"Zert," Casey interrupted, "I just want to remind the little ones that they're not supposed to kiss roaches unless they've been boiled. Don't do what Red did, OK?" Zert looked at the smaller kids and nodded. A few weeks ago, her warning—*Don't kiss a roach*—would have seemed insane. But it made sense now.

Red kissed brown roaches, black ones, skinny ones, fat ones, until by late evening, she had kissed one thousand four hundred and thirty-three.

At midnight, after kissing a baby roach that she found in a breadbox, Red began to feel sick. A bad stomachache, she thought. But red itchy spots popped out all over her, even on her fingernails. Her hair turned bright orange and fell out in clumps. Just before midnight, she died of pox.

John Gibson and Dawn Nelson gasped.

Meanwhile, Crunella and Prunella were wandering around town searching for someone to break their mother's spell. They spotted a sweet-looking woman, surely a mother, in front of Hatch's Corner Market.

Zert paused. Hatch's Market was the name of a store in Low City DC that he and his father had shopped at.

> *"I want to go first. I'm prettiest," Crunella said.*
>
> *"No, I want to go first. I'm the most beautiful,"* *Prunella said.*
>
> *They argued so long that the woman with her basket filled with all different kinds of delicious chips began heading toward the checkout line.*
>
> *"OK," Prunella gave in, for she saw that the woman would be leaving soon. "You go first this time."*
>
> *Crunella walked slowly up to the mother and batted her eyes and tried to look as sweet, pretty, and friendly as she could.*
>
> *The woman's sweet face contorted. "Argh!" she screamed.*
>
> *A store clerk rushed toward her. "What's wrong?"*
>
> *Speechless, the woman pointed at Crunella. The woman looked as if she was going to faint.*
>
> *Crunella scampered away, but the clerk chased her. Before she reached the safety of a shelf, he beat her with a broom.*
>
> *"Vermin," he yelled.*

Zert thought about how much Cribbie hated it when people mispronounced his last name, but he couldn't share this with the class. There was so much he couldn't share with anyone.

> *When Crunella found Prunella, she was hiding between some boxes of dodo pellets. The sisters looked at each other. Neither wanted to confess what she was thinking. Getting kissed by a human was going to be harder than they had thought.*

A short while later, a policeman passed by. "He's mine,"
Prunella said, trying to sound confident. She scuttled out
from under the box of dodo pellets toward him.

Her head still aching from the broom blow to her head,
Crunella yelled, "Be careful!"

Prunella swiftly climbed the cliff of the policeman's
pants and shirt and onto the plank of his arm. While she
waited patiently for the policeman to notice her, she smiled
ever so prettily.

As the policeman reached for a sack of meatloaf chips,
she saw his face convulse in horror. He swatted her, knocking
her to the ground. He stomped the floor and tried to crush
her with his big black shoes.

Barely escaping with her life, she scurried to their hid-
ing place, the box of dodo food.

While Crunella licked Prunella's bruises, they plotted
their next move.

Things did not go well.

Over the years, they traveled by lifter and 3-D Mag
Lev all over the world. They said "hello" to thousands of
men, women, and children. In one spectacular move,
Crunella dropped from the ceiling of a toy store onto a little
boy's arm. She hoped that the little boy would think that the
maneuver was as crunchy as the moon colonist action fig-
ure that he was holding. But he tried to pull off her wings.
Crunella almost didn't get away.

When Zert stopped to catch his breath, he looked around the
room. In his old school, kids would have been shuffling their feet,
playing with their RASM portals. But here, all the faces turned
toward him, listening.

Prunella said, "Crunella, I think we are on the right track. I think that we need to find a boy."

Crunella shook her head. "Not that boy. He was mean."

"We need to find the right boy," Prunella said.

"We need to give up," Crunella said, her voice despondent.

The sun had set when Crunella and Prunella left the Colorado town where they had spent the afternoon and started walking aimlessly into the forest. At first they were lonely for the sights, sounds, and smells of people, but then they decided that the forest was peaceful. No one screamed when they saw the two sisters. No one tried to smash them.

They spotted a campfire glowing in the darkness.

"Do we dare?" Crunella said.

"Try again?" Prunella finished her sister's sentence.

They looked at each other. "One more time," they said together and crept up to the campfire.

"Why, he's a little guy," Crunella said.

"A fairy," Prunella said.

"Yeah," Crunella said.

A boy, only a little taller than them, sat near the campfire. He was barbecuing a wormdog.

"Whose turn?" Crunella said.

"Yours," Prunella said.

"No, yours," Crunella said.

"Eenie, meenie, miney, mo, catch a witch by the toe. Prunella, you're it," Crunella said.

"No," Prunella said. "It's so quiet and peaceful. I don't want to get hit on the head tonight."

Crunella looked deeply into Prunella's eyes. Only the two of them knew how much each had suffered. "OK. Let's both go, Prunella."

Together, they walked toward the boy, smiling widely

but with their hearts full of fear. They had been bruised and stomped on so often.

Bezert Jackson Cage, a Rosie in Paradise, was cooking dinner and worrying about his homework. A short story was due tomorrow, and he had no idea what to write. He saw two roaches creeping toward him.

"That's it," Zert said. "I'll write about you for my English paper." He was so happy that he leaned over and kissed first one roach and then the other.

Prunella was happy because he kissed her first, and Crunella was happy because he kissed her longer. But all Zert saw were two long black shadows flying off into the night. The End

Beth whistled. The class clapped.

"Zert, your father told me you're a gifted writer," Casey said. "And it's true."

Zert blushed. "Thanks."

Millicent clapped him on the back. "Good job," she said.

"Millicent," Casey said. "Are you ready?"

Through the walls of the PeopleColor Schoolhouse, the sun shone brightly and cast the schoolroom in a greenish hue.

Millicent stood and faced the class. She patted her straight hair as if to style it as she said, "My story is called 'The Caterpillar's Bad Hair Day.'"

Zert laughed along with the rest of the kids. Until he remembered: He was going to get kicked out of this school.

In the old world, you couldn't get anywhere without an education. Here, he wasn't going to get to finish seventh grade.

Dumb Thumb.

36

I'LL SETTLE FOR LIVE

Zert's last week at school passed in a blur of insect husbandry and stories about Millard R. Dix. But Beth no longer accidentally stomped on his feet when she stood up, and he no longer felt John's eyes glaring at him. Rudolpho helped him rig an archery target so he could practice with a bow and arrow. And in art, he started carving his own sculpture. It was of Chub.

"Be at the campfire before dark," his father had said as Zert left Saturday midmorning to go to the parking lot. He had been standing at the door to their cave, wearing his tan sock shirt and holding the Cinderella broom in his hand.

"I'm not an idiot, Dad," Zert had said. "That's the third time you've told me."

"The vote is tonight, and if you're late, you'll give Don G. an excuse," his father had called as Zert had started down the trail.

"OK," Zert had called back. He had penned five roaches, three beetles, and six doodlebugs. Now he had to figure out a way to transport them to wherever they were going. He'd find a plastic bottle at the parking lot and pull it back to Paradise on a string. Plastic bottles didn't weigh much. Then, he and his father could drag it to the trickle, and they could float away and live happily ever after.

I'll settle for live.

As he and Beth hiked down the winding path, Zert was sorry that Millicent hadn't come with them. She'd had to stay behind to help her father dig up slugs. He wished he could have spent one last day with her before he and his father were voted out.

He wanted Millicent to see that he was keeping up with Beth. His lungs weren't burning. He wasn't even breathing hard. As his dad had promised, his feet were snug as two bugs inside his rat-skin boots. And with his rat cloak around his shoulders, he wasn't cold. The canteen that he brought still sloshed with water. And they were almost at the parking lot.

Beth cast an anxious glance at the sun. Even though she was barefoot, she wore a blue cloak around her shoulders. She had tied her hair back in a matching blue ribbon. "We better hurry," she said.

That's when he noticed that the sun was drooping in the sky. It was midafternoon already. The hike must have taken longer than he thought.

They bypassed the light pole and, a few minutes later, stood on the edge of the parking lot.

A sleek new Banana model lifter and another model called a Hummingbird were parked on the huge concrete slab. The lifters looked bigger, broader, heavier, and shinier than he remembered.

Bits of old foil gleamed in the sunlight, as if a treasure chest had spilled its contents. *Mongo is beautiful.*

"Zert, I found a newspaper," Beth called from a few paces away. "Help me turn the pages."

He stared down at the front page. The photo was of a boy a little older than thirteen whose hairline grew just above his eyebrows. He held a Shock Wave bomb between his teeth and the detonator in one hand.

"I want to see the ads," Beth said.

"Wait a minute," Zert said. He had to hop around the page to see the letters. Reading through a funny dance, he made out the headline: "Rogue Nations Conducting More Nuclear Tests."

"Oh no," Beth said, her bushy eyebrows drawing together. "Is that serious?"

"It says something about a war to control Venezuela." Zert looked up from the page when he heard feet pounding and branches breaking.

"What does that mean?" Beth asked as she turned to scan the parking lot. "What's that noise?"

A group of BIG boys wearing backpacks started to cross the parking lot. They must have parked on the hill. Some were holding nets; others fishing poles. They were dressed in blue uniforms: blue shorts and short-sleeved shirts with a splash of white at the collar. Boy Scouts.

So many kids together in one place. The epidemic must be over. St. Lulu's must have started up again. His class would all be wondering where he was.

He felt that familiar ache in his chest.

But in the BIG world, there would be a new quarantine someday soon. The war to control Venezuela might spiral into a global conflict. No matter what happened here, at least he would be able to enjoy the outdoors.

"Who are those weirdos?" Beth asked as they lay down on the edge of the parking lot to stay out of sight and to observe the boys.

"They're called Boy Scouts. I was one once," Zert said, gazing into her eyes. Ever since he had noticed the freckles on her face, he hadn't been able to look at her without seeing them. They *rosied* up the plain of her cheekbones and then spread all the way to her sunburnt nose.

"Why are they all dressed exactly alike?" Beth asked.

"It's the tradition," he said. He struggled to think of a way to explain uniforms. Rosies wore the outfits of a hundred pockets because that's what they had to wear, not for a purpose.

"Why?" Beth asked.

Zert wouldn't say an *If you!* no matter what. "To show they're a team."

"What did you do when you were a scout?" Beth asked.

"We helped the Nature Hotel maintain the outside-in trails." Zert smiled. Back then he had thought that the fake grass, Instant Trees, and indoor weather system were the real outdoors. "The rest of the time, I went to meetings and learned how to tie knots."

"But who are the scouts?" Beth asked in a puzzled tone.

Zert thought about her question. "They like the outdoors, like us Rosies."

Beth's dark eyes grew wide. "Those BIGS want to be like us?"

"Yep."

One of the boys took a soft drink out of his backpack and shook the can. When the boy opened the lid, the green, sticky liquid spewed all over his neighbors.

"What are they doing now?" Beth asked.

"The boy with the can is just horsing around," Zert explained.

He hadn't seen Cribbie stop up the drain with leaves and pour PeopleColor into the water fountain to get the birds to turn pink. But when the security guard told the scoutmaster that a boy had tampered with the fountain, the scoutmaster had headed straight over to Cribbie and Zert and said, "Leave, and don't come back."

"You mean?" Zert had asked.

"You're kicked out of scouts," Slem Pote, his scoutmaster, had said.

Cribbie told Zert about his joke as they walked home together. Cribbie had said, "I hated scouts anyway."

His thoughts returned to the parking lot when he heard the red-faced leader shouting at the boy. "Evange, one more prank like that, and I'm going to send you back to the bus. You'll miss the rest of our nature walk. You got that?"

Evange nodded, but when the leader turned his back, the boy

started laughing. Evange took one last long sip of his Vita Coke and set it on the base of a light pole.

"What's a nature walk?" Beth asked.

"They're going to walk around and look at nature."

Beth tilted her head and stared at him. "I don't get it."

Zert sighed. Trying to explain nature walks to Beth was like trying to explain water to a fish.

The leader blew his whistle. The Boy Scouts lined up.

"All right, Troop 55, break is over. Get ready to h—i—k—e." Just like Slem Pote, this leader stretched out the word "hike."

"I'm tired. Can't I go back to the bus?" a small boy whined. He was overweight, and his blue socks bagged over the lid of his boots just as Zert's used to. A net hung in one hand at the boy's side.

The leader ignored the boy with the sagging socks. "Remember, scouts, to keep your eyes and ears open. Now let's go."

The leader set off for a trail that veered off from the eastern edge of the parking lot, and the scouts followed in a ragged line. One by one the blue uniforms disappeared into the woods. The boy with the sagging socks was the last to set off.

"How can the scouts see nature?" Beth asked. "They're too tall."

"What?"

"I mean, those BIGS won't notice anything," Beth said.

"You're right." *BIG Zert didn't understand one thing about nature.*

A cloud passed in front of the sun, and suddenly, Zert shivered.

"My dad is going to kill me," Beth muttered. "I didn't tell him that I was going with you, and I'm supposed to help set up for the meeting." She sighed. "It took us *so* long to get here."

Zert looked at his dusty boots. So he had slowed Beth down after all.

Beth glanced over her shoulder in the direction of Paradise.

"Go ahead," Zert said. He wanted to find a water bottle anyway. If she went back, he wouldn't have to explain his plans.

"Are you sure?" Beth said, popping up and brushing off. "I hate to leave you, but the path is marked."

"No problem," Zert said, clambering onto his elbows, then his feet. By the time he turned to look at the trail, a cloud of dirt was the only sign that Beth had ever been there.

37

AN OLIVE GASH

"I swear, Mom."

Zert stopped pulling the water bottle and started crawling over tangled roots to head toward the boy's voice. A scout separated from the troop? Or another kid? Just a hiker? He peered out behind tufts of bearded stalks at a meadow.

The Boy Scout with the baggy socks stood alone in a clearing. He didn't seem to notice a giant anthill near his feet. He was probably one of those boys who could walk around all day with a toilet-paper tail without realizing it. Other than the clueless air that he had about him, he looked ordinary, with light brown hair, brown eyes, and brown skin. "I'm not making this up," the boy was saying into his I-ring.

Zert zigzagged across the field. When he got closer to the boy, he stopped to hide behind a pine cone.

"I was just swiping my net for fun. At first, I thought it was a butterfly. But it's a tiny human."

A jar had overturned in the clearing. At first Zert thought that the boy had trapped a bug. But then he realized that a Rosie was slumped inside. The man's long white beard spilled down onto the front of an old-fashioned vest. His cap had fallen onto his lap, revealing a red gash on his head. But his chest shuddered as it rose and fell, so the man was alive.

"I don't know where the troop is. I looked up and they were gone," the boy said into his device.

Thump. Thump. Thump.

Huge feet encased in gray boots with blue socks bunched underneath knobby knees carried towering legs toward him.

The monster, BIGfoot.

Zert had to stifle a scream.

The BIG bent down and squinted at the old Rosie. The Rosie's head stayed slumped against his chest.

Zert froze. He dared himself to keep as quiet and still as moss growing.

This close, the boy's face looked like a tract of canyon country. The pores in his cheeks were black holes. His nostrils were caves. His blue eyes were pools. His squirming wet lips were trickles.

"I'm not lying, Mom," the kid said into his I-ring. "I'm looking at the little old man right now. I'll show you. I'll bring him home. He can live in my old bird cage."

From the other end of the I-ring, laughter roared. "Ralphey!" a woman's voice shouted.

Ralphey frowned at the I-ring. "You never believe me, Mom." He sighed. "I can't help it that your screen is broken and you can't see him. Just a minute. I can't hear you." He took a step away from the jar and started pacing the clearing, hunting for better reception. "I told you. I don't know where my troop is."

Ralphey turned his back to the jar. "I'm not lying. You'll know that when I bring him home," he said into the I-ring. "I'm going to take him with me to the bus and wait for the other scouts."

Now or never. Zert ran as fast as he could. *Kapow.* He rammed his shoulder against the jar.

The jar swayed like a darting minnow's tail, then started to wobble back into place.

He shoved it again. This time, the jar toppled over onto the leafy ground.

Zert glanced up to see if Ralphey had heard the crash.

The boy was still talking on his I-ring. "I promise, Mom. I'll take care of him all by myself. I'm sure he'll eat birdseed."

Rosies don't eat birdseed. Zert bent down, placed his hands underneath the Rosie's armpits, and dragged him to a stand of dandelions.

As white pods rained down on them, the Rosie moaned. He wasn't dead. Not yet.

Once Ralphey discovered that the Rosie was missing, he'd start searching the meadow. Ralphey might accidentally step on them with one of his BIG boots.

Zert lost all sense of direction as he pulled the Rosie away as fast and as far as he could. He'd never be able to find the place where he'd left that water bottle now.

"Hey!" Zert heard Ralphey yell. "He's escaped."

Zert wanted to run, but he couldn't unless he dropped the old man.

Ralphey started crashing around, searching for the old man. The boy's feet pounded the ground like thunder gone wild.

Zert couldn't see over the tangles of brushwood. He couldn't make any sense of where the feet were, in which direction they were coming or how fast.

At any second, the sky would grow ridges, like an old-fashioned potato chip. The gray sole of the boy's boot would loom overhead.

He'd have no time to run away. The boot would descend, and his life would be over. His gravesite, the sole of the boy's boot, would have only a piece of squashed gum for a marker.

Thump. Thump. Thump.

Zert hauled the Rosie over the clumps of gray moss and bits and pieces of bark littering the lumpy ground. He dodged pine cones, gnarly roots, and sprigs of thistles. Luck was with him because he backed into a log with a knothole in its center, the perfect hiding place—at least for a few minutes.

Zert shoved the Rosie inside the knothole, squatted next to him, and tried to catch his own breath. It was musty and damp inside, but a red-and-white mushroom, twice his height, grew out of the worm-eaten wood. The umbrella-like mushroom was so cheerful he could almost pretend this was a game of hide-and-go-seek.

BIG kids didn't know how to treat animals, much less humans the size of insects. If Ralphey's sun-like eyes glowered down at them, the boy might tear off one of his arms or smush his head when he tried to capture him.

"Where are you, little man? I swear I won't hurt you. Come back!" Ralphey shouted.

The Rosie slowly lifted his gashed head. Kind eyes stood out from a face almost as wrinkled as the gray old-fashioned suit that he wore.

"Hello," the Rosie said.

Zert put his finger to his lips.

"Come out, come out, wherever you are," Ralphey called out. It felt like an earthquake as he stomped around.

Zert locked eyes with the old man, keeping his finger to his lips. When the old man nodded, Zert crawled to the opening and peeped out.

Ralphey was bent over and skimming his net in the grass. If it accidentally hit him or the old man, it'd chop off their heads.

"Come out, little man," the boy yelled as he patrolled the other side of the clearing.

The ground underneath them stopped quivering, but the boy moved so fast that he could return to the log in less time than it took to say *A blue bug eats blue blood* or one of the other tongue twisters that Millicent liked.

"Are you hurt?" he asked the old man.

"I don't think so," the man said as he patted his chest and legs.

"What about that cut on your forehead?" Zert said, pointing at the gash.

The man peeled the strip of red off his forehead. "A pimiento." He sniffed it then and took a bite. "Want some?"

Zert shook his head. Ralphey must have used an old olive jar to trap him. "So what happened?" He paused. "But remember. Keep your voice low."

"I was walking toward Paradise," the Rosie whispered. "The next thing that I knew, I was swinging in the air in a net like some circus performer." The man finished the pimiento and rubbed his stomach. "I could have toppled the jar, but I decided to pretend to be knocked out. I was waiting for him to look away, and then I planned to escape. Instead, I guess I blacked out. Not enough oxygen." He shrugged. "You came at just the right time."

"I want to be your friend, little man. I swear it," Ralphey called.

"The BIG's name is Ralphey," Zert told the Rosie. "I heard him call his mother over his I-ring."

"Ralphey likes me so much that he almost asphyxiated me," the Rosie said. He reached out and shook Zert's hand. "I'm Dr. Rosario, by the way."

"Dr. Rosario!" Zert said. "What are you doing here?"

"It's a long story," the doctor said. "And whom do I have the pleasure of talking to?"

"I'm Zert Cage," Zert said.

Dr. Rosario beamed at Zert. "Thank you for saving my life. It's a small life, but I value it very much indeed."

"OK. I'll agree to try to find the troop, but only if you'll admit that I'm telling the truth," Ralphey was saying to his mother with his giant voice.

As Zert listened to Ralphey's footsteps dying away, he felt a little sorry for the scout. The boy with the baggy socks had had the most magical experience of his life, and no one would ever believe him.

The woody room inside the log grew darker. He was sure that it was just a cloud passing over the sun. But it would also be night soon.

"Are you feeling well enough to walk?" he asked Dr. Rosario.

Dr. Rosario nodded. "A little bruised, but fine."

"Ralphey's gone. We need to get out of here." They had been inside the log an hour at least.

Dr. Rosario nodded.

Zert crawled out of the knothole and waited for Dr. Rosario. After a few seconds, he reached down and gave the doctor a hand.

He stood side-by-side with the doctor for a moment, staring at a lake of buttery sunlight that pooled the ground. Zert started to say, "Let's go," but when he looked over at the doctor, tears were spiraling through the doctor's wrinkles, dripping down his cheeks, and running off his chin.

"It's just as beautiful as I imagined," the doctor said.

The pine needles lining the trail swayed in a gentle dance. The pebbles sparkled in the fading light. An ant marched by, its antennae bobbing as it crossed their path.

"Bugs are not going to inherit the earth. They already own it now," the doctor murmured.

"Is that why you decided to come?" Zert asked. "To see Paradise?"

"No." The doctor shook his head. "I came to save this world from treachery."

PART THREE

38

A SLOW WALK AND A LONG TALE

White puffs of their breath ornamented the path as Zert trudged behind Dr. Rosario in the starlight. The doctor was so slow. At this rate, they wouldn't make it to Paradise until the middle of the night. He was going to let his father down. Again.

"You're Marin Bluegar's nephew, aren't you?" Dr. Rosario said. He wrapped his beard around his neck, as though it were a muffler, to keep warm.

"Yes," Zert said, his teeth chattering. He tied his rat cloak tighter, but it did no good. Only his feet were toasty, thanks to the warm boots that his father had made him. "Do you know my uncle Marin?"

"Yes, I do," Dr. Rosario said.

So Uncle Marin is alive. "My uncle was supposed to shrink with us, but he didn't," Zert said.

Dr. Rosario stopped to catch his breath. "I'm sorry to tell you that your uncle Marin and my son Benre have betrayed us all."

Zert groaned. He remembered the shadowy figure on the stairs in the doctor's house wearing the retro Hawaiian shirt. Benre, Dr. Rosario's son.

"The two scoundrels have made a deal with the holoshow *New Worlds*. I came to warn everyone here. We need to flee," Dr. Rosario said.

"I knew my uncle was up to something."

Dr. Rosario grunted and picked his way along the trail. "If this outfit *New Worlds* has its way, Rosies will become celebrity freaks. Tourists will overrun Rocky Mountain National Park trying to get a glimpse of us. We won't have the time or space needed to continue our important work," Dr. Rosario said.

Tourists would pop out from behind bushes and take his photo. No place would be sacred. Not Pancake Rock or PeopleColor Schoolhouse, not the turtle bath, not his corral.

"When are the tourists coming?" Zert asked, gazing at the pale trail that wound through the darkened field like an uneven part in a giant's hair. The path sparkled as though someone had smashed a communicator and scattered the crystalline dust.

"It may be much worse than that," Dr. Rosario said.

"What?" Zert said. "What are you talking about?"

"I should save my strength for the hike. There's no time to lose," Dr. Rosario said. "In fact, find me a staff. There's some frost on the trail. It's getting slippery. I can go faster if I lean on something."

Zert spotted a twig and handed it to him.

Leaning on the cane, the doctor shuffled along at the same speed as before.

››>

A few hours later, voices floated down from Pancake Rock onto the plain below. Zert and Dr. Rosario made their way slowly up the steps that were cut into the side of the rock.

"Your son will never fit in here." Don G. was badmouthing Zert again. "I knew that as soon as I met him."

"Don G., Zert saved your daughter's life," a woman said.

His teacher was taking up for him.

"He also attacked her with a knife, and now, on the night of this important vote, he's either run away or isn't even bothering to show up," Don G. said.

Because I'm crawling along with an ancient . . . who's here to save Paradise, by the way.

Dr. Rosario laid his hand softly on Zert's shoulder.

Zert reached for Dr. Rosario's hand and squeezed it.

"I told you, Dad. We were running late," Beth's voice rang out. "It was my idea to go to the parking lot."

"Something's wrong or Zert would be here," his father's voice wafted down.

"I'm here," Zert called from nearly the top step. But his throat was so dry his voice came out in a croak.

"We'll organize a search for him as soon as there's light. After we get back from risking our lives trying to find and rescue him, I vote we close our community entirely to minimized kids. Enough is enough, Rosies!" Don G.'s voice barreled down from the ledge. "We can't make the progress we need to here if we have to worry about our kids being corrupted by youth with BIG values."

"That's not the Rosie way," said another voice that Zert recognized. Artica Chang's.

"No more minimized kids," a few other Rosies yelled.

Zert stepped up onto the rock into the firelight. Behind him, Dr. Rosario had reached the top step. But he leaned on his staff to catch his breath.

Beth let out a hoot.

His father rushed over. "I was afraid that I'd lost you," Jack cried. He wore a rat-skin cloak, muffler, and hat. But despite the strange costume, Jack looked like Zert's own dear dad as he threw his arms around him. "I don't know what I would do without you," he said as he pressed Zert tighter to his chest. "You are more important to me than life itself."

Don G. approached them. "You are not more important to *me* than my life or my family's lives, Zert." He glared at Zert. "In fact, you are a drag on our survival."

"You've said enough, Don. G. We'll leave in the morning. You—" his father said, but his voice trailed off as Dr. Rosario stepped out of the shadows. Covered in dust from his head and long beard to his leather shoes, the ancient looked as if he had swallowed three bottles of white PeopleColor.

"Dad. I . . . um . . . ," Zert began.

"What's this I hear about a closed community? We created this world to welcome all," Dr. Rosario said.

Jack looked at Zert with questioning eyes.

Zert smiled. "You wanted to meet Dr. Rosario. So I brought him here," he said.

Don G. took a step back as if Zert had hit him. "How? What? Why are you here, Dr. Rosario?" Cleama Gibson gasped. Like most of the Rosie adults, she had on a gray floor-length coat and gray boots. But she also wore cotton-pad earmuffs that made her look as if she had an earache.

"Oh, my Rosies," Dr. Rosario said, "it seems that I arrived in time to stop another betrayal of our principles. Was that you, Don Gibson, who was proposing to reject all minimized kids?"

"We have to protect the mission, Dr. Rosario," Don G. said.

"But our mission is to help others, Don G.," Dr. Rosario said as the Rosies all gathered around.

Don G. frowned. "Easy for you to say, Doctor. To help others, our community has to stay together to survive."

Dr. Rosario took a deep breath and seemed about to speak when his knees buckled. Artica stepped up and took his arm, or else the old man would have fallen.

"What happened? Who's that man?" Dawn Nelson raised her head from underneath a pile of fur blankets where she had fallen asleep.

"Here," Artica said. He led Dr. Rosario over to a place in front of the fire. "You must be cold and tired."

Mary Kay Casey handed him a cup of hot root tea.

Harriet Chang settled a fur blanket over his lap.

"What happened, Doctor?" Artica asked as Dr. Rosario bent his knees slowly to lower himself onto the ground.

Bear Nelson propped up the doctor's back with a dandelion pillow.

"It all started"—smoke from the campfire enveloped him, and the doctor coughed—"when I was sick with a bad flu that turned into pneumonia. I was on the verge of death. While I was in bed, my son Benre took charge."

Zert settled in the circle around the fire, put his arm around his father, and snuggled close. Their cloaks weren't warm enough for this weather, but at least, even if they were kicked out tonight, he and his father had each other.

"I saved this for you." His father pulled a snail sandwich on acorn bread out of a pocket and handed it to him.

Zert took a bite of the sandwich and caught the powerful smell of fresh garlic. He finished it in three gulps. He looked at his father hopefully, but Jack shook his head. "That's all," his father said softly. "But I've got some wormdogs at the house."

Mary Kay Casey, who was sitting on the other side of Zert's father, passed him a parsley marshmallow.

"Thanks," he whispered to her as he popped the delicious morsel into his mouth.

"When my health improved, I found Benre rifling through my desk. I asked what he was looking for, but he was vague and evasive that afternoon. Later, a man with a foreboard that said 'World's Greatest Adventurer' visited our house."

Zert mouthed to his father, "Uncle Marin." Frowning, his father nodded.

"One afternoon, I came upon the man with the foreboard conferring with Benre in the secret map room. When I demanded to know what they were up to, Benre said, 'Dad, I have plans for your Rosies. Big plans. We're going to start with the settlement of Paradise. I've hooked up with the adventure show *New Worlds*. Marin Bluegar and I are going to make you all famous. And rich. We'll be moving to an Up City before you know it.'"

"I bet Uncle Marin thinks we'll help him," Zert said into his father's ear.

"He's wrong," his father hissed back.

"I knew then that my son had been totally corrupted. Although I acted as though I were playing along, Benre knows me too well. I found that the door to my room was locked that night and that my I-ring was disconnected. He kept me trapped in my house for several days before I decided that I had no choice but to escape."

Zert swatted away the smoke. When it refused to leave him alone, he hid his head in his knees and breathed in cedar and pine.

"I overheard him tell a supposed housekeeper he had hired that he was going to be out of town for a week and to keep me locked up. He didn't know that I kept an early prototype of the minimizer in my room. I could shrink. But I'd need help to reach you. Thinking of my Rosies in danger, I had no choice but to take a chance.

"I won't go into how disoriented I felt when I woke up on the floor of my bedroom, naked and a third the length of my pipe stem. Many of you here have experienced what I'm talking about. Suffice it to say that I was glad that, years before, I'd had a suit of Rosie clothes made on a whim. Once I'd dressed, I began to carry out the next part of my plan. I crawled onto my surprised cat's back and held onto her collar. I hated doing this, but I stuck her with a pin until she meowed so loudly that the woman whom Benre had hired to hold me prisoner opened the door to my room. The cat bolted with me hanging onto her back for dear life. When the woman saw that I was missing, she called Benre, but what could he do?"

Benre probably yelled at her, "Look under the bed and in the closet. Look everywhere!"

But BIGS can't see us, Zert thought proudly.

"The last part of my plan was the most dangerous. I had been unable to call Dr. Brown before I shrank, and now I was too small to use an I-ring. But Dr. Brown lived close by, and I was determined to make my way across town to his home in Foggy Bottom."

"I waited for my jailer to leave on an errand. When she did, I rushed through the front door as she opened it. It was dusk, and Dr. Brown's home was blocks and blocks away. It would take weeks for me to walk all that way on my own. Meanwhile, my Rosies were in grave danger. I needed to get to Rocky Mountain National Park to warn you."

The fire was dying, and cold was winning. But like everyone else, Zert didn't move. He inched closer to his father.

Dr. Rosario looked around at the smoky faces. At Don G., who sat across from him. At Mary Kay Casey, who sat next to Jack. She was covered in gray fur except for a stripe of green firefly essence on her forehead and glowing green beaded earrings. "There's not enough time for me to tell you about the next part of the trip. It involves a harrowing stint in a nursery, a ride in a Flayhead's pocket, my impersonation of a fairy, and a dive into a woman's purse. When I finally arrived at his home, Dr. Brown booked us for a Mag Lev trip to Colorado, and we landed in the parking lot late yesterday afternoon."

Dr. Rosario looked up at the sky for a long moment before he began again. "Dr. Brown held me on his palm as we said our good-byes. I felt the same things as all of you. Confusion. Awe. Thankfulness. Loss. Sadness."

The adults sitting around the campfire nodded.

Dr. Rosario sighed. "On my way to you, I was captured by a Boy Scout. It's ironic that Marin Bluegar's nephew, Zert Cage, rescued me. I would not be sitting here except for this brave young Rosie."

Jack squeezed Zert's shoulder again before speaking up. "I'm afraid we have some bad news of our own."

"Yes," Dr. Rosario said. "Let's hear it."

"My son has twice spotted a lifter with a *New Worlds* logo circling Paradise," his father said. "The floor is a microscope, so the BIG passengers can detect us. New Worlds has already begun their tours."

Dr. Rosario answered, "Ah, yes. *New Worlds.*" He exhaled slowly. "Dr. Brown heard a rumor that this nefarious outfit has planned something even more sinister than we originally thought. Their passengers may not be simple tourists but hunters armed with dart guns."

Zert felt his father stiffen.

"Dr. Brown didn't know if Marin Bluegar and Benre were involved in the change of format. I pray not." Dr. Rosario gave a quick shudder. "But the rumor Dr. Brown heard was that *New Worlds* revised the show. The new plan calls for hunters to capture us as trophies."

The Rosies around the campfire exploded in shouts of protest. "What?" Don G. shouted. "Don't they know we're human too?"

"What will they do with us after they capture us?" Mary Kay Casey asked.

"I don't want to dwell on this despicable plan. It's only more confirmation that we need to camouflage our village and leave as soon as possible. But before we begin preparations, I want to end by saying, Rosies, I'm grateful to be here and to be alive. When I see the grandeur of that purple mountain over yonder, I know that I'm ready to begin my new life." He paused. "With you, my Rosies."

The crowd started clapping. Someone had thrown a log on the fire, and it was now glowing brightly.

Zert's father no longer had his arm around him, but they were sitting close to each other next to the warm fire.

Mary Kay Casey sat on Jack's other side with Jack's hand on hers. She wore a brand-new pair of sturdy, rat-hide boots Jack had made for her by working nonstop over the last week. Zert looked into his father's eyes, and his father smiled.

Zert nodded. Mary Kay Casey was nice. It was OK with him.

Millicent and Artica sat across from them. They had a fur blanket over their shoulders. Millicent's blue night-suit looked like it had once been a bedroom slipper. It may have been the smoke that distorted his vision, but it seemed as if his best friend was smiling at him. In a new way. One that made his stomach tingle.

"So he's a jolly good Rosie," Artica cheered. Zert joined in. So did his father and Mary Kay Casey.

But not Don G. He glowered at the fire.

When the cheering stopped, Dr. Rosario put his hands together as if in prayer, and Mary Kay Casey stood up and marched to the outskirts of the rock. She tugged on the flagpole of the roach flag as if it were a lever.

Kabaam.

A blast of fall leaves shot out of the pipe in Pancake Rock. Then another one.

The leaves rained slowly down on the Rosie houses in the valley below until no hunter could see anything. Not even with a microscope.

39

CAMO ANTS
DARTING AWAY

"As your new leader, I say we go along snail trail 7, then follow the trickle to the stream," Mary Kay Casey said to the group of adults huddled around her. "We'll each carry a leaf overhead. In case we're tracked, we'll look like ants."

Don G. stood at the outskirts of the camp circle.

With a sock blanket draped over his cloak, Zert swung his feet over the edge of Pancake Rock along with the other kids. He drank hot blueberry tea and ate a mushroom biscuit.

"This is terrible," Millicent said. Her fur cap with a spiderweb visor didn't cover her ears, but her fur gloves and muffler and bedroom slipper night-suit looked warm.

"The worst," Beth said. "We've got to leave everything behind."

He had never seen her wear shoes before. Her feet, covered in fur shoes, were so big they looked like small animals.

"I don't know what to do," Ivy Potts sobbed. "This is my home." Underneath her fur jacket, she had on a knitted sweater. A matching knitted hat topped her head, and fur mufflers covered her ears.

"It feels bad, I know," Zert said. "But it gets better."

Beth glared at him and pulled her fur muffler tighter around her neck. "Easy for you to say. You don't understand."

If only he could find the words to tell her about his apartment and his purple couch and the photo of his mom. "I do understand," he said. "I had a pet named Chub. She—"

"You just got here," Beth interrupted. "This is our home," she said as she kicked her feet hard against the side of the cliff underlying Pancake Rock.

Millicent put her head in her hands and started crying. Her cap tumbled off and landed by the edge of the cliff.

Zert snatched it before the wind could blow it away. "It's not easy for me to say. I left one home before." He set the cap back on Millicent's head. "But the terrible feeling you have right now will go away." The leaves had covered Paradise, but he knew where the homes were. He knew where the corral that held his insect herd was. He could still see his favorite rock by the trickle.

He didn't want to leave either. But he had done it once before. He could make a new home again. Besides, they had no choice but to dart away, camouflaged as ants. They were being hunted.

"Kids," Casey said, clapping her hands, "head to the fire."

His father walked up to him. "We'll have to start our Cage & Father Bug Ranch somewhere else. Are you up for it?"

Zert nodded. "You've got a deal."

As the sun rose, the Rosies gathered in a circle around the fire. Beth stood across from him, her face solemn. Millicent dried her eyes. One Rosie woman began singing, and the others joined in. "O beautiful for spacious skies, for amber waves of grain . . ."

The last strains of the song had died away when Casey said, "Kids, put whatever you can in a backpack. We're leaving at dawn. We'll be back one day," she added. "But I'm not sure when."

"Dad," Millicent asked, "where are we going?"

"We don't know. We're explorers," Artica said. He straightened the cap on her head and shot her a big grin.

Mary Kay Casey clapped her hands, and her green earrings swayed in the wind. "Kids, return to the rock as soon as you can."

Dr. Rosario was nodding. He started to stand but fell back. His legs were too tired to hold him.

As Mary Kay Casey helped him get up, he whispered into her ear. She nodded.

"I have an announcement," Dr. Rosario said. "Don G.?"

Don G. stepped out of the shadows. He hadn't stopped frowning since the doctor had scolded him. His scowl had grown deeper when he heard the story of the hunters. Then after the villagers had voted to replace him with Mary Kay Casey as president, he'd moved to the edge of the circle and had been glowering at everybody.

"Will you accept the most trusted position that this community has to bestow and stay behind and guard Paradise?" Dr. Rosario said.

At first, Don G. stood frozen. But slowly his lips parted. His crooked smile gave him a mischievous look, as if he might even be fun to pal around with. "Yes. I will."

"And?" Dr. Rosario said. He winked at Zert. "Is there something you'd like to show the newest members of our community, the Cages, before we leave?"

The Rosies must have voted while he was talking to Beth and Millicent. He wasn't Abbot Number Two after all. He and his father had a community now.

Zert smiled up at his father. His father smiled back and whispered, "It was my great boots."

Don G. took a deep breath and turned to Jack. "Why don't you come with me?"

"Certainly."

His father had been wrong about a lot of things, but he was right about the most important thing.

Don't blow it, Zert lectured himself as he followed his father and Don G. down the side of Pancake Rock.

40

MISSION THUMB— THE SMALLEST FORGE OUR FUTURE

A black shadow swooped across the floor of the community center. Something dark, as large as a small lifter, flew overhead. Although firefly essence shone on the walls, the light didn't penetrate much of the room; the space was too vast.

"Don't worry. The fruit bats don't bother us," Don G. said, his voice echoing.

Zert shuddered. *I've never been so happy not to be a banana.*

The bat flew between floor-to-ceiling stalactites and stalagmites and disappeared into a crack in the crystal wall.

"No telling how deep that water is," Don G. was saying about a lake. "Or how many strange creatures live there."

Zert glanced at his murky reflection in the lake, still, quiet, and blacker than ink. As he followed Don G., he slipped on the bones and shells coated in phosphorescent slime and algae along the shore. A whiff of salt invaded his nose and mouth.

Don G. stopped in front of a slot in the rock that was shaped like a large keyhole. With the coming of morning, he had ditched the rat-skin jacket and was just wearing the Rosie standard-issue pants and shirt. His salt-and-pepper hair flowed down onto his shoulders. "This is what Dr. Rosario wanted you to see before you leave. It's our pride and joy. Our last resort."

Zert followed Don through the keyhole and entered a room darker than the previous one. He gagged as the latest smell hit him. It was damp, acidic, and vaguely rusty.

Water splashed nearby. A loud rustling startled him.

A city of bats must have been waking up. But when his eyes adjusted, he found that he was simply staring at a large brown stain on the wall. "What is that?" Zert asked.

Dark, torn wings were pumping. Antennae were bobbing. Bent legs were kicking. Hundreds—no, thousands—no, millions of insects clung to that wall.

"Roaches!" his father said, taking off his fur cap.

"We call this the Roach Palace," Don G. said. He stared at the wall as BIGs stared at the newest model of lifter.

"Roach Palace?" Zert marveled.

"The heart of our program is right here. These are the breeders," Don G. said.

He and his father looked at each other. This was the core of the Rosie mission, something this community didn't share with just anyone. The two of them had earned this privilege.

"We blind them to make it harder for them to escape," Don G. said.

"I told you so, Dad," Zert said. He knew he had seen a *B* on that blind roach's chest.

"Sorry for doubting you," his father said.

"If another Nuclear Mistake were to happen or if there was another world war, insects hold the key. No matter how polluted or troubled, we can always survive on roaches underground in caves," Don G. said.

Artica's vision of the huge insect farm, the reverence the Rosies had for Millard R. Dix, and the brown blob of a roach on the Rosie's flag—everything was starting to add up and make sense.

"But there's more, isn't there, Don G.?" Jack asked.

"Yes. In the event that the worst happens—a drought, a famine, a new disease—Dr. Rosario wants us to go public and offer the world a choice. We might rescue a city, a state, or an entire continent. We don't know yet," Don G. explained.

Zert's mind raced to a day in the future when a skinny Rosie kid named Zert Cage would travel to Low City DC and save Snow Blakely and some of his old friends.

On his life page for the sixth form, most kids had written things like, "Good guy. Zoink ball King." Someone had anonymously written: "Eats Too Many Chips." Not one of his friends had written, "SuperZert to the rescue." *Will I surprise them!*

"That's why it's so important that a bunch of idiots using dart guns don't take us all out," Don G. said. "And why it's crucial that minimized kids who don't know how to act don't divert us from learning all we can about the insect world."

Zert could feel Don G.'s eyes on him. "I heard about the trick the kids played on you. They were wrong," he said. "But when you, Zert, came here and acted as if Rosies aren't as good as BIGs, you were insulting a proud people. Do you understand me?"

"Yes, sir," Zert said.

"I was at fault too." Don G. winced. "This last night has been painful for me. I've been so focused on survival that I've forgotten our larger mission. Dr. Rosario is right. I signed on to help others, even bone-headed teenagers."

Zert nodded. That afternoon when Cribbie was at the door, he had opened it and maybe exposed Chub to Superpox. He'd never know if that's what happened or not. But he'd open the door again to try to help Cribbie. He couldn't live with himself if he didn't.

"As you know, Jack, the vote was unanimous tonight," Don G. was saying out of the side of his mouth. "I thought nothing could sway me to vote for Zert, but I did."

"Thank you," Zert said quietly.

"You—the newcomer—have helped save our community, Zert. I would never have guessed you would be capable of that. But you've shown us a few things," Don G. said. "And if you hadn't rescued Dr. Rosario, there's no telling what could have happened to us. I don't like being wrong, but I've had to face the fact that I've been wrong about you."

Jack said, "We're all wrong sometimes, Don G." When his father started cracking his knuckles, Zert guessed that he was thinking about Uncle Marin.

"Dart guns?" his father said. "I can't believe my brother-in-law would ever be so cruel as to turn hunting human beings into a sport."

Zert imagined his head on a plaque on a wall. *Here's my trophy. It's my nephew, Zert. I identified him by his freckles.* He was no fan of Uncle Marin, but he doubted that his uncle wanted a hunter to bag him either.

"I think Marin hatched a scheme to make money, and then it got out of his control," Jack said.

"I think so too," Zert said grudgingly. "Although what he did was bad enough."

"Your poor mother would be horrified," his father agreed.

"We should get going," Don G. said abruptly. He turned away and started heading in the direction of the crack in the cave wall marked by arrows and lit up with firefly essence.

"Sure," Zert said.

"Thanks, Don G., for showing us this," his father was saying as he walked beside Don G. toward the exit.

"If we had more time, there's actually a lot more to see. Now that we are close to their size, insects are teaching us how to fly, to walk on water, to hang on webs, and to climb walls. We are unlocking their secrets so fast, it's scary," Don G. said.

Zert had a hunch. "Are you a scientist?"

"MacArthur Fellow. Double PhD. If you had studied zoology, you'd know my name," Don G. said.

"Really?" Zert said.

"We have lots of scientists here. Artica Chang is a mechanical engineer. Bear Nelson is a cardiologist," Don G. said.

"Mary Kay Casey is an entomologist," his father said.

"Isn't that someone who studies insects?" Zert asked.

Don G. nodded.

No wonder his teacher's eyes lit up when she talked about bugs. *That reminds me.* Zert turned to Don G. "I've got five roaches, three beetles, and six doodlebugs in my corral by our cave. While we're gone, would you please take care of my herd?"

Don G. squinted in the dim light as he nodded at Zert. "Spoken like a true Rosie," he said. Without more, Don G. passed through the curtain of ivy to the outside.

Zert followed him through the hidden passage in the cliff.

The sun was shining brightly now. Light and shadow quilted the waterfall cascading down Pancake Rock. A bird as large as an eagle flew overhead. But its gray wings looked soft, and its head was light green. He adjusted for his size. The flying creature was a moth.

A tumbleweed of thistles rolled by, and for no reason, Zert thought of Dr. Brown's strange ink drawing and the way its wheels within wheels had started spinning.

Worlds within worlds. Paradise. Rosieland. Rocky Mountain National Park. The North American continent. Planet Earth. The universe. But he wasn't alone.

As the tumbleweed floated away, he linked arms with his father. Together, they started down the snail trail shimmering in the light of dawn.

ACKNOWLEDGMENTS

I wrote this book twenty years ago. So many people have read it during the years: Michael and Daniel Zilkha, Fred Leebron, Lois Stark, Franci Neely, Kim Morris, Melissa Fordyce, Michelle Cunningham, Laura Tolle, Lois Stark, Andy and Elena Marks, Ellen Susman, Lisa and Alia Eads, Claire, Georgiana and Craig Smyser, Dr. Gail Gross, Dr. Roberta Ness, an entire class at the Fay School, my daughter and son Elena and Will White, my niece Kaitlin Oliver, Molly Bordoff, and Shamsa and Salima Mangalji, to name just a few. I went about fifteen years without rereading the draft, but Stephen White, my youngest son, always said it was my best book. I took a peek at it a few years ago. By that time, my friend Carla Powers had come into my life, and she offered me the encouragement that I needed to get the book across the finish line. Amanda Jenkins did yeoman's work in making the book's characters come alive. I also am deeply grateful to Lucy Chambers, Alex Parsons, Stephen Roxburgh, and Jeff Smisek for their advice, suggestions, and friendship.

READING GROUP GUIDE

1. Describe key moments in the novel when you see Zert beginning to cross over from a rejection of his new world to an acceptance and understanding of it. What people or events cause him to change his opinion about Paradise and his view of himself in it?

2. Even though Zert liked his life in Low City DC and was connected to things there, he still felt frustrated, powerless, and stuck. How do you think becoming minimized and entering an unknown world eventually helps him become happier, stronger, and freer? How does he change from being someone who has things happen to him to someone who makes things happen?

3. Low City DC is portrayed as a place that has been ruined by war, pollution, crime, disease, and consumerism, essentially the destructive and wasteful nature of human beings. The author contrasts this with the clean, self-sustaining, natural "Paradise" of miniaturized people living in Rocky Mountain National Park. What statement do you think the author might be making about our world and the way we live our lives today? If we read this novel as a cautionary tale, what does it suggest about us and our role in the world? In light of this, what is the overall tone of the book? Does the author seem

to leave the reader with a feeling of hope or despair? Why do you think this?

4. The author presents a fascinating futuristic world in which she imagines innovative technologies that are used every day. What are some of the favorite technologies or inventions that you read about? Talk about the role of imagination in the book. How is the world of the Rosies just as imaginative as Low City DC?

5. Do you think Zert and Jack would have allowed themselves to be minimized if Cribbie had not gotten Superpox? Before becoming minimized, do you think Zert fully understood how this would change his life? Why or why not?

6. The author creates a sense of disconnect between Zert and Beth from the very first time they meet. Describe how this impacts the chapters that follow and why you think this might be important to the storytelling.

7. Zert sometimes hides his true feelings. How does this affect his relationships with other characters?

8. Loneliness is a prevalent idea explored in the novel. Zert experiences loneliness in his life in Low City DC and also later in Paradise. Talk about ways in which his loneliness is different in each of these places. How does he eventually overcome it?

9. How is Zert like or unlike Abbot? If Zert had run into Abbot soon after arriving at Paradise, what do you think he and Abbot would have talked about? If Zert had run into Abbot at the end of the novel, how do you think their conversation would have been different?

10. Describe other characters in the novel who, like Zert, don't really give things a chance at first. What does this say about the importance of openness and understanding?

11. Courage is a theme in the novel. In what scenes does Zert show courage, and how does this move the plot forward?

12. Zert has been around insects his whole life, but he does not fully appreciate them until after he is minimized. How does his attitude about insects evolve throughout the book? Talk about ways in which his openness to bugs moves the plot of the story forward.

13. Eating insects is a common practice around the world. Do you think you could eat bugs? How do you think Zert's ability to eat bugs informs us as readers?

14. How do you think Jack likes living in Paradise? Discuss ways in which Jack's love and loyalty to Zert throughout the book impact the outcome of the story.

15. Second chances play a major role in the book. What are scenes in which Zert gets a second chance? How do they impact him? How does he begin to learn to give second chances to others?

16. In one key scene, Zert saves Beth's life from a bassetduck, which to them, looks like a giant monster. No other character in the novel is able to help Beth in that moment. What are examples, throughout the book, that show how Zert has always been good with animals? What do you think this says about Zert's personality?

17. How would you characterize Don G.? Do you think he was wrong to be so closed off to minimized kids for so much of the novel? Why or why not? Discuss also the way the author uses the symbol of the Statue of Liberty throughout the novel. What statement do you think she is trying to make about welcoming others? In light of this, to what extent do you feel that nations and people in our own world should be welcoming to newcomers?

18. Knowing the outcome of the book, what would you say to Uncle Marin if you had the chance right now?

19. What do you think Zert will be like one year later? Why?

20. Do you think you would be able to live in a community like Paradise as a minimized human being? What, if anything, would you have done differently from Zert?

AUTHOR Q&A

Q: How and when did you first know you wanted to write *Surviving Minimized*? Can you share what inspired you to write a book about a teenager trying to survive in a miniaturized world?

A: I used to turn over rocks in my backyard and see the insects scurrying around underneath and dream about them. It fascinated me that there was a whole world underneath my feet that I knew nothing about. This book started in my backyard, but I wrote the first draft around 1997. After I finished it, I wrote thousands of more pages about the adventures of these small people. These other books are still under my bed, so to speak. At the time, I read this book and some of the others out loud to classes at a school near my house, called the Fay School.

Q: What inspired you to choose the dystopian setting of Low City DC as the world Zert came from? Do you have any particular interest in science fiction or with stories about the future?

A: Originally, I wrote this story in the present. But when I asked people to read the draft, their first comment was "I don't believe that a responsible father would encourage his teenage son to shrink." So, I rewrote the book and set it in a dire and terrible future. After that, no one questioned Jack Cage's love for his son or decision to escape.

Q: What kind of research did you do on insects when you were writing this novel? To what extent do you believe in using insects as a sustainable food source? Did you discover anything new in your perspective on entomophagy during the process of writing? Why did you want to explore this topic?

A: I read lots of books on insects. But the most surprising thing I found was that there are actual roach farms in China and that roaches are being raised for use in Asian medicine and in cosmetics. Also, experiments suggest that cockroach milk is among the most nutritious and highly caloric substances on the planet. Who would have ever known?

Q: How long did this book take you to write?

A: Before I got used to writing on computers in the late nineties, I wrote this book out in longhand four or five times. I would change the point of view from first to third. Then, I'd buy a brand-new notebook, and I'd change the point of view back again, and I'd write it out by hand one more time. After that, I let the book sit for over a decade. I started working on the draft again about four years ago. Thank goodness by then I was able to use a computer to write my stories.

Q: What was your favorite chapter to write in *Surviving Minimized* and why? Which chapters came easiest? And on the other side of the spectrum, were any chapters particularly challenging for you to write? If so, can you share what it was about these parts of the story that challenged you?

A: Getting Zert's character right was hard. In many drafts, he was such a smart aleck that no one liked him. I liked his sense of humor from the beginning, but I had to find a way to let him use it without making him sound bitter or too angry.

Q: What was one of the most surprising things you encountered as you worked on this novel? Did anything occur during the course of writing that gave you a different perspective on people and/or our place in the world? What did you enjoy most about the *process* of writing this book?

A: Writing with an outline is a good idea because it saves a lot of time. Unfortunately, I love writing freeform. I love it when I'm surprised by what happens in the next paragraph or the next chapter. I love it when I start typing and don't know where I'm going, but the character seems to know and directs me. I really love everything about writing the first twenty or so drafts of a novel. Draft 1,298 isn't as fun, though.

Q: The descriptions of Zert and Jack arriving as miniaturized humans in a new world are so vivid. Have you spent a lot of time in nature? What types of meaning do you personally attach to nature?

A: I have a trampoline in my backyard. It's underneath a group of tall oak trees, and I like to jump on it and watch the sunlight come through the branches and pierce the spiderwebs. This past weekend, I got caught up in a series on television, and I didn't spend as much time as usual outside. I am much happier if I go on a long walk at my neighborhood park or go for a swim and look up at the clouds.

Q: What do you hope readers take away from this book?

A: Insects may be the food of the future. Being the new kid in school is hard. And there are always new frontiers to explore.

Also, on a deeper note, the book is about bravery. When we're about to act in a brave manner, a determination or resolution carries us through. Resolution can be cultivated. I've written this book to remind kids of this. Kids need resolution to succeed in their lives.

Q: Would you tell us about a particular person or author who has had a fundamental influence on your writing or your philosophy of life? How does this inform what you create?

A: Author Justin Cronin told me that your answer is always in your book. If your character is looking for a way to communicate with his mother and he's forgotten his cell phone, reread the chapter. You'll find a pay phone on the wall waiting for him to use it.

It's also good advice for life. The tools are there to solve your problem. Just look around.

Q: Can you talk a bit about your writing process? How do you fit writing into your life? How do you get in the mood to write? Do you have any writing rituals?

A: I write at a newspaper during the week. It's a different kind of writing. I have to be sure I get the facts right. If I make a mistake about a date when something happened or misspell a name, I feel horrible. It's pure freedom when I get to the weekends and I start writing on my novels. Then I get to make stuff up.

It's fun to try to shine a spotlight on things at the newspaper using factual writing. But it's also fun to use my imagination.

I work on my novels every Saturday and Sunday that I'm in town. I exercise in the morning, and then I come back to my room and write for four hours.

Our house was flooded by Hurricane Harvey, but when we fixed it up, I got a study with a window that looks out onto a forest of trees. I sit in my comfortable chair and write. I love it. I don't feel good about myself if I don't spend time every week using my imagination.

Q: If a young person came to you for advice on how to get started writing, what would you tell them? What is the best—and worst—advice you've ever gotten about writing?

A: Best advice: write.

Worst advice: write with an outline. Again, outlines are great and save time. But they frustrate me, and one even made me cry.

Q: Do you have another book in the works? Anything you can reveal yet?

A: I have written three middle-grade books. In *Surviving the Second Alamo*, a young boy rebels against an authoritarian government that promises a risk-free lifestyle and perfect health. In *Surviving the BlitzCube*, a young boy gets trapped inside a game that his overprotective parent created to remind the world of the lessons of the Blitz. In *Surviving Roman History Camp*, a young girl thwarts a kidnapping at camp where holograms re-create the Roman games.

You can see by the titles what they all have in common.

Q: What do your children think about this book? In what ways did they help inform it?

A: Will, Stephen, and Elena, my adult children, will hopefully be rereading this book for the first time in a decade. Kelsi, my daughter-in-law, will be reading it for the first time.

Stephen always told me, "Write a book where the main character is someone I want to be."

I'm sure they'll tell me if I succeeded or not and if the book matches their memory of it from so long ago.

ABOUT THE AUTHOR

Andrea White is the author of four books of middle-grade fiction and currently serves on the editorial board of the *Houston Chronicle*. She lives in Houston, TX with her husband, former Mayor Bill White, and is grateful to share this book, which she penned 20 years ago.